(handwritten inscription) Len,

The Apostate

(handwritten) Who starred in my first Movie, then quit.

A Novel By

Paul Lonardo

(handwritten) Hope you finish my book *Paul Lonardo*

Published By
Barclay Books, LLC

BARCLAY BOOKS, LLC

St. Petersburg Florida
www.barclaybooks.com
A Spectral Visions Imprint

PUBLISHED BY BARCLAY BOOKS, LLC
6161 51ST STREET SOUTH
ST. PETERSBURG, FLORIDA 33715
www.barclaybooks.com
A Spectral Visions Imprint

Copyright © 2001 by Paul Lonardo

This novel is a work of fiction. The characters, names, incidents, places, dialogue, and plot are the products of the author's imagination or are used fictitiously. Any resemblance to actual persons, living or dead, or events is purely coincidental.

Printed and bound in the United States of America
Cover Design by Barclay Books, LLC
Author Photo Photographer Bill Kipp

ISBN: 1-931402-13-2

This book is dedicated to the memory of my father,

William Lonardo

1932-1976

Prologue

Massachusetts Bay Colony, Superior Court Of Judicature, May 1693

Magistrate Cromwell's voice was one of tolerance, but his eyes were stamped with conviction as he addressed the court. "Some persons will put an evil construction upon an innocent person, and then others, believing it, are apt to look upon all further actions with a squint eye, and through the multiplying glass of their own jealousies make a molehill seem a mountain." He let his heavy gaze fall upon Ann Hobson.

The accused witch shrank back in her chair and squeezed her clasped hands more tightly together in her lap. A murmur of anticipation circulated through the crowd of spectators gathered inside the cramped hall.

"In light of the recent reformation of this colony's official policy on witchcraft, this court, as sanctioned by his Excellency, Governor Phipps, of the Province of Massachusetts-Bay in New England, elects to reject the bill of indictment against the accused and move for a complete dismissal."

A sudden cheer rose up and the old widow's eyes rolled back in her head.

"All charges levied against Ann Hobson are disposed forthwith and the defendant is free to go about her business." Magistrate Cromwell punctuated his decision with a sharp strike of his gavel.

Ann Hobson collapsed to her knees and cried out in prayer through tearing eyes. Family and friends rallied around her in triumph. The magistrate could only watch the ensuing celebration spill out into the streets. Many people dashed out of the building, rejoicing throughout the town. Some remained in the courtroom and applauded the bench's ruling. Still others rushed toward the old widow to celebrate her freedom alongside her.

Masking his feelings of contentment, the magistrate began to rise from his bench. Just then a solitary voice distinguished itself above the others. The man's vehement shouts swiftly silenced the excited mob. As his words became distinguishable, Cromwell paused and turned in the direction of the complainant. "You're making a terrible mistake!" the man's voice boomed from the back of the great courthouse. "Remember how Satan tempted Jesus in the desert? 'When the Devil had finished all tempting, Satan left *to await another opportunity.*'"

A gaunt figure stepped slowly along the shadowy interior at the back of the hall.

"The gospel clearly instructs us, as in Ephesians 6:16; 'In all circumstances hold faith up before you as a shield. It will help you extinguish the fiery darts of the Evil One.'"

The man was wearing black, and so was not noticed by all until he was halfway across the room. Because of his attire, and the thunderous pitch of his voice, many of the spectators made him out to be a minister. He was toting a small black carrying case at his side, so still others supposed he was a man of medicine. They all gave him a wide berth.

The magistrate, however, knew the man to be neither a prophet of God nor a purveyor of science. Indeed, Cromwell saw this man as a bane to the present political and social climate of the colony. He was a witch-finder, a "pricker," who received a fee from local authorities for each witch whose presence he divulged. The sundry of needles and pins he carried in his leather bag were not intended to alleviate pain, but to inflict it. If no blood could be drawn after pricking the flesh of an accused witch, this was considered spectral evidence that the suspect was a consort of the Devil. In many cases, this testimony alone was used to both convict and condemn suspected witches. However, in light of the increasing social skepticism about witchcraft and the call for change in evidentiary law, The Pricker's services were considered bygone. He was now seen as a rogue who tortured innocent widows for a fee, and he was looked at with as much suspicion and contempt as those accused had once been.

Cromwell was embarrassed by the sudden jurisprudential shift regarding witchcraft. When the settlement was first granted its new charter by King William III., the colony made a moral pledge to God, which by the court's actions of the past year, it was now in danger of recanting. What made matters worse was the very real threat that this moral breach would seriously undermine the political stability of the state. And for this, Cromwell hated The Pricker.

When The Pricker stopped before the bench, Cromwell looked down at him with disdain. "None of the Governor's magistrates are unfamiliar with the scriptures you quote," Cromwell began. "You spoke your peace, Pricker. Now, be gone. Or did you not hear that the case against the woman accused by you of malefic witchcraft has been dismissed?"

"You can dismiss every charge of witchcraft if it makes you feel better. Overturn all the convictions. Liberate the imprisoned. Even evince contrition for those who have been executed. But understand this, Your Honor; you are playing right into Belial's hands." The Pricker raised one fist over his head and, in an even more exaggerated doggerel, said, "'Now the serpent was the most cunning of all the animals that the Lord God had made' . . . Remember, His grandest scheme is making humanity believe that He does not exist."

THE APOSTATE

"Pricker, the theological lessons you espouse have been reconsidered by this court, our findings reflective of the belief of the colonists that a kind of mass delusion has preyed upon us lo these many months. Through the power of God and rational thinking, all unsubstantiated invention has been thoroughly and effectively repudiated by this court and the law-abiding citizens it serves. Therefore, Pricker, the accusations that you have brought against Mrs. Hobson, including all spectral evidence, have been similarly disavowed. With the discontinuation of the Court of Oyer and Terminer, your livelihood, and indeed your very existence, have been discredited. You are a non-voice in this newly commissioned court, Pricker."

"You can silence my tongue of clay, but be aware that your skepticism has done nothing to disarm Satan. In fact, you have only succeeded in heightening the power of the Great Adversary and hastening this world toward Armageddon. Man's Common Enemy has achieved from these trials what had been his sole intent—planting the seed of apostasy in God's kingdom. Be assured that over time the Beast will see to it that this impiety is bathed by the waters of blasphemy and swathed in the blanket of moral apathy."

The small number of people who remained in the courtroom started to grow impatient. Some began to scoff and jeer.

"Hey, Pricker," someone shouted, "what are you going to do with yourself now that the Devil has been run out of Salem?"

"One day," The Pricker continued, "when hardly anyone is aware, the profanity of this day will come to fruition and its final yield will be complete apostasy. Humanity itself will have become so sinister that there will be no need for Satan anymore. At that point the Tempter will have become so powerful that not even God will be able to deliver us from His evil will."

A farm boy crept into the courtroom with a bunch of tomatoes basketed in the front of his shirt and stood beside a small gathering of similarly grinning boys.

"Satan will be back," The Pricker assured the court. "Maybe not in our lifetime, or our grandchildren's, but there will come a time when almost no one reads the word of God. And when the two factions that divide the world—the lamb and his followers and the dragon and his followers—become too close in number, it will be then that The Defiler will return. A century is a mere moment to Lucifer. And if the Father of Lies comes back before our Lord, it will be our children's souls that He harvests."

Suddenly an overripe tomato struck the top of The Pricker's shoulder, showering one side of his face and the front of the magistrate's bench with its juice. Magistrate Cromwell took the uproar of laughter that followed as his opportunity to make his exit. He only took one step before he heard something strike the top of his bench. Turning around, he saw that the black case belonging to The Pricker had been placed there. He looked up quickly, but The Pricker had already left the courtroom, with tomatoes, like a plague of locusts, following behind him.

Later that night, as his wife and children slept, Cromwell sat quietly in the darkness of his den, tobacco ash smoldering in the pipe bowl he held in his hand. On his desk in front of him, The Pricker's black case lay open, its needles and pins exposed. Cromwell contemplated the role that these instruments played in the Salem trials. He wondered how different, if any, his role—as well as those of the other magistrates who sat on the Court of Oyer and Terminer—had been from the devices of torture before him. In his rumination, some of the words The Pricker spoke that afternoon came back to him: *the dragon and His followers; complete apostasy; a time when no one reads the word of God; humanity itself will have become so sinister that there will be no need for Satan anymore; it will be our children's souls that He harvests.*

In the darkness of his den, Cromwell questioned if the right choice had been made to blame the errors in the Salem trials on The Church. If what The Pricker said about the relationship between man's apostasy and Satan's power were true, then the rift that The Church's acknowledgment of culpability would open and people's faith might just precipitate the fulfillment of this doomsday prophecy.

Whatever the future held, Cromwell knew that his own legacy, like that of The Pricker, would play a substantial role in the damnation of humanity if Satan's quest to destroy all that God created was to some day succeed.

PART I.

King OF Pain

They wring their hands, their caitiff-hands
and gnash their teeth for terror;
They cry, they roar for anguish sore,
and gnaw their tongues for horror.
But get away without delay,
Christ pities not your cry:
Depart to hell, there may you yell,
and roar eternally.

Michael Wigglesworth, *The Day of Doom*

I have stood here before inside the pouring rain
with the world turning circles running 'round my brain
I guess I'm always hoping that you'll end this reign
But it's my destiny to be the king of pain

Sting

11

Today

Chapter One

It was just after midnight when Chris lifted his head from the pillow and slowly began to raise his torso off the bed. He did not move another muscle until he was sure all the other boys in the room were asleep. Then he quietly crawled out of bed and put on his sneakers. He had not slept and he was still wearing the clean pair of jeans and T-shirt he had put on when he slipped under the covers two hours before. He spent that time staring into the darkness and waiting for the right time to make his escape. He tried not to think too much about where he would go or what he would do when he got there. He only cared about getting away, getting out of the clutches of his foster father and living his own life, wherever that might be.

The time was right, Chris thought, as he pulled his empty backpack out from under his bed. It was now or never. While it had only been a week since he had decided to run away, it had been a long time in coming. Ever since he had been adopted into the Crowley agricultural boot camp at the age of seven, this was a day that could not have come soon enough. The past week, however, had seemed harder for Chris to endure than the previous nine years. The brutal physical and emotional abuse he had been subjected to for so long had become magnified by his planned escape, so close at hand. He had come close to hastening his departure several nights before, after a particularly violent beating. But somehow Chris had managed to exercise enough self-control to wait until this morning, when he knew his chances for success would be much greater. On the Crowley farm, few distinctions could be made between days of the week, but the one difference with Sundays was that Chris's foster father would be groggy most of the day from a night of drinking. On those mornings, he did not want to be bothered by anybody, and odds were he would not notice that one of his boys was AWOL, at least not for quite some time.

Terrence Crowley was the town manager of Demater, New Jersey. All this title meant was that Crowley was the richest of the three farm families who lived there. And every Saturday night they would all get together at one of the farmhouses to play poker and get drunk. That night the game was at the Burns's, which happened to be the farmstead furthest from the interstate. This was essential to Chris's escape plan, because he wanted to make sure he put as much distance between himself and the farm as possible before the county sheriff, (who just happened to be his foster father's brother, Claybert) could be notified. Since both brothers were at the poker game, Chris was sure to be a long way from Demater by the time anybody even knew he was missing.

Now Chris began filling his pack with his belongings. He did not have much, so he had not done it in advance. Besides, if Growl had found it prior to Chris's leaving, he might never get away. His foster father would know about his plan and it would be the prod for sure.

Chris threw a few changes of clothes into his backpack, then he gathered his books—titles such as, *Summa Theologica, On Eternal Peace, The City of God, An Essay Concerning Human Understanding, The Social Contract*. There were a few others, but these were all that was left of a once large archive of treasured tomes. Chris could not help but think of his favorite high school English teacher. Mr. Lewis was a certified bibliophile who had been collecting books his whole life. He knew that Chris loved to read, and he would often give Chris duplicates of books he had, many of which he had seen Chris check out of the library numerous times. But Chris's foster father had destroyed most of them, calling them garbage and smut. Chris had always liked reading. He read anything he could get his hands on, but what he enjoyed most was finding out about how people lived and what they thought at different times throughout history. He supposed it was his way of escaping what his life was like at the present time.

Then Chris was ready to leave. He slipped into his battered denim jacket and pulled the backpack over his shoulders. The last thing he did was take out the picture of his biological mom that he always kept in his wallet. It was a black and white photograph, dog-eared, and full of creases. He held it up to catch the moonlight and stared at her image. He had to acknowledge that the smiling woman with light hair and soft, bright eyes was a virtual stranger to him. He did not even know her name. Yet, for all he did not know, she was still a big part of his life. She had guided him through the tough times at every stage of his development. He would often talk to her and she seemed to talk back. Whether it was a psychic link or something else, Chris did not know. What he was sure about was that whenever he was having trouble with something or someone, all he had to do was take out her picture and he could feel her presence, counseling him or giving him some piece of advice that always turned out to be right. In fact, it was his mother who suggested the week before that he leave the Crowley farm this morning. She was also the one who had encouraged him to be patient after his last beating and wait until Sunday before making his departure.

Chris was putting the photo back into his wallet when a tear came to his eye. He realized that the picture was the only thing he really needed. Perhaps the only thing he would ever need.

As Chris stuffed the wallet into his back pocket, he saw the empty bed in front of him and startled. It belonged to Growl, whose real name was Jimmy. Growl was nineteen, the oldest of twelve boys that Crowley figured he had saved from state dependency. None of the others got along with Jimmy because he was so devoutly loyal to Crowley, who favored the boy, even though he seemed to dispense more abuse on him than anyone else. Jimmy even had a room of his own, but he slept in here so he could keep tabs on what the boys were doing and saying. The room was large and sound carried well. It was actually four bedrooms combined to make one with the removal of the dividing walls. Since Jimmy was there, only as Crowley's watchdog, he was given the nickname, Growl. When the boys were younger they had devised an appropriate signal, barking like a dog, to let each other know when Jimmy was near. Each of them had their own unique bark, which individually identified the one who was giving the warning. Some of them imitated a specific breed of dog. At one time Chris could do a fairly good Rottweiler.

Just then the row of filament bulbs illuminated overhead. The bedroom lighting came down on Chris like an accusation.

"What do you think you're doing?"

Chris looked up instantly, and the sight of his foster father standing in the doorway confirmed what Chris already knew—Growl had tipped him off. The other boys began to stir in their beds.

The old farmer's eyes were red and glossy, and he swayed unsteadily on his feet. He was holding something behind his back, but Chris did not have to see it to know what was there.

The boy adjusted his backpack, pulling it higher on his shoulder, and stood his ground.

"You going somewhere, son?" Crowley said with mock interest.

"*I'm not your son.*"

"Maybe not, but your ass is mine until you turn eighteen. That means two more years of making sure the finish cattle are properly fed and fertilizing the crop soil with their crap. That's your only purpose in life. And you should be thankful to the livestock, because if they didn't eat and shit you wouldn't have any use at all."

Chris looked his foster father directly in the eye for a long moment, then said, "Get out my way." After a slight pause, he added, "Or, so help me God, I'll knock you on your ass."

Crowley snickered momentarily, but his crooked smile quickly faded and his face clenched like a fist. From behind his back he revealed the cattle prod he was hiding. It was actually a stun baton, a hard plastic rod a foot and a half long. Touching the contact prongs to living tissue and pressing a button on the handle delivered a 300,000volt electric shock. Just a half-second shock disrupted nervous system impulses controlling voluntary muscle movement, causing spasms and a dazed feeling that could last a quarter hour. It was much more powerful than a standard cattle prod, but Crowley used it on the kids in the home and the cattle alike. It had a custom-made rubber grip, a hand guard, and a wrist strap.

"Looks like somebody didn't learn his lesson the other night after I told him not to be reading any more of those filthy learning books," Crowley said. "I think it may be time to increase the voltage again."

The mere mention of the prod softened Chris's legs and stiffened his will at the same time. He shook his head and said, "You're never going to touch me with that thing again."

Crowley started forward, taking slow and deliberate steps toward Chris, the prod held out in front of him. Chris rocked back on his heels but did not budge. Suddenly Crowley stopped, an arm's length away from the boy.

"Take a look outside the window, boy," Crowley said tauntingly. "I don't know where you got that rust bucket from, but you ain't going nowhere in that. If you want to run away from home, you'll have to do it the old-fashioned way."

Chris hesitantly moved over to the window, making sure he kept one eye on his foster father, not wanting to divert his attention away from the cattle prod for too long. He only planned on sneaking a peek below. However, when he looked down and saw the silhouette of Growl holding a sledgehammer and standing beside the red Malibu, he could not turn his eyes away. Chris only had the car for a few days. He could not believe his luck when Mr. Lewis told him that he knew of someone who was selling the car for two hundred dollars, and asked Chris if he was interested. It was just about all the allowance money he had saved up, but Chris had jumped at the offer. Since then he had kept it hidden behind the old barn, where he thought it could not be seen from anywhere on the farm.

"Go on, Jimmy!" Crowley yelled.

Among the many things that were going through Chris's mind at that particular moment was how Growl could have known about his plan to leave. Like the other boys, Chris had learned not to say anything when Growl was around. In fact, he had not told anybody what he was planning today, so how Growl could have found out about it was puzzling to Chris.

All at once Growl raised the hammer and began to beat on the trunk and roof of the car in a wild frenzy. The metal crimped and dented from the blows. Glass shattered.

"NO!" Chris yelled. Then suddenly he felt a powerful surge of electricity enter his body from behind his neck. He dropped to his knees, feeling the disorientating effect of the current on his brain. He turned around and saw Crowley standing over him and sneering as he brought the prod down on him again. Just as his foster father was about to administer a second jolt, Chris brought one arm up to fend off the assault. The contact prongs glanced off his forearm and he received only a mild shock. Chris swiftly forced the elbow of his other arm into Crowley's groin, driving the sadistic farmer back and buying himself some time while the tingling feeling throughout his body dissipated.

Crowley let out a loud wail, but even while stooped over and in obvious pain he came after Chris, who, now standing, was able to avoid the reach of the flailing prod. But Chris soon found himself backed up as far as he could go, with the window behind him and Crowley approaching.

"Jimmy said you were talking to that picture of your whore

mother again," Crowley hissed through clenched teeth. "More big talk about you leaving and what you'd like to do to me if you had the chance." Crowley saw the look of understanding flash across Chris's face. "What's the matter, you think I wouldn't find out? This is my town. Me and my brother's. He's got his way of dealing with delinquents, I have mine." He raised the prod high. "Let's see what you're gonna do now, big man," he said as he thrust the weapon toward Chris's head.

Chris quickly removed his backpack, initially to use defensively, as a shield to ward off Crowley's blows. Then, instinctively, he swung the backpack across his body and knocked the prod out of his foster father's hands. With no hesitation, the boy swung it back the other way, this time catching Crowley on the side of the face. The heavy books inside bloodied the man's temples. Chris wound up again and, with everything he had, he slung the backpack a third time, striking Crowley square in the face. The pointed edge of one of the books—Friedrich Nietzsche's *Beyond Good And Evil*— entered the farmer's left eye socket and ruptured his eyeball with an audible pop.

Crowley howled in agony as he reached up to cover his injured eye. Watery red blood ran out between his fingers like pink tears. Chris, however, did not relent. He grunted as he hurled himself upon the partially blind man, not fully comprehending the amount of damage he had already inflicted upon his foster father, and not really caring. All he saw was that the drunk farmer was still standing. In the frenetic rush of his adrenaline-assisted rage, he shoved Crowley so hard that he knocked the older man out of his slippers and catapulted him through the air. Crowley struck the bedroom window with sufficient force to shatter the pane and propel his body, screaming and bleeding, out into the night. Three stories down he fell, hitting the cobblestone walkway below in a shower of broken glass.

Almost instantly, Chris felt nauseous and weak as the chemicals that had been coursing through his body suddenly deserted him. He was not sure what to do next. He stood there for several moments, still woozy from the high voltage shocks he had received. Then he noticed the other boys standing around the broken window, looking down at Growl bawling over the lifeless body and murmuring to each other as the cold December air whipped into the room. His foster mother was also standing nearby, barefoot and wearing a tattered gray terry cloth robe. Her arms were crossed as she stared at Chris with an expression of both horror and relief. She too had suffered, but not only for herself. The guilt she harbored over her inability to stop the violence that her husband inflicted on the boys was etched on her face, and Chris could see how it had compounded over the years, making her look twice her age. With Crowley's demise, Chris knew that part of the conflicting emotions that his foster mom would be feeling now was exoneration for the years of abuse that the children had endured. Now her eyes caught on the prod lying on the floor between them. Without saying a word, she reached down and grabbed the device, handling it as if it were a live snake. Stepping over to the window, she tossed the prod down upon the man who had wielded it with such cruelty.

Chris kissed her on the cheek, then paused. He knew what he had to do now, but it was not going to be easy leaving his foster family. At length, with tears in his eyes, he stepped past them on his way to the door. Nobody spoke. However, they all followed him out of the room and down the hall, stopping at the top landing, as if they could go no further, prisoners in their own home. They watched him descend the stairs and pause at the bottom.

Chris turned to look back at them one final time. They seemed so lost, in a kind of domestic shell shock. They had all been through a war together, and they did what they had to do to get through it. They would be just fine, Chris thought before pulling the front door open and walking out of the farmhouse forever.

As Chris walked to the 1970 Chevy Malibu, he saw Growl sobbing fitfully by Crowley's corpse. In his grieving state,

Growl was oblivious to Chris, the sledgehammer at his side. Chris quickly surveyed the damage to his car and determined that it was drivable. Then he tossed his backpack into the back seat through the broken rear window and forced open the damaged driver side door. He brushed the broken glass aside, sat down, then turned over the 350 engine.

He could not remember driving away from the farm until he was found himself on westbound I-78, halfway to the New Jersey-Pennsylvania line. Chris simultaneously became aware that Claybert would have already organized a dragnet for his capture. As he pressed his foot harder on the gas pedal he looked in the rear-view mirror and noticed that a small gash had opened up on his forehead, blood running down his temples. Then he realized that his hands had also been cut, dried blood sticking to the steering wheel. He thought that he must have gotten sliced by pieces of glass that were being blown around by the wind entering the car through the broken back window.

As he was wiping the blood with a clean shirt he removed from his backpack, Chris found that he was able to think coherently again. The first thing he wondered about was where was he going. He did not know, but on some subconscious level, he understood that the reason he was leaving Demater, New Jersey was not simply to escape the abuse of his foster father—he was dead, after all.

Chris paused, noticing his wallet on the passenger seat. It was open to the picture of his mother, and she was staring up at him with her soft, bright eyes. Chris smiled. Now it was just the two of them, he thought.

He stared out at the open highway, not knowing where he was going, but trusting that he would get to the place he needed to be.

Chapter Two

After her last patient left that day, Saney let out a deep sigh of relief and deposited herself onto the futon chair in her office, unsure if she would ever be able to move again. She was thinking that the janitor might just find her in that exact spot the following morning unless she could summon the strength to get to her feet.

The paint on the frosted glass door that read DR. XENIA WIELAND had not even dried yet and Saney was ready for a vacation. She was just grateful that the day had finally ended. She had just seen ten patients in a ten-hour period. Incredibly, they had all been walk-ins. And when she was not in a session with somebody she was making appointments. She hadn't had a chance yet to interview for a secretary, and the phone had rung nonstop all day. She was already booked solid through the holidays. *Insane* was a legal term that Saney did not like to use, but that's just what the whole day had been like for her.

She had only arrived in Caldera the previous week and had not been expecting such a hefty caseload so soon. She thought she would be spending the first few weeks (at least) with prefatory matters and PR work, taking ample time to ingratiate herself with the people of Caldera, but not actually seeing patients.

Another part of her was just as excited as she was flabbergasted by the overwhelming need that the people of this burgeoning city had for her services. After all, she had come here specifically to test her theory—which she had first proposed in her doctoral thesis, but had never been fully validated to her liking—that people living in areas of intense and rapid growth were more prone to a wide range of psychological problems and psychoses than people in relatively static social and economic environments. Before Saney arrived in Caldera, she was confident that she would uncover plenty of credible evidence to support her supposition, but she had not imagined anything like this.

It truly was an opportunity of a lifetime. Saney would be conducting a clinical research study that could merit publication by the American Psychiatric Association, while at the same time doing what she loved most—treating patients. She was fortunate that such a psychosocial phenomenon had occurred in her lifetime so that she might be able to study it firsthand. With relatively few exceptions, such as San Francisco during the California gold rush, and perhaps Las Vegas, boomtowns were more mythical than real. Typically, your garden-variety thriving American metropolis like New York City experienced growth and expansion in fits and starts over a period of many decades.

Rome may not have been built in a day, Saney thought, but Caldera came awfully close. Starting out as a mere highway rest stop where truckers could load up on caffeine and sugar on their way to Albuquerque, Phoenix, and Southern California, Caldera had quickly become a sparkling jewel on the High Plains of New Mexico. The entire state population numbered around two million, with Caldera's 30 square miles, comparable in size to Manhattan, accommodating nearly a quarter of that. While straining under the weight of its own prosperity, the city continued to grow. And with all it had to offer, it seemed as though it would continue expanding indefinitely. With a strong and varied economy, it was fast becoming the state's leading center for business and commerce, anchored by competitive manufacturing and service industries. The metropolitan area was ranked high among the nation's best places to live. Its cultural center featured numerous theaters and museums that were nourished by a swift and convenient transportation system. From well-kept recreational facilities, shady parks, upscale shops, first-rate hotels, and five-star restaurants to a state-of-the-art hospital and a sound school system, Caldera lacked for nothing. Combining all that with an ideal climate of warm, sunny days and cool nights, it was easy to see why people were flocking here. But Saney knew there was often a high price to pay for that kind of success.

All at once Saney became aware that she had not eaten all day. Her hunger took precedence over everything else and somehow she managed to force herself off the chair, out of the high-rise building, and into a cab.

She had a million and one things on her mind as she sat in the back of the taxi on her way home. One of the two moving trucks she had commissioned to drive her belongings across most of the country had not shown up yet, so her patients had to sit in a futon chair that had been left behind by the last tenant in the office suite. The rest of her office furniture consisted of several items she borrowed from her apartment, including a stool and a folding table, which numbered among the few items her movers did not lose. She was determined not to let any of that bring her down. She would simply make do with what she had while she waited for her beautiful antique chaise lounge to arrive with the rest of her office furnishings.

Things were no better at home, with her clothes still in suitcases and the boxes containing some of her most prized antiques sitting in a truck somewhere between here and New York City.

Then there was the dream she'd had the night before. She could not remember any details, but when she woke she had been too frightened to fall back to sleep. Not only that, all day she had been unable to shake the cold feeling in her bones that the nightmare had left her with. On top of everything else, she was planning on returning her mother's call from the week before and letting her know where she was.

Saney was just staring blankly out of the cab's window, lost in her own thoughts, when she saw the sign for DELUDER BAKE SHOPS.

"Oh, could you please pull over here?" Saney yelled, struck by a sudden craving for a spinach pie. Her mouth was watering as the cabby, without saying a word, crossed two lanes of traffic and double-parked in front of the bakery. They were almost broad-sided by another taxi, whose driver leaned on his horn for a long time, then made a rude gesture with his hands as he passed. But for Saney, it was worth it.

She had been in another Deluder bakery yesterday near her apartment building. She had gone out to get a little exercise by taking a walking tour of her new surroundings. She'd only made it two blocks before she'd spotted the bakery and had decided to put off her fitness regiment for another day. And boy was she ever glad she had. There, she'd had the biggest, fattest spinach pie she'd ever had in her life. It was the size of a loaf of Italian bread and it was absolutely stuffed with spinach. She could not wait to get her hands on another one and eat it while watching Ray Milland in *Golden Earrings* tonight on Classic Cable Cinema.

"I'll just be a minute," she said as she got out of the cab. From the sidewalk the smell was overwhelming, and before Saney even walked into the bakery she could practically taste the thick, tasty dough with enough spinach inside to gag Popeye.

Once inside, she became aware that this bakery, although with a similar interior layout, was clearly bigger and newer than the one she had been in yesterday. She was relieved to find that it also shared the same menu. She did not know what it was about the bakery that drew her to it, but it was obvious she was not alone in her appreciation. The place was crowded. In fact, they were taking numbers. Saney pulled number forty-five.

They were serving seventeen.

She looked out at the cab still double-parked outside. This was going to be one expensive spinach pie, she thought, as she turned her attention on the bakery's clientele. The majority of people all fell into the same socio-economic class, as might be expected in a city as prosperous as Caldera. They were all well dressed and maintained an air of refinement even as they waited for their cakes, biscuits, and breads. Very similar were they in comportment to the Manhattanites that Saney had lived and worked around the previous two years. Here, however, only the women were wearing earrings, and both sexes seemed to have manicured fingernails.

There was one man who specifically caught her attention. He was standing against the far wall, near the door. Saney was not even aware that she was staring at him. Like the others, he was dressed nicely. While achieving a look of confidence, he also had a bearing about him that underscored a grounded sense of himself—a combination that was rare in men with money and looks. And whoever he was, he certainly had plenty of the latter. But there was something else about him that made him different, though Saney could not specifically identify what that was.

Saney began to wonder what she was doing. The romantic side of her could not be so easily suppressed, she supposed, a little embarrassed for indulging herself in such fantasy. Was not she supposed to be a new millennium woman, who need not submit to such a retrogression of gender roles? No, that was actually her mother's idealization. And Saney knew her own intemperance was just an innocent way of passing time in a crowd. But whether it was harmless fantasy or a pathetic waste of time, Saney had to admit to herself that she still had hope of finding someone she could spend the rest of her life with, and she was not about to apologize to N.O.W. or her mother for that. While Saney continued to watch this man, he kept his eyes on the digital number display and did not let them stray to look at anything or anybody, and he certainly did not notice Saney.

When a voice called out for number twenty-four, the man suddenly rocked forward on his heels and began to pick his way through the throng of people. He moved cautiously. Saney could not help smiling in amusement as she watched him track his way to the counter as if he were navigating a minefield. With practiced precision, he was able to make it all the way to the front of the bakery while managing to avoid even the most incidental contact with the other patrons.

Unable to stop a psychoanalytic perception from forming, Saney guessed that he might be suffering from some sort of somatoform disorder, trying to elude a host of communicable germs that are readily transmitted between large numbers of people who are gathered in a relatively small space.

Saney stepped forward as well, getting as close to the counter as she could. She was able to get within earshot and heard the man order two strips of pizza and a box of biscotti. His voice was not commanding, but it was not subdued either. There was no fluctuation in his pitch, but it was not a monotone. It was as if he thought speech was simply meant to convey information and nothing more.

As he paid for the items, Saney made sure she was standing close enough to him so that there would be no way he could avoid her as he was leaving. In fact, she was so certain that he was going to turn around and run right into her that she braced herself for the impact. But somehow he managed to dodge her, making a sharp pivot on his inside foot and twisting impossibly at the hip while at the same time dipping his shoulder to utterly miss her. At no point did he say anything or look at her. Then he just wiggled his way through the crowd in the same fashion and out the door.

Saney noticed that a man who must have just come into the bakery was looking directly at her. He was standing by the door. He had an amused smile on his face and a small sty in the corner of his right eye. She quickly turned away from him in embarrassment, realizing how she might look to someone who was secretly watching her. She might appear to have a personality disorder of her own—first nearly getting herself killed so she could have her daily spinach pie fix, and then blocking the exit so some guy she was fixated on would notice her. If Saney had observed someone as she'd just described herself, she would likely have recommended a swift committal to a well-guarded and well-padded institution.

As it was, she shrugged it off, but deep down she held a lingering hope that she might run into Number Twenty-Four again somewhere.

When Saney's number was finally called and the man behind the counter asked what she wanted, she replied, "Two pizza strips and a box of biscotti, please." The words just came out of her mouth before she could stop them. She must have still been daydreaming about Number Twenty-Four, she thought.

"Is this your first time visiting us here at Deluder Bake Shops," the man behind the counter asked.

"Yes," Saney said, then faltered. "No . . . Well, it's my first time at this location. I've been to the one over on Glenmere. How many Deluder bakeries are there, if you don't mind my asking?"

"Not at all. There are now thirteen Deluder Bake Shops throughout the metropolitan area."

"A baker's dozen," Saney said, smiling.

"Precisely. The one you visited previously was our first shop. This is our newest."

Even this man looked like every other guy in the bakery, and in Caldera for that matter, Saney thought. He was natty and on the not-so-tall side.

Suddenly she realized what it was about Number Twenty-Four that further set him apart from other men in town—he had to be over six feet tall. Saney was nearly six feet tall in her heels and she had to raise her head quite a bit as Number Twenty-Four passed to look into his eyes, which were hazel. Finally a man in Caldera that she did not have to look down on, she thought.

"The reason why I asked if you'd been here before," the man

continued, "is because first-time customers are given a box of biscotti of their choice, free with any purchase. Since this is your first time here, you may select either the butter rum, vanilla wafer, or chocolate almond."

"Butter rum sounds fantastic," Saney said, then removed a twenty from her purse and placed it on the counter.

"Butter rum it is," the man said. "Just like Mr. Bloom. And let me tell you, they are fantastic, although most people select either the chocolate or vanilla."

"Mr. Bloom?" Saney repeated.

"Yes, Mr. Julian Bloom. I don't suppose you know him, but he was a customer who was in here just a short time ago. He ordered the *exact* same thing you just did, right down to the butter rum biscotti." After handing Saney her change and the bag containing her order he said, "Thank you. Enjoy. And please come again."

"Thank you," she said and walked out of the bakery feeling like a schoolgirl because she had learned his name. Julian Bloom. Julian Bloom. She kept repeating his name in her head so she would not forget it. *Julian Bloom. Julian Bloom.*

She did not know what she was going to do with this bit of information, but she felt an odd exhilaration just the same. Stopping at the bakery certainly proved worthwhile after all, she thought as she got back into the waiting cab.

Julian Bloom. Julian Bloom.

Chapter Three

As soon as he leaned back in his chair he heard something in his back pop and he grimaced. "You're going to have to learn to sit up straight, old boy," Julian told himself, "if you want to continue walking upright."

He lifted the frames of his reading glasses and rubbed his eyes. He had been leaning over the computer for so long he did not realize how late it was. Feeling like a little snack, he remembered he still had a pizza strip left over and got up to get it out of the refrigerator. He was crossing the living room of the small rented house when, wearing only a pair of wool socks on his feet, he stubbed his toe on one of the many unpacked crates and boxes. Julian yelped like a kicked dog and hopped to the other side of the room. Leaning against a large stack of boxes for balance, he rubbed his throbbing toe and looked back at the living room floor to see what it was he had nearly tripped over. A small case, bound in dried and cracked leather, was lying only a few feet from him now after being booted across the room. With the heel of his foot he nudged the case. He heard a soft metallic clanking as its contents rattled around inside.

As Julian went to straighten up, his fingers rustled the edge of a small, but ornately wrapped Christmas present that was sitting atop the stack of boxes. He had placed it there after finding it on his doorstep earlier that day. There were no markings of any kind to indicate where it had come from or who had sent it. Julian feared that it was some kind of advertising gimmick, and opening the present might instantly enroll him in the Jelly Of The Month Club. So he just ignored it.

However, it did remind him of the office Christmas party on Sunday night, which he still was undecided about attending. He had only been in Caldera for a week and he was just starting to get familiar with the local environment and the matters of chief concern to him and his organization. All Julian wanted was to take his readings to determine the possible sources of local contamination. In comparison to that, the party was of little consideration. There was still a lot to do yet, and Julian figured that if anybody could find fault with him for being hardworking, then so be it.

Julian realized he was doing it again; trying to justify his social detachment. He got that way whenever he was working on a new project and felt any kind of interpersonal pressure at all. His typical reaction would be to instantly immerse himself in his work so deeply that he could not even think about anything else. And that was what he was doing now.

As he absently rubbed his toe, he thought about Caldera. While he knew that it was not at all unusual for a city that was experiencing enormous population growth to require a little assistance in keeping up with environmental mandates, the preliminary findings that Julian had recorded were especially alarming. He wanted to take more time to re-test the air, water and soil samples to be sure he was getting accurate readings. He was even thinking about having the same studies conducted by another agency to confirm his results. Things were that out of whack here.

Especially disconcerting to Julian was the saturation of lead and mercury in the atmosphere of a city that did not burn its garbage. Then there were the dozen other dismaying findings that Julian had detected elsewhere in its ecosystem. The soil and flora, for example, were both showing an inexplicable low-level infusion of sulfur. Acid rain would be the most obvious culprit, but there again, Caldera had no oil or coal-burning factories to hold accountable, not to mention its meager annual precipitation.

While nothing was conclusive yet, Julian's initial calculations were not promising, to put it mildly. He knew, however, that in order to facilitate any major change in how the people of Caldera viewed their environment, he would first have to increase his already painstaking research and fact-finding efforts. The tedious nature of his work did not put Julian off in the least. He was used to it. Nature and its complex beauty had always fascinated him, so environmental activism was a logical career choice. He often likened his job to that of a nurse, except that he got to work outdoors. Earth was like a sick patient, and she needed constant care. While there were many others who shared his concern, when Julian was busy working, he felt like he was the only one on that particular shift. The fact that he worked alone heightened that sense of exclusiveness. Julian was never a "people person" and everybody at Project Earth knew it, but when they needed to have the planet's pulse taken at some particular point on her surface, he was the one they called to read it, and he was more than happy to go.

Julian had traveled the world. In the United States there was hardly a square foot of ground that he had not traversed at one time or another. He moved around so much he had not been able to keep a permanent address for more than a year since he signed on full-time with Project Earth right out of graduate school. However, it was looking more and more like Caldera was going change his living arrangements for an indeterminable amount of time. But he would not know exactly how long he would need to stay until he got back out into the field and took a second set of readings.

Right now, however, all Julian could do was yawn in exasperation. He had been putting in some late nights since he'd arrived, pouring indefatigably over the data he had collected during the day. Maybe, Julian thought, it was beginning to catch up with him. He had a big day on tap tomorrow as well, when his data collection and analysis would be interrupted by a meeting with the local Project Earth board members. Julian thought it was a good time to knock off for the night. Those meetings always had a way of wearing on him. It was the only aspect of his job that he found personally disobliging.

But, Julian had to concede, it was all part of what it took to clean up a city's environment and make sure it stayed that way. In the end, it was all worth it. Every place he visited became a branch on the Project Earth tree—a testament to the impact of the organization's dedicated members and concerned citizens everywhere. If a problem were thought to exist in a given region, Julian would come in to conduct his analysis. Then, based on his data, the source of the problems would be pinpointed and comprehensive objectives would be established to offset them. Finally someone from the main office would fly in to oversee the project on an interim basis. That person was the conduit to area politicians and legislators, the one who would try to convince them that they would have to step up their environmental protection standards if they did not want to see the complete melt down of their city. This person was also the one who actually saw to it that the set up of the new Project Earth Chapter—utilizing volunteers from the community—went smoothly. Ron Tasker was the lead man on this project, and the man to whom Julian would be reporting his findings. With his toe still a little numb, Julian finally made it to the kitchen. He removed the unwrapped rectangular pizza slice from the refrigerator and, without even thinking about heating it up, bit into the thick tomato sauce and chewy dough. Even cold, it hit the spot. He only wished he had gotten more of them from the downtown bakery. Then he remembered the biscotti. The box was on the counter, and although he was never very fond of the crunchy Italian cookies, he ate them anyway. To his surprise they actually were quite tasty. He did not remember them being so sweet. Considering that they were free, they were that much more satisfying. A free box of biscotti seemed to be the way they welcomed strangers in this town, and that was all right with Julian. He made a mental note to go back to the bakery the next chance he had.

With his appetite sated, Julian shut down his computer and got ready for bed. The cool sheets felt good on his body and he fell quickly into a shallow, troubled sleep. Within minutes he became an unwilling participant in a frightful dream from which he tried but could not escape. In it, he was running. Being chased. Something was gaining on him, but looking back he could see nothing. Only the blurry landscape rushing by, like a Saturday morning cartoon—all shapes and whirling colors. Suddenly someone appeared in front of him, running as someone would in a dream, half floating legs taking short strides but covering enormous ground. Somehow Julian was keeping up. Then the person in front of him turned his head around and Julian saw the face contort in abject terror. Julian must have been wearing the same expression, or maybe there was a mirror in front of him, because the face staring back at him was his own. Julian wanted to open his mouth to scream, but when he did, no sound emerged. Then the face of the Julian in front of him voiced the scream that he was trying to usher forth. A cord of saliva stretched from the top jaw to the bottom lip. The shriek persisted, growing in cadence until it finally popped the thin nightmare bubble that Julian's mind had formed while he slept.

Julian woke thinking he had been screaming out loud, but he could not be sure, and he could remember almost nothing of the dream that had provoked him to cry out in the night. He sat up in bed for a moment, staring into the darkness and listening to the silence, which was broken only by the low humming of his computer, which Julian thought he had turned off before brushing his teeth and retiring.

He got out of bed and walked into the living room, awash in the iridescent light from the computer monitor. He was reaching for the OFF switch when he noticed something written on the screen. He stopped suddenly.

no one will ever hurt you again

Julian quickly reasoned that he must have written those words in a half sleeping state before he went to bed, and then neglected to turn off the computer. Now he did turn it off.

Walking back to the bedroom, he heard a strange sound coming from the basement. Something was striking the ground and making a soft, reverberating echo with each deliberate impact.

Julian had not even known there was a basement in the house, but as the sound persisted he was able to identify the small door to the basement that he had previously mistaken as a closet. Julian turned the handle. As the door swung open, a wedge of darkness greeted him. He flipped the switch on the inside wall and a single bulb illuminated a flight of wooden stairs with no handrails. The light was dim, barely able to hold the surging darkness at bay. Julian paused, listening silently. Whatever it was had stopped. He waited there a moment longer. When no further sound came from the basement he considered just closing the door and going back to bed, but he knew he would not be able to fall back to sleep until he had a closer look. He took the first step cautiously, the riser creaking beneath his bare feet. The wood was coarse and cold, and as he descended, the frigid air rose gradually up his body. When he reached the landing, his teeth were chattering.

Then the sound came again.

Julian looked around but saw nothing, but it was obvious now what was making the sound. Then Julian saw it—a child's rubber ball. It emerged from the darkness to his left, as if someone had tossed it. It bounced slowly in tiny looping arcs atop the dusty cement floor directly toward Julian. By the time it got within a few feet of him it had slowed considerably, and then it just rolled the rest of the way. The ball was bright red. It was barely moving by the time it kicked off the side of Julian's foot and scuttled to a stop nearby.

It was happening again, Julian thought with trepidation.

He looked up and peered into the darkness in the direction the ball had appeared. With more than a little hesitation, Julian stepped forward until he found the pull string for a hanging bulb. The light source, however, revealed only an unfinished basement and four empty walls. There was nothing to see except a few rusted metal support beams, an old boiler, some copper piping, and a bright red ball.

Julian was not quite sure what made him look down at the floor at that moment, but he almost jumped out of his skin when he saw the tiny bits of fingernails scattered near his feet. They looked like they had been bitten off and spit out.

When Julian left the cellar in darkness again and went back to bed to try to get some sleep, he knew that while he might have been able to explain away how he had left the computer on and how the message had gotten scrawled on the screen, the bouncing ball in the empty cellar and the fingernails on the floor could not be so readily dismissed.

It was happening again, he thought, and Julian was scared for the first time since he was a boy.

Chapter Four

Chris's head had dropped back against the car seat and the jolt back to consciousness strained a muscle high up on his neck. Now he opened his window and stuck his head out, hoping the rush of cool air on his face and the noise would keep him awake. He knew he would have to pull over to get some rest. It had been a long time since he woke from a ten-hour snooze behind an abandoned barn in Charlottesville. It had been the same amount of time since he last had anything substantial to eat.

He kept fairly close to the speed limit, not wanting to draw any more attention to himself than he already had by driving an old red Malibu pockmarked with dents and no rear window. Somehow he had avoided the law thus far, though the drive was not without its mishaps. He'd had to change a flat just after he had crossed the Tennessee border, and later had spent two hours in gridlock as a result of a major pile up during rush hour in Knoxville where I-81 and I-40 intersect.

By now, Chris was ready to pull into the first town that had a motel. The Chevy was comfortable enough, but Chris preferred an actual bed where he could really stretch out. He didn't even care if it cost him every penny he had left.

Just then Chris came upon a sign that read, WELCOME TO NEW MEXICO, LAND OF ENCHANTMENT, and he suddenly felt like he had arrived, or at least like he was done running for the first time since his journey had began, although he had experienced such intuitive thoughts before, on every other occasion he'd had his mother's picture in hand. This time he had not been consulting with her when the notion came over him to stop. He did not think much more about it, concentrating instead on what he saw beyond the dashboard—a vast arena of twinkling lights. It appeared on the edge of the distant horizon. As Chris drew nearer, he could see the outlines of tall buildings and an expansive city that straddled both sides of the highway. He was not too sure of his geography, but whatever city it was, Chris knew he would be calling it home for a while.

To the right was a large sign that read, CALDERA NEXT FIVE EXITS. Beside it was a smaller sign, old and dilapidated and hanging askew on a rotted post—Caldera, Population 345.

Chris slowed and took the first ramp down into the city. He could not believe its immensity. It was even bigger than Newark and Jersey City, the only other big cities he had been in. There was a lot of activity for this time of the morning, Chris thought. It made driving difficult for him because he did not know where he was going. There were road cones everywhere he looked, and tall cranes frozen and silent before half-finished buildings. A city this size might be just what he needed to safely lay low for a while, and with people so different from one another, he knew he would go virtually unnoticed. In a place like this, he would fit in by not fitting in, and then he would become free to move about without suspicion. At the very least, Chris figured he could pick up some part-time work and save enough money to get his car fixed before moving on. But there would be time enough to think about that after he got some sleep.

Chris drove slowly along the city streets until he found exactly what he was looking for. A green neon motel sign in the shape of a cactus with a blinking pink arrow beneath it. The Bonanza Motor Inn boasted COLOR TV and FREE HBO.

There were few cars in the lot and perhaps a couple dozen rooms. He pulled into a spot directly in front of the office door, whose chimes on the inside handle announced his presence as he entered. The office was so small that he had only taken two paces before walking right into the counter. No lights were on and there was a pervasive odor that Chris could not readily identify. A door behind the counter was closed.

Suddenly the tiny room was flooded with so much white light that Chris became temporarily blinded.

"Why did you come here?" a timorous voice said.

Chris, squinting and pressing the side of one hand against his forehead to simulate the bill of a cap, saw that the door behind the counter was cracked open only enough to accommodate the face of the man who had spoken. He was older, balding, the hair on the side of his head sticking straight up. His beard stubble was white. His eyes were blinking forcefully. His tongue was darting in and out of his mouth. None of these things he seemed able to control.

"I came in to get a room."

"No. Why did you come *here*?" The muscles on the man's cheeks and around his lips contracted spasmodically, contorting his face into grimace after grimace.

Chris thought about it for a moment, then said, "I saw the sign."

The man's eyes widened, but continued to blink incessantly. "I know who your father is," he said in an accusatory tone.

"What?"

"I know who your father is. You get out now. You're not welcome here. You hear me? GET OUT!"

Chris heard the click before he noticed the shotgun barrel poking out of the darkness. The man's arms were jerking rapidly and Chris was afraid the gun was going to go off by accident. He quickly grabbed the door handle and pushed. But the door would not open. An electric pulse of terror surged through his body, then he realized that the door had to be pulled open, which he did. It was all he could do to keep from

39

screaming.

As soon as Chris was outside, he recognized the smell he had first identified inside the motel office. It was bread. The smell of a bakery. And then he jumped into his car and turned the engine over. With his back tires spinning out behind him, the Malibu slued out of the parking lot and into the street.

Now that he was out of range of the shotgun-toting motel owner, Chris began to wonder why the man was asking about his father. Did he know his foster father? Did he know Chris was involved in his death? Was there a WANTED poster of him in the post office already? It did not make sense. These were the kinds of riddles that his mother had always provided the answers to. He took her picture out now to coax some kind of feedback from her, but none came.

He returned it to his wallet, and when he next looked up, the traffic light ahead was turning red. He had to stop short to keep from rolling through the intersection.

As he sat waiting, the scent of baked dough and confection could not be disregarded. He looked up and there it was—a bakery right on the corner. From this position, Chris spied two men in white aprons as they emerged from a side door. Each was carrying a tray of bread out back behind the shop.

Chris, even in his sleep-deprived state, was unable to resist the enticing aroma. He pulled his car into the rear of an adjacent Sunoco, killing the lights and the engine. From this position he could see an open dumpster behind the bakery and the two white-aproned men walking back with empty trays. Chris quietly got out of his car. There was an air hose nearby which he retrieved and then hunkered down behind the front end of his Chevy, pretending to be checking his tire pressure.

Peering over the hood, Chris watched the bakers reemerge with two more trays full of bread, which were hot and steaming, fresh from the oven. A third man, who was much older than the bakers and wearing a suit, was trailing them.

"I cannot sell that bread now," the man in the suit yelled. "I *will not* sell it. And this will happen every time the recipe is not followed precisely."

The bakers dumped the trays of bread into the dumpster, then had to walk by the irate man in the suit to get back inside the building. But the man did not move out of their way. One baker managed to slip by him, but as the second one attempted to do the same, an arm flashed out and struck him on the side of the face. The baker recoiled and staggered backward through the side door.

Chris was shocked by what he had just witnessed. He felt an instant hatred for the man in the suit and an instant affinity with the baker. He watched the man in the suit stop just inside the door and turn around, looking over in Chris's direction before finally retreating into the building and slamming the door shut behind him.

After a few moments had passed and Chris was sure they would not be returning, he stood up and casually proceeded toward the dumpster behind the bakery. Without hesitation, he reached into the refuse container and picked out a loaf of bread as if he had every right to do so. It was still warm and smelled like cinnamon. He ripped off a corner and greedily stuck it into his mouth.

Soon after he'd began chewing he just stopped, and his jaw slackened. What Chris was eating did not taste bad—in fact, it did not have a taste at all. What made the bread so unsavory was the feeling it had in his mouth. Chris did not know what a mouthful of maggots felt like, but he imagined that this would be close. The chewed dough seemed to be moving, breaking apart into still smaller pieces and wriggling around on his tongue. Chris pitched forward and opened his mouth, letting the half-swallowed hunk of bread fall to the ground.

Looking down at it now, Chris realized that it was just bread after all. His stomach, however, could not be so easily convinced, and it clenched, as if trying to turn itself inside out. There was not a thing he could do to stop from retching, which was made even worse because he had almost nothing to disgorge.

He tossed what was left of the loaf back into the dumpster and was wiping his mouth when he saw someone out of the corner of his eye. It was the man in the suit, standing in the open doorway at the side of the bakery, staring down at him.

"I gather the bread was not to your liking, young man?" said the man in the suit. "I *told* them that this would happen if they did not follow the recipe precisely."

He continued to stare at Chris with no expression that the young boy could read; he did not appear to be angry, repulsed, or sympathetic.

"Young man, I would like to help you and I hope you will allow me to do so. As a local businessman I am fortunate to be in a position to serve the people of this community in ways beyond simply slaking their appetite for baked goods. Our success in greater Caldera has enabled us to extend charity deep into the community. For example, food is donated and shelters have been built for the disenfranchised in the name of our bake shops." The man in the suit stepped in front of Chris and put an arm on the boy's shoulder. "It appears that you are in a transition period yourself and could use a little assistance."

"I don't need any handouts," Chris sneered and pulled away from the man.

"Some people might not be so understanding, seeing you as you are . . . desperate, filthy, and trespassing. They might even be inclined to call the police. I, however, would like to make an offer to you. I can give you a place to stay and a job. Both for as long or as short a time as you like. What do you say to that?"

"You struck that baker!"

"I'm afraid I did. You are right. I was wrong for doing that and I've since apologized to him. It was totally uncalled-for. My desire to give the public the best goods and services possible is no excuse for what I did. Now how about it?"

Chris needed time to think. He was confused. His lack of sleep was starting to become a factor. Maybe that was why he could no longer perceive anything from his mother, he thought. If only she could get through to him now. She would know what to do. Chris felt the mounting pressure to make a decision on his own. He knew he did not like the man in the suit and did not want his help. On the other hand, he could use it. Besides the sleep, he could also use the money. And the man had promised that he would not notify the police. Besides, it would only be for a short time. Just as long as it took to pay for the damage to his car, anyway.

The man must have read his mind, because he smiled and said, "You will find that it is all for the best. What is your name?"

"Chris."

"How would you like a nice home cooked meal, Chris?"

"That sounds great, but I could use some sleep."

"You will be able to rest comfortably for as long as you want. You can eat when you awaken. Come with me now. I have a car waiting out front."

"Wait," Chris said. "What about my car?"

The man looked around toward the gas station where Chris's Chevy was parked.

"Oh, yes. Your car. You seemed to have had a little . . . mishap. Well, I can arrange to have that taken care of for you. It'll be completed before you even awaken."

"I want to earn the money to have it fixed," Chris insisted.

"If that is what you desire, Chris, we can employ you at one of the bake shops. The work is hard, but it pays very well. It is our belief that minimum wage produces minimum effort. And you can work as many hours as you want."

The man motioned to Chris to follow him inside. They wound their way through the rear of the bake shop, past many aproned bakers, and continued uninterrupted to the front of the bakery, where several other workers, dressed in red and black uniforms, were getting things ready for the start of the business day.

"Rebecca," the man said to one of the girls without stopping, "I'll be on the road most of the day. You know how to reach me if you need me. OK, dear?"

"Yes, sir," said Rebecca, a young woman with fair skin and fiery red hair. Chris looked back at her and she smiled. Then they were outside and Chris was whisked into a big black car. The seats were made of the softest leather Chris had ever felt. As they pulled away from the bakery, Chris saw the sign on the front of the building: DELUDER BAKE SHOPS.

The car's windows were tinted, and looking through the glass as they drove through the city in the predawn darkness made Caldera look even stranger to the boy. The man in the suit did not say a word as he drove, and Chris had time to wonder if he had made the right choice.

"Hal, you listen to me," the county sheriff said, "this little bastard killed my brother. It's been forty-eight hours and the state police haven't done a goddamn thing. They had their chance, now I'm going after him myself. My way."

Claybert Crowley, seated now, was somewhat restrained, though still visibly agitated. He was unshaven and in street clothes. Seated across a large mahogany desk, wearing a blue monogrammed silk robe, was county attorney, Hal Smith. They were in the D.A.'s sumptuous, black walnut-finished home study.

"NO, YOU LISTEN TO ME," said Hal Smith, rising to his feet. "I will not allow a one-man lynch mob to go scouring the country looking for this kid. And I certainly am not going to waste all of this county's time and money when the state police are better equipped to handle this kind of thing. Believe me, they're not sitting on their hands on this one. In fact, they had an unconfirmed sighting of the boy yesterday on I-40 in Tennessee. When they do catch him, and they will, he'll be extradited and the trial will take place right here in our court. Until then, I have other criminal matters that need tending to. There have been nine farmhouses burglarized this month alone. Someone poisoned Lyle Trainor's feed with cyanide and killed fifteen of his best milking cows. And Mrs. Meehan's granddaughter was raped at knifepoint over the weekend. I've got more than enough on my plate and I don't need to be doing work that the state police should be doing. And I don't appreciate you banging on my door at four in the morning, shouting loud enough to wake the whole house, and stinking of liquor. I have a good mind to have you arrested on a disorderly. Now, if you'll excuse me, I have a busy day ahead of me."

Now Claybert rose, swiping his arm across the desk in the same motion. He was a large man, six and a half feet tall and as wide in the body as a stuffed grizzly. The large limb displaced everything in its path. Papers, lamp, telephone, and FAX machine all went crashing to the hardwood floor. He leaned across the desk and the D.A. recoiled.

"The kid throws my brother out a third floor window and kills him in cold blood and you tell me stories about rapes and robberies and Lyle Trainor's cows. You got some nerve, Hal, you ungrateful son-of-a-whore. It was my brother who got you your job. He got me into office as well. We owe it to him to get this kid ourselves."

"Clay, I'm very grateful to your brother and your family. I'm just trying to do this thing the right way, that's all. Go through the proper channels. Protocol. All that crap that I'm supposed to do as the district attorney. Can't you understand that?"

"I understand this: There's not going to be any trial. I'm still the sheriff around here, and if I have to hunt down that kid and kill him myself, then that's what I'm gonna do. And don't you dare try to stop me."

Claybert turned and lumbered toward the closed door, pulling it open so hard that it struck the interior wall with enough force to splinter the walnut finish.

"Claybert," Hal yelled after him, "come back here. For Christ's sake, Claybert."

The D.A. could only shake his head as he surveyed the localized destruction Claybert had caused. As he began the task of putting his desktop back together, it seemed to him that he was always cleaning up after something one of the Crowleys had done. Sure, they had helped get him into the D.A.'s office, but he had been paying the price ever since. Now, for the first time, Hal Smith questioned if it was all worth it. One thing was for certain—he knew that the destruction that was going to follow would be much more widespread by the time this whole thing was over, and Hal did not know if he would be able to clean that up.

Chapter Five

Her back hurt and her feet were starting to blister. She stopped suddenly, looked at the heavy brush all around, and began to think about heading back. There was nobody in sight, and every direction looked the same to Saney. She did not know why her patient had insisted on having their session in the woods. She was even less clear why she had consented.

Only the occasional trill of insects broke the preternatural quiet. It was midday, but little direct sunlight escaped the high canopy of leaves. Inch by inch, the shadows began to lengthen. Suddenly the feeling came over her that she was being watched and she got a little scared. Then, when she heard the snapping of twigs and the brushing of leaves—the sounds of somebody walking through the woods—she got a lot scared. She thought she caught movement out of the corner of one eye, but when she looked in that direction there was nothing to see but trees and brush. Despite what her eyes told her, the feeling was strong that not only was somebody out there watching her, but moving toward her as well.

Now completely terrified, Saney started to shift forward, moving slowly at first, but with increasing speed, until finally she broke into a full run. The woods raced past her at dizzying speeds, but she knew that whatever was chasing her was keeping up.

Then, when Saney turned to look over her shoulder, her legs buckled. She fell headlong, striking the ground on her right side before skidding to stop. Inexplicably, the earth and the brush continued to rush by.

Then she saw it. It came into full view, standing over her, an abomination too profane for words. The texture of the figure's dark flesh was corrugated with deep furrows. It was not immediate, but Saney quickly came to the realization that whatever it was she was looking at was made of wood—an eight-foot tree that followed the physiological contours of a man, exactly. It had a long crooked nose and a sharp chin. Its eyes were narrow slits and it had a hollowed-out knothole for a mouth. But its bark was pliant, for beneath its surface it twisted and shifted subtly as if by unseen muscles. It's chest expanded. Between its legs was an upraised knob-like branch. When Saney felt the creature's hot breath in her hair as it leaned close to her, she opened her mouth to scream as loud as she could.

Saney woke with her cry echoing around the bedroom. In front of her, an antique mahogany George III chest-on-chest caught the first rays of dawn. As she stared at its dark surface, the swirls and patterns in the wood seemed to become animated, trying to form images. Saney quickly turned her eyes away and got out of bed.

As she showered and dressed, Saney reflected on the images in her dreams and what they meant. She even wondered if she had chosen a career in psychiatry in order to prevent her own insanity, to learn how to use the mechanisms of this branch of medicine so that she could better understand what she had gone through in the woods that afternoon in her childhood. While she was aware of the events that had spawned the bad dreams of the past few nights, her deepest fear was that the trauma of the incident would suddenly and completely overtake her one day when she least expected it, and just when she thought she had it all under control. She knew that the memories would always be with her, to some degree, for the rest of her adult life, but she could not help feeling perplexed and a little agitated by the nightmare just the same.

Perhaps it was just her psyche reminding her of the incident so that she would not repress it completely. Nobody was more aware of the psychological dangers this defense mechanism could cause a person, and it actually made good sense that she did not distance herself too far from the past ordeal.

Before Saney left her apartment that morning on her trek to her downtown office, she determined that she was not going to completely forget about the emotions that had resurfaced in her sleep. She would talk to somebody about it. A therapist. Perhaps her mother. Even a stranger. She knew it did not matter. But the fact remained that there were a lot of other people in the city with much more serious problems who needed her help, and they would take priority. She would be fine.

As she waited for the elevator in front of her tenth story apartment, her mind was curiously blank. When the doors opened and she stepped inside she did not even notice the man standing in the far corner.

"Polly?"

Saney was so startled she reacted as if he had yelled in her ear.

"I'm sorry," the man said. "I didn't mean to alarm you. I thought you were someone else. I can see now that you're not, but the similarity in the profile is uncanny. Sorry again."

"That's okay." She was about to turn away when the man extended his hand.

"I'm Ron, by the way."

He was handsome, with dark hair and gray eyes. He wore an expensive suit that matched his eyes. The designer label was meant to impress. Saney was not. She hesitantly took his hand, but when she attempted to pull hers away again, she felt his grip tighten. When he finally loosened it, she jerked her arm back so hard that her elbow struck the wall behind her.

"It's nice to meet you . . ."

"Xenia," she said, with an obvious edge in her voice. She had always insisted that people call her by the moniker, Saney. This time she did not.

"I have a friend in the building," he said. "I don't live here myself."

Saney felt like yelling, HALLELUJAH! Then the elevator began to slow.

"Xenia is a beautiful name. It fits you very well. Is it of German origin?"

"It's Hungarian, actually."

"Really! Is that where your parents are from?"

"Yes. I was born there as well."

"How interesting. So are you considered a resident of Hungary?"

"I came to this country on a student visa to attend New York University. I've been here ever since." She knew she was probably telling this guy more than he needed to know, but she did not want to be standing in the elevator with this guy in complete silence either.

"Have you been naturalized yet?"

Why doesn't this elevator stop already? "I have my final hearing in about two weeks."

"That's fascinating. I've been practically every place you can imagine, but I've never been to Hungary and I can't recall ever meeting a native Hungarian."

The elevator doors finally opened and Saney made her escape. She stepped through the door into the foyer and thought she was home free, when she suddenly felt a strong hand lock around her elbow, forcing her to stop.

"I hope you don't think I'm being forward, Xenia," Ron began, "but I was wondering if you'd like to get together for dinner some time." He reached into the inside pocket of his jacket with his other hand and removed a small card. "You don't have to answer right now," he continued. "That's my voice mail number. As much as I travel, it's really my home number." He gave a little laugh, then smiled winsomely. He was still holding the card out in front of her, and after a long moment, when she still did not give any indication that she was going to take it, he just stuffed it into the side compartment of her purse. Then he released her arm and walked out of the building ahead of her.

Saney stood there a moment, incensed and utterly repulsed. Despite his looks and well-groomed exterior, she thought he was probably the most vile man she had ever come across in her life. Her experience as a psychiatrist taught her that it was impossible to tell anything about a person based on what they looked like. Words to live by, she thought, dismissing the encounter as an unfortunate occurrence.

She thought she had put the man out of her mind, but Saney was still feeling uneasy when she got into her cab. The guy had given her the creeps, much the same way that her early morning dream had. She asked the driver to turn the heat up all the way, but even that could not suppress her goose bumps.

Perhaps she needed to speak to someone sooner than she thought. If she was not in the right frame of mind, she knew she would be of little use to the people she treated. All she had to do was talk to someone about her problems and they would go away. Wasn't that how it was supposed to work? she thought as she was driven to her office where people paid her all that money to listen to them talk about their problems.

Saney was still a little anxious when the taxi pulled in front of her office building. She only wished she had stopped by the bakery to get something sweet in her system and maybe get her day back on a more positive track. She settled for microwaved water, Folgers, and NutraSweet, hoping that it would have the same effect.

It did not.

He did not want to chance losing the Hungarian, so he

decided to follow her. When she paused before getting into her cab and looked up in his direction, he thought she had spotted him. She looked a little scared, but Ron knew she would not have been able to see him through his Jaguar's tinted windows.

As he tailed the unsuspecting cab through the city, Ron reflected on his good fortune. Not only did Xenia represent the forty-seventh and final piece in his European sex puzzle, but she was one of the most beautiful woman he had ever seen. She had big brown eyes and shoulder length chestnut hair. As for her body, what little he could detect beneath her pants suit looked very promising.

Outside the U.S., Ron was rarely in a position to sleep with a woman so physically appealing. When he met a woman who was from a country he had never been to, he was never picky. He could always upgrade if a better one came along, but in this case, he knew that if he ever did get another opportunity at a Hungarian woman, there would be little chance that she would be more attractive than Xenia.

He already knew where she lived. He knew her floor from where she had gotten on the elevator. He even knew her last name was Wieland, because as he'd passed the apartment mail boxes in the foyer he'd glanced at the names of the tenth floor residents and saw only one with a first initial X. Now, as he watched her exit the taxi in front of a large downtown skyscraper, his file on Xenia Wieland was nearly complete. He now knew where she worked, so if she did not call him, he would know where to find her at all times. What made it even more exciting for Ron was that the clock was ticking. He only had a few weeks before she turned into a pumpkin and became just another American girl. He would give her one week to call him and give herself to him. That would be the easy way. After that, the final week would be his to just take her. That would be the hard way. And to Ron, it did not matter, the easy way or the hard way, so long as he had his way.

With that thought, Ron smiled broadly. He was glad he had taken this assignment in Caldera. The Eskimo woman he had met at the airport the previous night would have made the whole trip worthwhile in itself. He got a Manitoba Province upgrade out of it, and now a Hungarian falls into his lap. It just goes to prove once again, he thought, that sometimes the best things in life happen when you least expect them.

With his mind and his libido at ease, he could once again concentrate on his work. He had meetings to attend all day, and now he would be able to sit through them with renewed vigor. He checked his watch and realized that he had more than enough time to grab a quick shower and relax for awhile. However, when he got back to his place and removed the Canadian woman's driver's license from his pocket, the trophy sparked within him a more passionate need to continue to push himself forward, onto the next conquest, like some out-of-control hobbyist/collector. As satisfying as the Eskimo pie had been, it was nothing compared to what was to come. He had work to do that he knew was far more important, but he quickly became overwhelmed by a gnawing, all-consuming sense of anticipation, and he wound up putting aside Caldera and Project Earth, opting instead to take a look at the Big Board.

He had not been able to focus on his work since he'd arrived here. Maybe he was just having too much fun, he thought as he called up the file, "world conquests," on his computer.

Instantaneously, a directory of subfiles appeared. The names of the thousands of women he had slept with and their countries of origin were cross-referenced every way imaginable. First he clicked on GEOG. Then, from the numerous choices that followed, he selected EUROPE and a map of the continent emerged. All of the countries were shaded gray except for Hungary, which remained white. He clicked on it and an empty screen appeared. He paused, contemplating if he should go ahead or not, then touched a button that brought up an information grid. He typed in XENIA WIELAND and then pressed another button.

IS THERE ANY OTHER INFORMATION AVAILABLE? flashed across the screen. Tasker typed NO and the computer gave this reply, CROSS REFERENCING. A second later, the computer generated an image of Europe. Only now, Hungary, like every other European country, was shaded. Tasker then went back and clicked on WORLD from the geographical listings. A representative map of the entire planet was displayed. But for a few small countries in obscure regions of the world, the entire globe was shaded.

Tasker just stared at the screen, as if in a trance. All of a sudden the shade on Hungary disappeared. He clicked on the country and found that Xenia's name had been deleted. He tried to type it back in, but when he did this, his own name appeared instead. After a second attempt and the same results, he clicked back onto the world map, and what he saw made him cringe.

One by one, all of the countries lost their highlight and reverted to white. Instinctively, Tasker banged the laptop with the back of his hand, thinking that would straighten the problem out. He clicked on Italy and his name came up there as well. Egypt. Brazil. Ireland. All of them featured his name and vital stats.

He did not know what was happening. Had his computer succumbed to a cybergenic virus? Was this a belated version of the Y2K "millennium bug" that doomsdayers had theorized about? Was he about to lose all the information of his sexual globetrotting that he had compiled—his life's work? Would he have to start all over again, woman by woman, country by country? Or maybe it had all been a fantasy to begin with, he thought with dreaded horror, the way he had been fantasizing about Xenia.

But he had been to all of those places, he reasoned, and he remembered a lot of the women, so it could not all be a lie. Even false memories could not seem *this* real. But he pondered the possibility anyway.

"NOOO-OO!" Tasker screamed out in frustration without even realizing it as he stood with the PC raised above his head. Just as he was about to smash it to the floor, he noticed that the screen was once again dominated by shades of gray. He lowered the computer and saw that it had been restored to the way it was before it went haywire. Even Hungary was shaded.

It was not a virus or Y2K after all. His mind had just played a trick on him. Tasker took it as a warning that he was getting too cocky, too sloppy. He placed his computer back on the desk and removed Xenia's name. Hungary was no longer shaded. Not yet. It would have to wait.

But Tasker would not wait too long.

Chapter Six

After the meeting broke up, Julian took extra time to gather up his things and file them into his briefcase. He was hoping for an opportunity to talk to Tasker alone, to reiterate some of his concerns. Julian had not held anything back. He had given the board all the data he had gathered, had specified the dangers that the city's rapid growth would have on the natural environment if left unabated. However, no one seemed overly concerned. The meeting was more of a formality than a real attempt to right Caldera's environmental wrongs. The city mayor, in fact, openly frowned with suspicion, calling for further testing and tangible proof of all the problems that were suspected. Julian could not believe it. Taking that kind of position was more than a little careless . . . it was downright dangerous. But Julian did not say anything. While he was confident he could provide them with the proof they asked for, he wanted to make sure he had the backing of the man who would have the greatest influence on the success of Project Earth in Caldera.

When Julian looked up again, everyone had cleared the room except for an attractive blonde woman from the Environmental Protection Agency. Tasker had her attention and it was easy to see why. He was outgoing and gregarious, a real people person and a ladies man, the complete antithesis of himself, Julian thought. The only thing the two of them had in common besides Project Earth was a life in transit. It seemed that everywhere Julian found himself, Tasker would be there as well. But he was usually heading up several projects at a time, so he was constantly flying back and forth all over the world.

Finally the woman left and he and Tasker were alone.

"Say, Ron," Julian said as he approached Tasker, "you got a minute?"

Tasker hesitated, then looked at his watch. "Yeah, sure," he said with some degree of uncertainty. "What's on your mind?"

"Look, Ron, I know it's not my place to say, and I'm probably out of line for saying it, but I feel compelled to tell you that you really need to go after these guys. Push hard for strict legislation and tight control on this one."

Tasker just looked at him coolly. "I have a handle on it," he said. "But I don't think it's time to hit the panic button just yet."

"According to the data I collected, the levels of toxicity in the air, soil, water, and vegetation in and around Caldera are all through the roof—everything from carbon dioxide to radon." Julian began pulling data sheets out of his briefcase for Tasker's benefit and placed them on the conference table in front of him. "As you can see they're all highly irregular."

Tasker did not so much as glance at the material. "Well, maybe your instruments are faulty. Have you ever thought of that?"

"I intend to take all new readings, but I think it would be wise if we had the Agency for Toxic Substances and Disease Registry conduct separate field tests."

"What I recommend, Julian, is you check your instruments, then take the readings again. And while you're out there—since they want to see some physical manifestation of these environmental ills—go and find a two-headed turtle or something. Isn't that your area of expertise? If there are no critters being harmed, then people won't be harmed either, right? And if things really are as bad as you say, then there's got to be something out there to prove it." Tasker picked his briefcase off the floor and then paused, looking at Julian as if to say, *Is that it*?

"I think we should get started right now filling out the paper work and getting all the necessary signatures to petition for Superfund money."

"Julian, that money is allocated for the clean up of hazardous toxic waste sites and to prosecute violators."

"And to safeguard the public against immediate threats from pollution."

"Nobody but you sees this situation as an immediate threat. Now, I can see you're going at this thing full throttle. And your enthusiasm is commendable. But take my advice and ease off a bit. Things will work out best for everyone if we take one step at time. OK? Now if you'll excuse me, I have another meeting to get to."

After Tasker walked out of the room, Julian collected his data sheets and stuffed them back into his briefcase. *Ease off*, he thought. What kind of advice was that? In the hallway, Julian saw that the elevator was full, and resigned himself to wait for the next one. Before the doors closed, he caught a glimpse of Tasker. Standing beside him, Julian noticed a tall man wearing a dark suit and a black overcoat. He seemed to be looking right at Julian. He had an odd smile on his face and a mole of some kind in the corner of one eye.

"Keep me posted, Julian," Tasker yelled as the doors closed.

More people were waiting on the floor now, and when the sound of dual electronic chimes announced the arrival of two elevator cars moments later, Julian lingered back. He watched as everyone herded into the same elevator and then he jumped into the other one. His peripheral senses immediately informed him that he was not alone. He could smell the strong but pleasant scent of a woman's perfume, but he did not look around. He just shifted to the other side of the car after pressing the first floor button. The doors closed and the woman's perfume became stronger and more pleasant. Then Julian felt the floor push against his feet and he knew he had gotten on the UP elevator.

Resigned to the fact that he would be getting down to the first floor the long way, Julian just stared up at floor numbers going by.

"Number twenty-four," the woman said, and stepped a little closer. She was peering at Julian. Her scent was intoxicating at this range.

"Number twenty-four," she said again. "I knew it."

Finally Julian turned around to face her. "Excuse me?"

"You were number twenty-four. At the bakery yesterday. I was forty-five. Small world, huh?"

"Yeah," was all Julian could think to say.

"It was pretty crowded in there. Is it always like that?"

Julian shrugged. "I wouldn't know."

"Oh," the woman said, surprised. "How was the pizza?"

Now it was Julian who looked surprised.

"I happened to overhear you order," the woman added.

"Yeah, it was good. Real good."

"I love their spinach pies. I bet everything they make is good." Julian hoped she would keep talking because he did not know what to say next.

Suddenly the elevator came to a stop. The doors opened and three people rushed in, wedging themselves between them. However, because of their height, they could still see each other's face. She took her time getting out, and Julian dared to follow her progress as she moved away from the elevator down to the 42nd floor hallway. Julian was delighted and amazed to find her looking back at him. She was smiling. It was warm and angelic. The warm smile of an angel whose name he did not know.

Then the doors closed and she was gone. However, her lingering fragrance stayed behind, and at that moment Julian realized he had made a mistake. He should not have looked at her so long.

Now he was glad he did not know her name. The dreams he

had been having, along with the message he found on his computer, the ball in the basement and the fingernails all served as reminders to Julian that even the most superficial bond between him and the woman could have disastrous ramifications. That was just the way it was, starting with the death of his parents when he was an infant and then *every single person* he had ever cared for after that, as if he were some flesh and blood idol who bore bad luck to anyone he came in contact with. Any person who was unlucky enough to develop any type of relationship with him at all had the life expectancy of a goldfish.

A competing emotion told him that it was crazy to be living that way, and he was getting tired of it. For the longest time he considered it something he just had to live with, like any other hardship or disability. Maybe now he was thinking that it was time to take control of his life. But Julian had been through this before too, and each time somebody ended up dead. There had been times before when he would get so lonely that he would ignore all the risks. The last time was when a business associate wanted to set him up on a blind date and Julian foolishly consented. He took the woman out once, but the day before they were supposed to go out a second time, she fell ill, diagnosed with a blood infection. A week later, she died when the bacterium attacked her heart.

Now, he was being foolish again.

Still, as he was walking out of the building to the parking garage, he could not help feeling cheated, knowing that he would never get to know the woman on the elevator. The smell of her perfume was in his clothes, but he kept telling himself that it was better this way, and that if he attempted to become further involved with her, it would not last, like all the others before. And when it finally did end, there would be a lot of spilled blood.

A.J. zipped himself into his full-length Tyvek suit beside the open trunk of City Car 49. As he slipped on his silver booties he drew in one last mouthful of smoke. Then he crushed out his cigar in the dust and popped two aspirins, swallowing them dry. After he pulled the cartridge respirator over his nose and mouth he stuffed his arthritic fingers into a pair of heavy rubber gloves. With a flashlight in one hand and a .45 automatic in the other, A.J. padded slowly down the side of the slope where he was parked.

He was on the farthest outskirts of western Caldera, where the city gave way to the plains. As A.J. descended down into a shallow gorge, the city, which loomed in the distance like a mirage, slowly disappeared from his view altogether. It was here that the environmental specialist for the Caldera Public Works Department found what he was looking for. The cement pipe was five feet in diameter, but it would narrow considerably as it neared the city and joined its sewer lines deep underground. The pipe was originally constructed to serve as an aqueduct to carry water from the Canadian River into a tiny town called Caldera, to help its growth. But before the pipe could be completed, Caldera was all grown up. Natural springs were discovered and the aqueduct was no longer needed. Now all it was used for was sewage overflow relief.

A.J.'s job was to determine if the pipe should be sealed off or destroyed altogether because of the fear that the only purpose it served was helping a certain species of small, brown, furry and four-legged vermin to proliferate.

Right away he noticed the grease marks along the inside edge of the pipe entrance, betraying the presence of *rattus norvegicus*. However, he was more concerned with the area around the pipe, and after only a short time of surveillance he found it honeycombed with rat runs. A complete infestation. Even where he could not see the small holes in the earth, he knew they were there because of how the ground had settled in places, becoming uneven and rutted.

Perhaps this was all vacated real estate, A.J. hoped, and they had since moved on to another city where there was a better supply of food and more suitable harborage, like Santa Fe or Albuquerque. But there was no real chance of that, he concluded. He knew Caldera was more than capable of supporting large numbers of rats for a long, long time.

A.J. could have just baited the entire area with blocks of Talon, but the little bastards had probably become resistant to the bloodcurdling anticoagulant. Besides, he had planned on investigating the inside of the pipe. At least part of it, anyway. It was something nobody had done up to this point, and it was long overdue. The rat problem was so far out of control, A.J. felt that if he did not try to do something about it right now, the entire city might be completely overrun. It was just what he had been afraid of, and now it looked as if he was about to substantiate his worst fear. He had tried talking to his boss about hiring more men and stockpiling supplies and safety equipment in case of such an occurrence, but he had been given the old it's-not-in-the-budget song and dance.

A.J. did not quit there, however. He had gone over his boss's head, seeking to generate political interest by appealing to both state and federal officials. The few legislators he had found who shared his concern did not dare stir up civic panic, which a rat infestation was sure to evoke, especially in an election year.

So here he was, about to walk into a sewage runoff pipe by himself so he could get some kind of tail count on the rat population in Caldera. Since nobody else was willing, A.J. became the city's only hope.

He was not surprised that he had yet to spot one of the small-eared, blunt-snouted rodents. Inside the pipe, however, it would be like night, and activity would be rampant.

As he took his first step inside the pipe, A.J. prepared himself for the worst. There was no telling what he might find. He had heard stories of gigantic rats dragging the carcasses of much larger animals into their harborage to devour at their leisure. Local folklore attributed the super-sized rats to the atomic age and the testing that went on near Alamogordo in the

40's.

Being a confirmed rat-catcher, A.J. maintained a wary respect for these enduring creatures, while being simultaneously fascinated by the lore the simple rat conjured. Despite their notoriously unpleasant features, such as their slender scaly tails, long sharp claws and chisel-like teeth, he could not help admiring their cunning and opportunistic ability to survive.

Taking another step into the pipe, he immediately noticed the drop in temperature. Outside, beads of sweat had been trailing down the side of his face, and the clothing he wore under the Tyvek suit had begun to dampen. Now his perspiration was replaced by goose bumps. Even through his protective outerwear, he could feel the stagnant, damp air all around him.

He proceeded cautiously.

Chapter Seven

When Saney got back to her office she still had some time before her next appointment. But all she could think about was her encounter in the elevator with the man from the bakery. She could not believe she had run into him again. She wondered what he was doing in the building, and regretted not asking. She had been in such a talkative mood, too. She had contacted a psychologist earlier that morning to set up a consultation for herself. The woman, Tana Ouhrabka, was also new in the area, and come to find out, she lived in the same apartment building as Saney. So they had decided to meet for lunch and talk. She was on her way up to Tana's office when Julian got on her elevator.

She almost laughed when he first got on and stepped all the way over to the other side of the elevator. Thinking about it now, she did laugh. She was sure he had no conscious knowledge that he had done that. It was a conditioned response. But to what? She wanted to find out. She wanted to find out a lot more than that, too.

Try to keep some composure. She chastised herself for being childish and unprofessional. She needed to be thinking about her patients. But it was all happening too fast, and she was utterly powerless to think about anything else. Her main concern was how she and Julian Bloom were going to officially meet, random encounters not withstanding. Saney regarded herself as old-fashioned when it came to which gender should be the aggressor, but because of Julian's obvious reticence, she thought she might be able to relax her principles in this case.

Suddenly there was a gentle knock on her door and she got up to open it. An older man stood in the doorway, his features warped by abnormal involuntary muscle contractions.

"Mr. Todd?"

"Hank."

"Okay, Hank. You can call me Saney. Why don't you come in and have a seat."

As Saney moved away from the door, Hank took a few cautious steps inside, then just stood there looking around the room.

"Is there something you're looking for, Hank?" Saney asked.

"Don't you have one of those long couches you're going to make me lay on?"

"No," Saney said, suddenly glad that her Victorian chaise lounge had not yet arrived. "We're going sit in regular chairs."

Hank chose to sit on the stool so Saney dropped into the futon and raised her hands disarmingly. "Now then, Hank, what is it you would like to talk about?"

"Well, originally I wanted to find out why I've been having these bad dreams about the end of the world. But now I know."

"Know what, Hank? Why the world is going to end or why you are having these dreams?"

"Both."

"And why is that?"

"Because Christ has returned."

"And how do you know this, Hank?"

"I saw the Son of God in my motel."

"What was He doing there?"

"He wanted to rent a room."

Saney was already making a diagnosis in her head—positive symptomatic schizophrenia—though that conclusion was purely speculative at this point. After treating patients for almost two years in New York City, she thought she had heard it all. However, what she was hearing after only a few days in Caldera made Manhattan seem like Disneyland. She could not fully explain to herself what was going on in this city, but she had a real bad feeling about it. She was sure a clear picture would emerge from the unsettling puzzle pieces of personalities she was working with. It was just going to take her a little more time to put them all together. Mr. Todd was just another piece in that puzzle. And while he fit perfectly with the other pieces she had so far, there was still no clear picture.

Yet.

Chris stirred from a dream-fraught sleep. He slowly came fully awake, unsure of where he was at first. He was in a bed so large he could not see the end of it until he lifted his head off the pillow. Then he got a taste of a something foul in his mouth and he recalled the bread he had eaten from the bakery shop dumpster. Now everything came back to him and his initial instinct was to get out of there as fast he could. The man in the suit had promised to have his car repaired by the time he woke up. Chris could only hope he was a man of his word.

He took a moment to survey the room. Like the bed, the furnishings were large and extravagant—polished wood floor, wall hangings, ornate sculptures, original framed paintings, and priceless bric-a-brac.

He crawled to the end of the bed and jumped off. The floor was cold. He was undressed, wearing only his underwear, but his clothes were folded neatly on a fancy chair beside the bed. The first thing he did was reach into the back pocket of his jeans and take out his wallet. He breathed a sigh of relief as he removed the picture of his mother. He looked down at it now, staring hard into her clear, bright eyes as if waiting for some kind of signal. Like the last time, he did not get one.

Chris stuffed the picture back into his wallet and quickly dressed. Then he stepped over to the closed bedroom door. When he tried the handle he found that it was locked and he was unable to open the door from the inside.

Just then came the sound of footsteps on hard wood. Chris turned his ear up and listened as they grew louder, just outside the bedroom door. Looking quickly around the room, he made a dash for the window closest to him. He parted the heavy velvet drapes and jumped up onto the wide sill just as he heard the sound of the lock being keyed. He swept the drapes closed and remained motionless as the door opened.

For a long moment there was no sound. Chris wondered if he had been spotted, his pursuer slowly sneaking up on him. But even with the sunlight streaming in on his back, Chris was certain that he could not be seen through the drapes. The fabric was simply too dense and dark to allow even the most meager ray of light to escape it.

Then came a loud metallic clank as something fell to the floor. This sound was followed by the frantic retreat of footsteps moving quickly down the hallway. A trailing voice shouted, "He's gone! He's gone!"

Chris peaked out from behind the curtain. The door was open. On the floor in front of the threshold was a brass breakfast tray. Scattered all around it was an assortment of fruit, a puddle of orange juice, and an overturned bowl of what looked like bran cereal.

Chris was not sure if he could make it out of the cavernous mansion and to his car (assuming it had been repaired and returned) without being spotted, but he knew he had to try. He grabbed a handful of strawberries on his way out of the room and moved swiftly, but cautiously, down the hallway.

The doors to all the rooms he passed were closed. Then he came to the staircase. It had two sides, both wide and arching downward at a steep angle. As he descended, the front door loomed just ahead, across a marble floor foyer, with nobody to block his path. As he neared the bottom, however, Chris found himself entertaining thoughts other than that of escaping. He started to ask himself questions like why he had been locked in his room, why had he been invited here in the first place, and why the motel owner had threatened to kill him. For some reason he could not just leave this city behind for some other destination without these answers. So instead of heading toward the front door, he turned left at the bottom of the stairs.

A heavy wooden door opened inward on a wing of rooms whose immensity in size and grandiosity humbled Chris. All the doors were open and he took a peek in each one. There was a great banquet hall and ballroom made to accommodate a large gathering. There was one room whose walls were lined with more books than Chris had ever seen in any library. He thought of Mr. Lewis, and was tempted to go inside and peruse the titles. But he resisted and continued on. Then, down the end of the hall, he was confronted by a closed door. He proceeded toward it casually and stopped before it, listening for any sound or voice on the other side. He could detect neither, so he tried the handle. The door was unlocked. He cracked it only wide enough to see inside.

It looked like a private study and home office. Right now it was empty. Chris swung the door open a little further and stuck his head in before stepping inside and closing the door behind him.

The chamber was meager in proportion to the other rooms, though no less decorous. It was elegant, comfortable, and functional, with everything that was needed to run a business, or a small country, at the fingertips of whoever was seated in the high-back leather desk chair. The room was dominated by an ancient and absolutely monstrous desk that had any number of draws and cabinets. The desktop was cluttered with papers and electronic equipment. There were inlaid shelves built into the walls. The books, though numerous, were nothing compared to the ones he had seen in the library room. Many of them were old and covered with fancy binders. Again, he thought of Mr.

Lewis. And then he turned away. In one corner at the back of the room was yet another door. Chris found it unlocked as well and stepped through it.

On the other side Chris was greeted by the shimmering water of an Olympic size pool. With no natural light entering, he flipped on several lights switches as he made his way further inside. He passed a sauna, steam room, Jacuzzi, and a room with a massage table and numerous bottles of scented lotions. Further along was a larger room, complete with barbells, weights, various workout machines, and a regulation boxing ring. Beyond that were adjoining rooms that housed billiard tables, Ping-Pong, pinball, video games, and the like. The last room was a swanky lounge. Behind the long bar, the entire wall was lined with glass shelves that quite possibly supported a bottle of every type and brand of liquor in existence.

By this point, Chris had already ranged so deeply into this wing of the estate that he did not think he could possibly go any further. He was about to turn around when he heard the sound of garbled voices. He looked up and spotted a narrow door on the side of the bar. The voices were coming from the other side. As Chris drew nearer he realized that the sounds he was hearing were actually moans, though whether in pain or ecstasy, he could not decipher. The door was already ajar, so all he had to do was push it open a little wider to spy the interior.

He saw very little. It was almost completely black inside. One thing was for certain, however, the moans were clearly of pleasure. Intrigued, Chris stalked through the room, which had a dungeon-like atmosphere. The air was cool. On the near wall he detected what apparently were several pairings of chains and manacles. Then, just ahead he encountered what could only be a gigantic bed. A dim red light emanated from somewhere above, dispersing its murky radiance only a short distance in all directions. But it was enough the reveal to Chris a bed that was very likely larger than the entire room that he had shared with his foster brothers in New Jersey. It was draped in yards of velvet, with red satin sheets beneath the purple coverlet. Closed-circuit televisions descended from the ceiling above the bed. Chris could not clearly make out the writhing images they displayed from where he was standing.

The bed itself was actually so big that Chris did not notice anybody on top of it at first. Finally he saw the convulsing mass of naked bodies, and the longer he looked the more of them he saw. There had to be a hundred of them up there, the entire staff of the mansion, Chris thought, participating in a orgy while the boss was away.

"Chris, come closer," said a female voice above the din of rapture and slapping flesh. "I have something to ask you."

Chris hesitated, but slowly moved toward the colossal bed until he saw the face of a light-haired woman looking at him amid the grinding, trembling bodies, slick with perspiration. What Chris saw going on atop this impossible mattress distracted and shocked him. As far as he could tell, anyway, there were only women on the bed. All were nude. All were beautiful and seductive. They were touching themselves and each other in pairs and in groups. This tableau of unbridled feminine lust galvanized Chris to the spot.

"Fuck me, Chris," the blonde woman urged him, and as Chris focused on her he recognized the clear blue eyes as those of his mother. The realization left Chris numb and sick to his stomach. Then she suddenly shifted forward and began crawling across the bed on her hands and knees toward him. Tongues, lips, and hands caressed her as she passed. Rebecca, the girl from the bake shop, had been lying under her. She sat up and smiled at Chris.

At the edge of the bed now, his mother reached for him. She was panting as she began to help him off with his shirt. Chris caught a glimpse of himself on one of the TV screens and he pulled away from her at once, angrily tucking his shirt back into his pants.

"Fuck me," she whispered as she sat back and opened her legs wide for him. "You know you want to." She started to giggle.

Chris shook his head in dismay and started to back away. "You're not my mother," he said. He closed his eyes and told himself that it was not real.

"I can see your erection," Chris heard her say, and she continued to laugh.

He turned away and began to shuffle quickly out of the room on weak legs, very much aware of his sexual arousal.

It's not real. None of it is real.

But even when he was safely in the next room, Chris could still smell the musk of sex. It was in his clothes. But he kept moving, and when he eventually found himself back in the main corridor where this excursion had begun, the man in the suit was standing there in the shadows waiting for him.

"What's going on here?" Chris asked.

"I'm afraid I don't understand?"

"For starters, you can tell me why you locked me in my room."

"I'm sorry if that startled you. Your door was locked as a precaution, for your protection, and no other reason, I assure you. As I told you, these doors are open to all those in need. When the homeless shelters are full, we accommodate the overflow in our guest rooms. Again, I'm sorry for the inconvenience and any anxiety it may have caused you."

Chris did not know how to respond. He was still very much unnerved by what he had just seen (or thought he had seen), but the man's words and the way he spoke them eased his mind more than he would have thought possible.

"As promised," the man continued, "your car has been repaired and is in the garage waiting for you as we speak. Although I must inform you that the car's original shade of red could not be perfectly matched. In any case, it's ready and you are free to go if that is your desire."

"I want to pay for the work that was done to my car."

"That won't be necessary. Consider it a charitable donation."

"No," Chris insisted. "I want to work off my debt."

"As was also promised, there is plenty of work for you to do. You are welcome to stay here as long as you please and you may leave at any time."

"I want to compensate you for your hospitality as well."

"If you feel it necessary."

"I do."

"Then let me officially offer you an entry position with Deluder Bake Shops. Welcome aboard, Chris."

When the man in the suit extended his right hand Chris took it.

"Now come, let's go to the kitchen and get you something to eat. Then I'll show you the rest of the grounds before you start your new job."

Chris nodded. He was surprised that he was not more uncomfortable with this than he was. He knew he could leave at any time, but now that he had a debt to repay, he could not just walk away. So it was without the help of his mother that he determined to stick around Caldera a little longer.

Chapter Eight

As A.J. continued to move forward, he listened for their high-pitched squealing. So far the pack had eluded him. It was a good sign, but he needed to go a little further into the pipe before he called it quits. He had the hammer of his revolver cocked and kept his pace slow to increase his response time. He knew that as soon as he did hear them, it might already be too late.

The flashlight beam cut a narrow swatch through the darkness and dissolved completely ten paces in front of him. A.J.'s throat tightened when he looked over his shoulder and saw that the pipe entrance had diminished to the size of a pinhole. He had never been claustrophobic, but he found himself trying to occupy his mind with more pleasant thoughts. He visualized himself fly-fishing from the deck of the Hyde Drift Boat he always wanted. He saw it sitting in the South Fork of the Snake River while he waited for a nice trout to sip his #22 midge. It was a perfect day. The sun was warm. The sky cloudless. His dog Leon was snoozing on the deck by his feet. Everything was perfect as well; the midges were hatching by the tens of thousands, his knots held, the trout were feeding ravenously at the surface and he was about to pull up a record-breaking 27 lb. brown trout.

Reality quickly set back in, however, and A.J. found himself in a dank underground cement pipe which was sure to be teeming with rats, walking slightly bent over now as the passage narrowed and wearing a cumbersome space suit.

Passing the light around the walls, ceiling, and floor of the pipe, A.J. saw no apparent signs of nesting. It was peculiar that the ground around the pipe entrance could be so riddled with rat runs, yet there was no indication that the animals had been inside thus far.

Then, just as this thought occurred to him, he happened upon what at first appeared to be a dead end, or at least a cave-in. Whatever it was, it was blocking his passage. As A.J. drew nearer, he saw that the pile was more expansive than he first thought. All around this barrier were small blunt shapes, about the size of black-eyed peas. A.J. gasped, knowing exactly what he was facing, but unable to believe it.

As he stepped nonchalantly through the solid and liquid rat waste, he realized two things: first, since the rats were using this section of the pipe as their toilet, they must be entering from the other end, in Caldera; and second, there were many times more rodents than he had initially feared.

A.J. was so astounded by what he was seeing that he continued to push his way forward and up the mountain of rat turd to survey its size. By the time he crossed the colossal dung heap and made it to the other side, A.J. was in a full state of shock. Hundreds of thousand rats had created this, he thought, perhaps as many as a half million. Suddenly he did not need to see any more. The further he ventured into the pipe toward Caldera, the more perilous it would become for him. He already found out all he needed to, though getting the public to believe him and convincing the politicians to do something about it was quite another matter altogether.

He was turning back to head out of the pipe when heard a low rumbling sound coming from his direction of escape. The pipe began to quake gently from the impact of a legion of tiny feet. Their high-pitched squealing coalesced into one feverish wail as the army advanced. They were cornering him in, A.J. realized, and he took a moment to consider his only two options. He could try to make it out by shooting his way through the pack in front of him or he could head deeper into the lightless tunnel and hope to find another route to the surface.

The squealing and marching grew louder, the clicks of their claws on the cement suddenly becoming all too distinct to A.J.'s ears. He looked down at his flashlight and revolver. Both were useless. The batteries were waning and he may as well have been carrying a squirt gun filled with jelly. He knew he did not stand a chance. He turned and started running blindly down the tunnel toward Caldera.

Then, because of the darkness and his speed, he was not able to stop in time to avoid what was now in his path. He saw it only a fraction of a second before he tripped over it. He tumbled headlong and collided against the side of the cement pipe. His right elbow and arm took the brunt of the impact and his gun went flying. It discharged as it left his hand, sending a screaming bullet ricocheting into the darkness. The flashlight, also shaken loose during the fall, skidded a few feet away from him, the faint beam pointing in the direction of the object he had just stumbled over. A.J. squinted, trying to determine what it was in the dimness. What he finally saw lent some credence to all the folklore he had previously dismissed.

He recognized the denim fabric and immediately perceived part of the shape. It was a human leg. Then the rest of the body came into focus. However, this man, though obviously dead, did not appear to have been scavenged. At least not yet. There was a small open wound in the middle of the chest that did not look to be attributed to rat bites, though it was actually too dark to be sure.

In the meager light, A.J. began to see the outline of other bodies as well. He blindly reached back, feeling along the cement with his gloved hand, and came in contact with something that may have been a shoulder. A little further away, he touched the side of someone's head, brushing the ear as he passed. It was a woman. Her hair was long. It was sticky with hair spray, and it smelled just like the kind his Jeanie used. He probed the chin and jaw line with his fingers, then leaned in as close as he could to the corpse's face. It was her.

"Jeanie!" he cried.

His wife had been dead ten long years, but she looked the same as she did the last time he had seen her, the day of her interment in her family's mausoleum in Yazoo City.

She was not dead after all, he thought distractedly. Somehow she had come back to him.

A.J.'s head was swooning. He called her name again. As he gently pulled the body of the woman he believed was his deceased wife closer to him, one hand randomly found the same inexplicable cavity in the center of her chest. Then, without warning, rats began to rain down on him from above. Through cracks in the concrete, they poured into the pipe unceasingly. A.J. struggled to get to his feet amid the rising swarm that tore at his Tyvek suit and the tender flesh beneath with keen claws and gnashing teeth.

His flashlight was completely smothered, as was his gun, and his Jeanie, now under three feet of dark, squirming bodies. They were up around A.J.'s crotch, and he could feel their pointed teeth prick his legs as he uselessly slapped at the ones that tried to climb further up his torso.

In the pitch blackness, as he was being chewed alive by vicious rats, A.J. did not think it could get any worse. That was when an entire section of concrete above him came crashing down.

Julian had been disturbed enough by what he had found the previous week, but what he was *not* seeing today was even more distressing. While the earlier data had been consistent with the logic that a decline in amphibian life occurs predominantly in regions downwind of highly polluted and densely populated areas, what he was encountering due west of Caldera was as disconcerting as it was paradoxical.

He gently rolled the third set of toad bones he had discovered that afternoon into a separate Glad-Lock Zipper Storage Bag. Like the other two, this specimen was a "true toad," a member of the Bufonidae family, and the presence of teeth marks and scratches on its skeleton made it a certainty that the animal had been preyed on. But the *by what*, as well as the answer to the question of whether predation had occurred after the toad's death or if an attack had caused its demise, had yet to be determined.

Habitat loss and pollution might be contributing factors to blame for the decline of certain species on the plains east of Caldera, Julian thought, but certainly they were not responsible for both the scarcity of amphibian life here and the ravaged remains of the few specimens that he did come across. The waters of the nearby Canadian River, associated lakes, and runoff streams were ideal breeding grounds for all amphibious creatures.

Julian was sealing the plastic bag when he heard a dull pop followed by a sound like a distant bottle rocket going off on the Fourth of July. Both these sounds were so muted that he could not be sure which direction they had come from. He waited, listening patiently for them to come again so that he might identify them. They did not.

He had started packing the third set of bones into his field bag when the sound of a voice screaming filled his ears. It too was muffled, but as Julian looked around he suddenly realized that the scream, like the sounds before it, was not coming from any linear direction; it was coming from under the ground.

He tried to hone in on the exact spot the scream was emanating from, but it proved difficult. He took long paces all around the area, hoping to lock in on it. With each step he could feel the ground beneath his feet give slightly. The earth was so soft that his body weight pushed his shoes half an inch into the sandy top soil.

Then suddenly his right leg sank into the ground above his

knee. He attempted to pull it free, but his foot had gotten wedged between something unyielding. Julian redoubled his effort, using his other leg for leverage to try to push himself up. He managed to succeed, but the instant his right foot broke free of whatever was clutching it, the ground beneath him suddenly gave way. And then he was free-falling, dirt and sand filling his nose, mouth, ears, and eyes. It seemed like he would plummet forever, into the very bowels of the earth.

All at once he just stopped. His back struck something solid and pain rocked his entire body while he was slowly being buried by falling dirt and debris.

He rolled to one side, coughing and wincing in agony as the dust settled. Julian could see sunlight streaming down from the opening in the ground above him. It was midnight everywhere the light did not stretch, but he saw movement in it, a streaming swirl of motion. It was as if a river were flowing by him, but there was no water. Then several of the bristly bodies came into focus.

Rats.

They were running away from the light, too many to guess. But they dispersed quickly, leaving behind something that was large, white, and covered with dirt and blood. Someone was moaning. Julian put his own pain aside and got to his feet. He brushed several dead rats off the man's body and checked for a pulse. It was weak, but he was still alive. Julian realized that what he did in the next few minutes would determine if the man stayed that way or not.

Looking up momentarily, Julian saw that he had fallen into a sewage drain of some kind. The ground was only a few feet above the broken concrete overhead. Then he looked down, and near his feet he spotted his field bag. There was enough chemicals and sterile materials inside to serve as a makeshift first-aid kit, so Julian immediately set to work to try to save the man's life. He just hoped it was not too late. Even if he did all that he could to buy the man a little extra time, Julian knew that he needed to get him to a hospital.

He was in such bad shape, however, Julian was not sure anything could be done for him.

Chapter Nine

Julian stepped lightly into the curtained cubicle of the ICU. The first thing he noticed was a large flower arrangement on the floor. There was no card. He had to step around it to approach the bed. For the next few moments he just stood there, looking down at the patient. He was not sure this was the same man he had pulled out of the drainage pipe that afternoon. Besides that, Julian did not know what he would say to the man if he had not been asleep or unconscious from the painkillers at that moment. Suddenly he began to question why he had come there in the first place.

He wondered if it was out of genuine concern for the man, or if maybe his visit had been prompted by Tasker's challenge to determine if what was happening to the amphibious community of Caldera might carry over into the human population. If it was the latter, Julian thought it was a poor excuse for a visit to an intensive care ward.

Now he felt like he had no right to be there. He stopped just short of leaving and instead asked himself if there might be another explanation for his desire to get out of the hospital.

He did not have to think too long. He knew there was.

There was no cause to feel guilty, he told himself. That was too convenient of an excuse. He was not responsible for this man's condition, nor should he regret wanting to get to the bottom of Caldera's environmental problems. He knew he was only troubled by the fact that he might end up actually liking the man. And therein lies the real reason he wanted to leave now. The same reason he wanted to leave every other place he had ever lived. The same reason that kept him from getting close to people. The same reason why he shied away from that woman in the elevator. This time, in anger and defiance, he fought that same impulse.

The man's chart was hanging on the footboard. Julian reached down and picked it up. Albert James "A.J." Brackenwaggen was his name, and then Julian dared to read the rest of the information on the chart.

He was fifty-five years old. He was five-feet-nine inches tall and weighed two hundred and ten pounds. He was a city resident and an employee of the Caldera Public Works Department. He was an environmental specialist. He had been born in Mississippi. He was a widower. He had no children. He had a history of high blood pressure and hypertension. He suffered a mild heart attack nine years ago. He was on medication for all these conditions. It indicated that his blood had been thinned considerably by a long-term daily intake of aspirin, and he nearly bled to death today as a result. Finally, it said he was being treated for *leptospirosis*. Julian was familiar with its epidemiology and was not surprised that A.J. had contracted it. *Lepto* was a serious vermin-borne bacterial infection that could springboard the development of many other serious inflammatory conditions, including meningitis and liver disease. Heavy doses of doxycycline and penicillin were being used to remedy the condition.

Suddenly the man in the bed made a horrible sound deep in the back of his throat. Julian looked up and was surprised to see that the man's eyes were open and lucid.

"I'd rather be fishin'," said the man in a raspy voice. Then, after a pause, "Are you the man who saved me?"

"I'm Julian."

"I'm grateful."

"A.J., I'd like to ask you a few questions, if you're up to it."

"After what you did for me, I'd tell you who I voted for in the last election, how much money I made last year, and my Internet password."

"Good," Julian said with a laugh. "I'm a herpetologist. I work for Project Earth, an environmental organization. Like you probably are, we're concerned about what's going on in Caldera. I'm not quite sure what's happening here yet, but whatever it is, it's bad. I intend to find out what's going on and put a stop to it. And I could sure use your help."

"To be honest with you, you're the first person who wanted to listen to me. I've been after my boss, and everybody else in this town with any clout at all, to get their heads out of the sand on this thing before it's too late. That's all my life has been about since my Jeanie passed on. It's all I think about. I don't feel the pain of missing her so badly when I'm busy battling rats and politicians, *and* trying to tell the two part. I've been telling everyone who will listen that the only problem facing this city goes by the name *rattus norvegicus*."

"The Norway, or brown rat," Julian said.

"You know your mammology as well."

"I've always been a big Dolly Parton fan."

"I only hope you're better at your job than you are at telling jokes," A.J. said, allowing himself a brief smile.

"I just told you everything I know about the Norway rat. Maybe you can tell me if they could be responsible for eradicating a large population of amphibious animals. Some of the remains, which I was fortunate enough to come across, had been picked clean to the bone. I know rats are attracted to uncontained garbage, but are toads a typical food source."

"I've seen them chew on everything from cereal to soap, from lollipops to rubber balls. They've been known to feast on furniture, motor oil, lead pipes, grain, birdseed. You name it, they eat it. They sometimes cause fires by chewing the insulation off electric wires. To thrive, they need three things, called the "rat triangle:" food, water and harborage. The runoff pipe offers all these, and access to more in Caldera. The colony is too immense to ignore. Not only are they formidable, but they're highly aggressive. Not a good combination if you're a member of any other species."

"What do you think needs to be done? Extermination?"

A.J. made another noise deep in his throat. This time it was a laugh. "The rat war," he said, "can never be won, only mitigated. The problem with Caldera's rapid growth is that the rats flourish also, and breed unabated. Consequently, they must compete for a limited food supply. As a result, they become more aggressive and vicious in their feeding practices. The city *must* cease its rapid expansion projects. I've tried to convince them but they won't listen to me. Maybe you, Julian, and your organization, can succeed where I failed. Scare the hell out of them. If they have fear, they might listen. And beware, some of the big developers will try to discredit you. They stand to lose everything if they cannot expand their businesses. This entire city was built on greed. It festers in it still. All those young folks with their fancy clothes and sports cars, living in expensive homes or condos. There's something unnatural about it all, I tell you."

Julian nodded in agreement. He and A.J. were on the same page all right. Caldera had a secret to reveal.

"There's one other thing," A.J. began. "When I was in the pipe, I saw something." Then he fell silent.

The look of apprehension on his face prompted Julian to ask, "What did you see?"

"Dead bodies. One man . . . And one woman. I think there may have been others. Between you and me, they both had small circular wounds in their chests that I could not account for, but no other signs of attack."

"Nothing like that was mentioned in the papers."

"I know how it sounds. It's okay. Everybody else thinks I'm crazy."

"I don't think you're crazy."

"Just before they attacked me, I asked myself what could sustain such a large number of rats, and have them proliferate at this rate. Then I saw the bodies. I wondered how many more there might be in the pipe. . . . It's a big city, Julian."

Julian did not know what to make of A.J.'s assertion. Rats have been known to nibble on the ears of sleeping infants, but A.J.'s premise that they were feeding on the people of Caldera was, well, hard to swallow.

"I suppose I shouldn't give a rat's behind if the whole damn town went to hell. I don't even know why I'm still here. I suppose I originally came to Caldera just to get away. I left everything that I loved behind. I buried my Jeanie and I sold my old fishing boat, thinking that life in a small town would be just what I needed to take my mind off my old life. But I've found that you really can't run away from your past. It eventually catches up with you. Now, with everything suddenly growing and moving so fast around here, I find myself thinking more and more about Jeanie and wanting to get back on my boat with my fly rod. So, I guess what I'm trying to say is that I'll help you. Just as soon as I can get out of this bed."

"It's a deal," Julian said.

"Not so fast. There's something you can do for me first."

"Name it."

"Get me a cigar. Anything. I'd even take one of those cheap Tiparillos or El Productos, if that's all you can find."

Julian put a finger to his chin thoughtfully. "That's got to be against hospital rules," he said. "I'll see what I can do. But on one condition."

A.J. gave him a wary glance.

"When you do get out of this hospital, you have to promise to take me fishing with you. I've always wanted to go on a fishing trip."

"You got it," A.J. agreed, then added "as soon as you get me my cigar."

Julian left the hospital feeling optimistic about both A.J.'s recovery and Caldera's future. Even the presence of the media outside A.J.'s room did not discourage Julian. Naturally, they wanted to underscore the hero angle. And while Julian played that aspect down, insisting that he was just in the right place at the right time and that anybody would have done the same thing, he saw the news cameras as an opportunity to publicize their cause, as he and A.J. had talked about. He mentioned his work and how it related to A.J. and his injury. And while he did not come right out and say that there was a rat infestation problem in Caldera, he did make it perfectly clear that what had happened to A.J. could also happen to them.

Julian went straight home from the hospital. He was anxious now to sort through the reams of data he had collected that afternoon so he could compare them with his initial findings. As soon as he clicked on his laptop, the icon indicating that he had e-mail appeared. He ignored it at first, eager as he was to get going on his work. However, at the back of his mind, a totally un-Julian notion occurred to him. It was as enticing as it was fanciful. He was thinking that the woman on the elevator had somehow gotten his e-mail address and was trying to contact him. It was preposterous, but the next thing he knew he was opening his mail.

A few key strokes later, a very short and very provocative message was revealed, though not the kind he had hoped for.

To: jbloom
Subject: carelessness
From: nicholas
You're getting careless. But I'll take care of it like I always do.
Your One And Only True Friend,
Nicholas

Julian stared at the screen in disbelief. The message on his computer a few nights ago was, most certainly, residue from a nightmare, but this e-mail had far-reaching implications. It came all the way from his childhood.

No one else knew who Nicholas was. No one knew that Nicholas was his imaginary friend when he was a boy. No one knew that he used to receive phone calls and letters from somebody named Nicholas his entire life. Until it all just stopped one day about a year ago. Julian thought one of two things had occurred. Either he had been spontaneously cured of the mental illness he was suffering from, or his imaginary friend had succumbed to his own mortality. Perhaps he had crashed his imaginary car into an imaginary tree, or his imaginary heart had failed. Or maybe he was eaten by imaginary rats.

Whatever Julian thought might have happened to Nicholas, he was obviously back now, and he was on-line.

Julian decided to scroll down to the bottom of the letter to see if there was any additional information on nicholas or the transmission of the document. Only then did he notice the postscript further down the page. It read:

P.S. I hope your new friend likes the flowers I sent him. I couldn't find a DON'T GET WELL card, so I didn't leave any. I suppose they could be used for his funeral. This way, at least he gets a chance to enjoy the beauty of his own floral arrangement before he's buried beneath them.
I told you, no one will ever hurt you again.

Julian asked himself why this would be happening to him all over again after so much time. But he knew the answer to that question too, just as he had known what had been compelling him to leave the hospital before A.J. awoke.

It was A.J. It was that woman on the elevator who he could not take his eyes off. It was his whole way of thinking. His entire perception of things. He was being suffocated by his own fear and loneliness. And he was sick and tired of it all. He was sick of being afraid and he was tired of being alone. It prevented him from meeting people, from getting to know anyone, from sharing a life with someone special, from falling in love and having a family—everything that Nicholas did not want him to have.

Now it had to end. Julian made up his mind once and for all that he was not going to let things go on this way any longer. Nicholas had to be stopped. And if Nicholas was inside his own mind, Julian would have to confront that too. Whatever it took. He was through running.

It was decided, then. Despite the potential danger it posed to himself and all the people he came in contact with, it had to be done. Then the face of the woman he had met in the elevator came to his mind.

Whatever Nicholas turned out to be, Julian was scared. But somehow the thought of the woman made him feel confident and brave. Tomorrow he was going to find out who that woman was. He knew she had gotten out on the 42nd floor, so she either worked there or knew somebody that did.

She could have been meeting her husband for lunch, Julian thought, then remembered she did not have a ring on her finger. That was not something Julian generally took notice of, but he had this time.

Boyfriend, perhaps?

No, he thought. And not just because of the way she looked at him. It was something else. Something he could not fully explain.

Tomorrow would be the day. It could not arrive soon enough for Julian. But first there would be a long night. Certainly sleepless. He had been having terrible nightmares lately, and tonight, on the verge of his new resolve, Julian knew it would only get worse.

Chapter Ten

There were only eight suites on the floor, so he thought his odds of running into her were pretty good. Two were doctor's offices. The others included a physical therapy facility, an orthodontist, a psychology group, a telemarketing firm, a tax lawyer, and an employment agency. The doors and front walls of the suites were made of glass, but after making two fruitless passes up and down the hall, Julian decided to adjust his strategy a little. He was probably starting to look conspicuous and he already felt plenty foolish. Judging by the woman's curious and thoughtful demeanor and her perfect smile, Julian figured she was either a psychologist or an orthodontist, so he decided to concentrate his efforts on these two suites. Fortunately they faced one another across the hall and were close to the elevators.

After a few moments of loitering, Julian surprised himself when he just walked right into the Caldera Psychological Associates office, intent on following through on the pledge he had made to find out about Nicholas. He was also hoping to run into that woman again.

With his heart racing and a sinking feeling in the pit of his stomach, he approached the reception counter. Julian's initial instinct was to just turn around and walk right back out, pretending that he had meant to go into the orthodontist's office, but had accidentally come in here by mistake.

"Can I help you?" a woman behind the counter asked. She was standing with a file folder in her hand.

Julian's heart was trip-hammering uncontrollably and he was perspiring as he leaned forward and whispered, "I'd like to speak to one of the counselors here."

"Do you have an appointment?" she whispered back.

"No. I need to make one."

"Okay. Let me give you one of these to fill out." She handed him a clipboard with a pink sheet of paper pinned to it and a pencil on a string. "Carol just stepped away from her desk for a moment. My name is Tana. I'm a therapist here. I actually have a few minutes for a brief consultation before I see my next patient. If you could complete that form and give it to Carol when you're finished, she'll take you around back and I'll see you."

As Julian began to fill out the form where he stood, the receptionist returned. It was basic information, and when it was completed he handed it to Carol, who showed him into a room where Tana was waiting for him. Carol gave her the pink form that Julian had filled out and then left, closing the door behind her. Tana glanced briefly at the form before looking up suddenly, as if something there had shocked her.

"How tall are you?" she asked.

Julian did not recall seeing a request for that information on the questionnaire. "Uh, I'm about six-three, I guess."

"Please, have a seat."

Julian hesitated. Tana was partially blocking his way, but he sidestepped around her so she did not have to move. He did not see the mindful expression on her face as she watched him pass. She followed behind Julian and took the chair opposite him.

"So, Julian, what brings you here?"

Julian thought about this a moment, wanting to come up with the best words to explain his delicate two-pronged incentive.

"Well, to be perfectly honest," he began, "I need to talk to someone about some problems that have come back into my life since I moved to Caldera. But I was also hoping to find a woman here."

"In Caldera?"

"In this building. On this floor."

Tana listened to him with an expression that was both patient and eager.

"There was a woman I had spoken with briefly on the elevator the other day. She got out on this floor. I don't know her name. I thought maybe she worked here."

Tana's smile widened. "You *are* him," she said. "I thought so, but I wasn't sure." She glanced down at her watch and softly said, "This is going to be interesting."

"Excuse me?" Julian said.

"Oh, I'm sorry. You talking about Xenia Wieland. She likes to be called Saney. She's a friend of mine. Well, we just met, actually, but we seemed to have hit it off. Anyway, she came in on Tuesday to talk to me. She's a psychiatrist."

"How do you know who I am?"

"Saney spoke about you," she said matter-of-factly.

"She did?"

"And I really can't say too much more than that. Counsel-client privilege." Tana laughed enjoyably.

"Pardon my ignorance," Julian said, "but if she's a psychiatrist, why would she need to talk to you?"

"Same reason a barber doesn't cut his own hair, I suppose. We wouldn't want to subscribe to the Flo-B approach to mental health." She threw her head back and laughed even more indulgently.

Suddenly there was a knock at the door.

"Come on in," Tana said, raising her voice to be heard.

Julian assumed it was Carol with some document that required Tana's signature, so he did not turn around to look at first. But Tana had a peculiar smile on her face, which made Julian just curious enough to swivel his head slightly in that direction. He did a double-take when he saw that it was the woman Tana called Saney. He instantly jumped to his feet and stood there staring at her. She had stopped just inside the room and was looking back at him with a similar look of surprise.

"Sorry, Tana," Saney said, "I didn't know you were with someone. I'll wait outside."

"Actually he's here to see you. But why don't I have him explain." Tana walked toward the door. "I'll be by the reception desk." She whispered something else into Saney's ear as she left, then closed the door behind her.

Saney slowly made her way further into the room and halted a greater distance away from Julian than he would have preferred.

"Number twenty-four," she said, "so we met again?"

"I'm Julian."

"Hi. Saney. Nice to meet you."

Julian took her hand. It was as warm as her smile. An awkward silence followed.

"This is a little embarrassing," Saney said. "I wasn't expecting to see you. But, in a sense, I did have a feeling we'd meet again. It's sounds kind of strange, I know."

"Actually, no. This is not like me either."

Saney recalled what Tana had only a moment before whispered to her as she was leaving the room: *You guys were meant to be together.*

Julian looked around anxiously, then said, "Is there somewhere else we can go to talk? I'm not really comfortable here."

"How about we take a walk. The weather's rather nice. And there's a bakery only a few blocks from here. Your favorite."

"My favorite?"

"Yeah. A Deluder Bake Shop. The man behind the counter mentioned your name last time. I figured you must go there a lot."

"That was the first and only time I'd ever been in one of those places."

91

"Hmm. He must know you from somewhere else."

Julian just shrugged and followed Saney as she turned and started for the door.

Tana did not ordinarily smoke at work. She was usually able to wait until she got home, and then she would blow through an entire pack of Virginia Slims. But she just found out that her last patient of the day had canceled, so when the urge came upon her she just snuck off into the hall to take in a lungful. As soon as she stepped into the hallway, she saw a man turning away and heading for the stairwell.

"Ron," she called out, recognizing the khaki green waist coat.

He stopped and, with one hand still on the doorknob, turned around. "There you are," he said, a broad smile sweeping across his face. "I've been looking for you."

"Are you spying on me?"

"You caught me."

Tana walked over to him and put her arms around his waist. "You said you were going to call me." Smiling playfully, she reached behind him and grabbed his butt.

"Things have been hectic at work," he began, and Tana raised her eyebrows dubiously. "No, I'm serious. That's why I thought I'd sneak over while I had the chance and surprise you."

"We could go to my office for a nooner," she said, pressing her pelvis against him.

Tasker pushed her away. "I don't have the time for *that*. I wish I did."

"How about right here, then," she said as she grabbed his crotch.

He pulled back further. "I promise, I *will* call. First chance I get." He managed to extricate himself from her grasp and open the door behind him. He paused on the threshold and looked back at Tana. "I thought I saw somebody go into your office. Is that a patient of yours?"

"Oh, no. We're just friends. Though we actually just met."

"So you and your new friend have hit it off pretty good then, huh?"

"You could say that."

Tasker looked down at the smoldering cigarette in Tana's hand. He pointed to it and said, "Those things will kill you."

"You have to die from something, right? Might as well be from something you enjoy. Although I can think of something else I'd rather die doing." She winked and walked her eyes up and down his body.

"I don't know what they did to make you girls up there in Canada so damn horny, but I like it." He stepped away from the door and it closed behind him.

Tana laughed, though it quickly faded. She had not really expected to hear from him again. He seemed like he was only interested in sex, but maybe she was wrong about him. She knew she had made a mistake giving herself up to him so easily, and she regretted it, even if he was great in bed and great looking. Still, she thought, he was not as good-looking as Saney's tall boy. Tana could not help thinking that the two of them were perfect for one another. Under any other circumstance, she never would have imagined herself saying such a thing. They were really only meeting each other for the first time at this very moment, and she had only known Saney for a few days herself. It was unusual, to say the least, but it seemed right to her. Whatever that was worth.

As Tana walked back toward the suite, Saney and Julian were exiting.

"So where are you kids off to?" Tana asked.

"To the bakery," Saney said. "Do you want anything?"

"Just the details when you get back." Tana started to laugh. Julian seemed to have found it amusing as well, but Saney just pushed him forward, away from Tana and toward the elevators.

"You kids have fun, you hear?"

"Sure, mom," Saney said, and Tana laughed even louder. They would hear her howls of amusement echoing down the elevator shaft for several floors before dissipating completely.

It was a short walk to the bakery, but it allowed enough time for Julian to begin explaining how his imaginary friend from childhood had resurfaced. He told her about the mysterious deaths, the letters and phone calls, his resulting self-imposed isolation as well as the recent nightmares and e-mail. He maintained a safe emotional distance by keeping the tone of the conversation professional, although he spoke with deep sincerity and passion. The one thing he neglected to mention to her were the strong feelings he had for her, which even he did not fully understand. He did not feel right keeping this from her, but part of him was still afraid something bad might happen. Something that called itself Nicholas.

When Julian finished, he looked at Saney, truly expecting her to be put off by what he had told her. She was silent for awhile, as if she was trying to decide if she was going to help him or tell him that he was a lost cause, beyond all hope.

"Strange," she said. "All of my patients, I mean *every single one*, have mentioned nightmares of the intensity you're experiencing. Most of them had never been bothered by bad dreams to this extent prior."

"Prior to what?"

"Prior to coming to Caldera, apparently," she said. "But the incidence and variety of phobias and hallucinations accompanying these nightmares have left me nothing short of dumbfounded."

Saney stopped short of volunteering any information about her own nightmares, and the wood monster that was pursuing her. Maybe she was embarrassed. She was, after all, a professional who was being confided in because of her stability and rationale. She did not want to make it seem as if the inmates were running the asylum, but she thought she should at least be honest with him, the way he had been honest with her. She knew she would eventually tell him everything, but for now, this would have to do. "What troubles me most," she continued, "is that many of these people just arrived here, like us, so they haven't had a chance to fully experience the growth that Caldera has undergone. Yet they're suffering the same profound psychological effects as any long-term resident. It's as if this city is acting as an accelerant, distorting and magnifying people's fears."

"That's kind of how I've felt," Julian said. "Only about the local ecology. And you're right. It just doesn't add up. You think it might be organic? A toxin of some kind that influences brain chemistry."

Before she could respond, they were at the bake shop. Their conversation abruptly ended at the door, as if they were embroiled in some insidious plot that no one else knew about and only they could unravel.

They were both glad that the line was relatively small. There were two young people behind the counter, a boy and a girl. Saney was reading the daily bagel specials on the chalkboard near the door when the boy asked to take their order.

"Two pizza strips please, a regular milk, and whatever the lady wants."

With her back to the counter, Saney said, "I think I'll be daring and take a chance on the spinach bagel." Finally she turned around. "And throw in a spinach pie for later. With a small ginseng tea, please."

The boy did not move, and he never took his eyes off Saney, who smiled at him and said, "That's all, thanks." The boy gave no indication that he had even heard her. He just stared, transfixed, as if she were the snake-haired Medusa.

It was as if her picture had come to life and he was staring at his mother in person.

"Excuse me," a disembodied voice said.

"Huh?"

"The lady said, *that will be all*," said the man with the woman who looked like his mother.

"Oh. Sure." Chris started to turn away, but he could not stop staring at the woman. Someone else's order was on the counter in front of him and he did not realize that it was there until the back of his hand struck the red and black paper bag. Its contents spilled out onto the counter and one of the Styrofoam coffee cups popped its lid, spraying the hot liquid everywhere. The woman let out a soft yelp as some of the coffee splashed on her legs. It instantly soaked through her linen pants suit and scalded her.

Chris immediately apologized and retrieved several towels. The man took one from him to assist the woman while Chris patted down the counter.

"What's happened here?" It was the man in the suit, standing directly behind him.

"Just a little accident," the woman said. "No harm done."

"It was my fault, sir," Chris said nervously as he continued to clean up the spill.

The man in the suit stepped behind Chris, who could not help flinching when the man raised his right hand and placed it on his shoulder. "It's okay, Chris," he said. "Accidents happen. We can only hope to learn how to avoid them in the future." Then he looked directly at the woman and smiled contritely. "I'm terribly sorry about this, Ma'am. I'll be glad to pay whatever it costs to replace your outfit."

"That really won't be necessary. Thank you. It's really old and very worn."

"Such things are often more valuable and precious. Allow me to at least pay for the dry-cleaning."

She thought about it a moment, then nodded in consent. "If you really insist."

"I do," he said, then put both hands on Chris's shoulders. "Chris here can pick up the garment at your residence first thing in the morning and have it returned to you by day's end. Won't you, Chris?"

"Yes, sir."

"Good," the man in the suit said before turning back to the woman. "Now please accept your order without charge and give Chris your address so we can put this whole matter behind us."

"Thank you," the woman said.

"My pleasure. And please come again." He smiled, nodded at the man she was with, then turned and walked into the kitchen.

Chris watched the woman take a business card out of her purse and write something on the back. "Here you are, Chris," she said, placing the card on the counter between them. Her eyes fixed on his and she said, "My name is Saney. I live just five blocks north of here, on Glenmere. What time did you want to come by?"

Chris could only manage a nod.

The woman smiled. "Why don't you come by at eight-thirty. How's that?"

Again he just nodded.

"I'll just write that down for you." She did, then picked up the card and tucked it into the breast pocket of Chris's uniform shirt. On the pocket was a logo of a little devil holding a pitchfork whose tines skewered loafs of bread over an open fire.

"That's cute," Saney said, staring at the logo. "I never noticed that before." Then she looked at Chris, smiled, and said good-bye.

The man was also smiling as he removed the two bags from the counter and walked out of the bakery with the woman who looked like his mother. It was like a dream to Chris, but the voice of the next patron in line brought him back to reality.

Chris looked at the person in front of him and knew right away that he had seen this man before. It was not unusual. The same people came in all the time. This particular guy was easy to remember. He had a sty in the corner of his eye and for some reason he was smiling all the time. He smiled as he placed his order, and as Chris filled it, the boy slowly came out of the fog he was just in. It would not be until much later that he would discover the business card in his pocket and realize that it was not a dream at all.

Julian could barely hold back his laughter once they were outside. "That was about the strongest case of puppy love I've ever seen in my life," he said.

"Ah, leave him alone," Saney said. "He's just a kid." Suddenly she turned and looked back at the bakeshop sign above the door. She saw the same little devil logo inside the oversized D in Deluder that she had noticed on Chris's shirt pocket.

"Oh, Saney," Julian began. "Before I forget, or lose my nerve, there's something I want to ask you. I have a company Christmas party Sunday night that I wasn't even intending on going to, but I thought that maybe if you went with me I wouldn't feel quite so out-of-place. It's really more of an informal get-together, a way to meet some of the local politicians and people who share our concerns. I know it's awfully short notice."

Saney had to consciously control her adolescent delight. She deliberately paused before she said, "That sounds like fun," hoping she sounded more poised than she felt.

Julian smiled oddly.

"What is it?"

"Nothing. I guess that's just the affect you have on people."

Saney smiled back. Neither of them spoke any more about Chris, but for no tangible reason, they both had a feeling that the boy was an integral part of the whole unknowable future of Caldera.

PART II.

Elephant Shoes

Faith and reason are like two wings on which the
human spirit rises to the contemplation of truth;
and God has placed in the human heart a desire to
know the truth—in a word, to know himself—so that,
by knowing and loving God, men and women may
also come to the fullness of truth about themselves.

-*FIDES ET RATIO*, Encyclical Letter of The Supreme Pontiff
John Paul II.

When the stars threw down their spears
And water'd heaven with their tears:
Did he smile his work to see?
Did he who made the Lamb make thee?

- *The Tyger*, William Blake

Chapter Eleven

So far, the red Chevy Malibu with New Jersey plates had not been spotted by law enforcement agents anywhere west of Tennessee all the way to the Texas line. While Claybert combed through every rest stop and motel along the interstate looking for Chris, he used all his influence and his police fraternity privileges to make certain that the boy had not been picked up already or written up for speeding and let go anywhere along the way. If the boy did turn up somewhere, he wanted to be the first one on the scene. He had dibs. But now into Texas, the sheriff was just free-floating across the country, just like the kid, not knowing where he was headed.

As Claybert drove aimlessly through the panhandle, with no particular destination and very little gas, he began to wonder if he would ever come across the orphan murderer who killed his brother. It made him mad as hell to even consider the possibility that the little fiend might actually get away with what he did. Right now, however, the gas gauge, whose needle had been pinned in the red zone for the last fifty miles, drew most of his attention and his ire. Spotting a sign on the highway indicating that there was a gas station at the next exit, he took it and pulled up to the pump.

As he was filling the tank, he took a quick look around at the desolate landscape. The expansive desert plains left him with a feeling of isolation and dread. It only reinforced his fear that the boy had simply vanished into thin air, never to be seen again. Then, much to his appreciation, he noticed that a small bar (a *saloon*, he reckoned it was called in these here parts) was attached to the gas station. Being sober for way too long, Claybert could not resist the opportunity. He paid for the gas and then stepped into the adjoining bar.

The place was practically empty, dark and rank, country music coming from an old juke box. None of these things bothered Claybert, except for the country music, which was all he could get in his car since he'd crossed the Appalachians. He turned the radio off completely when he went through Little Rock and had not put it back on since. Still, the shady hole was a welcome relief from the heat and sun he had been driving in all day.

He barked for a whiskey on the rocks and the bartender hobbled over on one bad leg carrying a bottle and a dirty glass. He placed them both down on the bar in front of Claybert, but did not let go of them until the sheriff slapped a fifty and his badge down next to the booze.

"Leave it," he instructed the bartender, then poured himself a shot. He threw back three quick ones, pausing before the fourth to take a look around the bar. There were only three other people inside. They were all standing around a pool table in the back, shooting and drinking beer. There were two young roughnecks in leather jackets, chugging Lone Star Beer and posturing for the girl who was among them. She had piercings clustered all over her face—ears, nose, lips, eyebrows and one on her tongue. She had dirty blonde hair, and when she saw Claybert watching her she looked over at him and smiled. She also had a silver hoop in her navel. She whirled around and bent over the table to take a shot. The denim shorts she was wearing rode up the crack of her ass, the cotton so thin Claybert could see that she was not wearing underwear. Tufty, light-colored pubic hair peeked out around the thin fabric near her crotch and he caught the gleam of yet another metal piercing. Her legs were long and tanned. She seemed to pause in that position a long time before the smack of the billiard balls was heard and she stood up again. She looked back and smiled even wider at Claybert when she saw that he still had his eyes on her.

He swallowed another shot as she walked around to the other side of the table, watching Claybert the whole time. The dark-haired fella put an arm around her shoulder. Both of the brutes were looking over at Claybert now, amused and sanguinary expressions on their faces. Then the light-haired one leaned over and said something to the dark-haired one and they both laughed as they continued to stare at him.

"Yeah, it looks like we got ourselves a genuine dirty old man," Dark Hair said loud enough for Claybert to hear.

Claybert poured himself another drink and watched as Dark Hair made his way to the bar.

"Three more beers, pops."

As he stood beside Claybert and waited, he eyed the money and the badge on the bar.

"You a cop?"

"What's it to you?"

"Thought maybe you'd like to buy some time with Sandy over there," Dark Hair said, then reached down and placed his hand on the fifty. "Saw the way you were looking at her."

Claybert lowered his big right hand down on the top of the kid's wrist, applying just enough force to keep him from moving. In the same motion, Claybert reached for something behind the bar with his other hand. He came away an instant later with a small basket full of darts. Black Hair wriggled his fingers helplessly under the giant hand.

"Hey, what are you doing, man? Let me go."

Claybert removed one dart from the basket and raised it above his head. Dark Hair could only scream as the dart came down and the tip bore through the back of his hand and into the scratched and stained wooden surface beneath. As Dark Hair wailed in agony, Claybert quickly removed a second dart and stuck it through the punk's other hand, pinning him to the bar. The sheriff frisked him, since he was already in the position, and removed a wad of money, several vials of colored pills, and a small bag of weed, all of which he tossed onto the bar.

With this one out of the way, Claybert whipped out his .45 and turned around just as Light Hair was approaching with his own gun drawn.

Claybert fired first.

The round tore into Light Hair's upper arm and he dropped his weapon before it could be discharged. Bits of leather and a piece of his formidable biceps spattered the girl behind him. As Light Hair sank to the ground with a yelp, the girl started to scream.

Dark Hair began kicking the bar. "I'm gonna kill you, you cocksucker!" he yelled. Claybert just poured himself another shot of whiskey and drank it down. Then he pulled the bloody bill out from under Dark Hair's hand. It tore around the point of the dart and he just tucked it back into his wallet.

Claybert looked at the shocked bartender. "The boy's are buying my booze," he said, motioning toward the wad of money. "Keep the change." Claybert grabbed the bottle to take with him, but as he turned to leave someone came out of the men's room holding a .38 loosely in one hand. The sheriff was already in a firing stance, but he eased off when he saw that the man was old and perhaps senile, with a severe nervous tick. The gun was shaking so violently in his hand that he would not have been able to hit water if he were standing on a beach. He did not look to Claybert like he was going to be any trouble to anybody but himself. He was not even looking in Claybert's direction, just staring off distantly.

Suddenly Dark Hair managed to pull one of his hands free from the bar, the tip of the dart still protruding from his palm. He was then able to use his full body weight to pull his other hand free. In a rage, he whirled around to face Claybert.

The eyes of the man who came out of the bathroom went

wide with terror then. "It *is* Him!" the man shouted. "The Christ child! He's come seeking vengeance because I turned Him away from my motel!"

Claybert was so taken in by the man's abject fear that he almost did not turn around in time to avoid Dark Hair's flailing arms. Claybert took one step back and, with an amazingly quick display of hand speed, managed to get in four solid blows to the side of Dark Hair's head with the butt of the gun. As Dark Hair fell unconscious to the floor, Claybert turned back to the old man. He continued to rant about God, Satan, Armageddon, and a kid in an old red Chevy, but the body-pierced whore in the back drowned most of it out with her squawking.

"SHUT UP!" Claybert yelled as he spun around and fired one time. The girl was instantly silenced as the slug tore through the center of her neck and severed her spinal cord. He fired once more, this time hitting the jukebox and muting the endless opus of the mundane that droned from its speakers. Then he turned and approached the man with the twitching face. Claybert grabbed him by the collar and pushed him up against the wall.

"Tell me about the kid in a red Chevy," Claybert said. "What did he look like?"

The man closed his eyes. Viscous, white foam escaped from the sides of his mouth as he spoke. "Blond hair. Blue eyes. Scared. He doesn't know the power he possesses."

"Where is he?" Claybert asked.

"New Mexico. A place called Caldera. It tricks you. Uses you. You can't tell the difference between good and evil. Don't go there. Armageddon is already underway. The casualties are already mounting. There's nothing anybody can do now. I tried to escape, but I have nowhere to go. Satan took my soul. He'll take yours too."

The man reached into his jacket and pulled out a prescription, but it promptly fell out of his trembling fingers. Claybert saw that there was no cap on it and that it was empty when it struck the ground.

"Only God can save us now," he said, and began to convulse

in Claybert's arms.

The New Jersey sheriff released the man at this point and he fell to the floor, where he began to shudder violently. Thick strands of saliva, now tinged with blood from biting his tongue, poured from his mouth.

"There's no way out of this," he gurgled as he guided the barrel of the .38 into his mouth with an unsteady hand. He chipped a few teeth before he finally pulled the trigger. The smell of gunpowder and blood was strong, but it was curiously more pleasant to Claybert than the scent the bar had before all the carnage.

Gimps, prostitutes, thugs, and pill-poppers; what a town, the sheriff thought as he headed for the exit. He holstered his piece, pocketed his badge and carried the whiskey out with him. Leaving the bar like he was walking out of a Quentin Tarantino movie, it barely registered in his mind that two people were dead, two others were seriously injured, and he was largely responsible for it. He was so blinded by his quest for vengeance that he did not grasp the irony of a lawman killing and maiming in the name of justice. He was entirely without remorse. Whether it was called revenge or justice or something else altogether, Claybert felt the need to destroy Chris and everything in his path more intensely the further west he went.

Outside now, the Texas sun had a sobering affect on Claybert. He stuffed himself into his cruiser, got back onto I-40, and opened his road atlas.

New Mexico.

Caldera.

C-5

And there it was. Just a few hundred miles further west. Claybert may not have known where to find Chris, but Rand McNally sure did.

One small break was all he needed. Just like in police work, a witness or snitch is usually all it takes to bring the guilty to justice when hard evidence is hard to come by. Claybert's luck was suddenly changing, and Caldera had better brace itself, he thought as he barreled along at ninety plus miles per hour, because he was not about to leave any stone unturned until that boy got what he had coming to him. And that was a world of hurt.

Chapter Twelve

Saney was experiencing such divergent feelings and becoming so confused that she did not know what to do. While she had become more intrigued by Julian and wanted to spend all the time she could with him, she knew her work would never allow it. Her first obligation should be to her profession, and the people of Caldera her top priority. That settled, at least temporarily, she immediately started going through her patient files.

While she was setting up her laptop, she flipped on the TV and turned to the Classic Film Network. It was airing *Stagecoach*, one of her favorite movies, and she became immediately absorbed by it. She told herself that she was only going to watch it up to the Indian attack scene, but by then she was too engrossed in the story and wound up watching it to the end. Saney gasped when she finally looked up and saw the time. She had not done any work yet, and it suddenly occurred to her that finding out what was wrong with the collective psyche of Caldera was proving to be more of a challenge than she anticipated. Every time she started to get into it, something would come along to distract her, whether it was the whirlwind of emotions she was experiencing since meeting Julian, her own hectic daily work schedule, or a classic movie on television. That kind of procrastination and lack of focus was not like her at all. She did not like it, and she meant to do something about it.

Saney turned the television off, determined to pull an all-nighter if she had to. She even made a pot of coffee so her efforts would not be thwarted even by old-fashioned sleepiness, and then she set to work.

She went through each file one by one. The notes she had taken were meticulous and it was slow going, but within no time some unsettling patterns were already starting to emerge. Aside from the pervasive accounts of unsettling daydreams and harsh nightmares, there was a disturbing escalation of violence and antisocial behavior. Also, many of her patients described not feeling like themselves anymore.

The problem Saney had was trying to determine if the city's rapid expansion had any bearing on these permutations in the dynamics of personality or if these distortions were latent personality buds that were now blooming in her patients. If it were the latter, explaining how the entire city could be going through this at the same exact time would prove to be even more complex. However, like emigrating compatriots who settle in the same foreign city or town, such quirks of personality could have been born out of some shared anguish caused by residing in a city in constant flux.

Saney was debating this cause and effect dilemma when the phone rang. She had her machine on mute so that her attention would not be diverted away from the task at hand. She planned on waiting until she had made a decent amount of headway in her observation and analysis before playing back the message to find out who had called.

But when the machine answered, whoever was calling hung up right away. She glanced at the digital display of the recording device for the first time all day and noticed that there were nine messages on it now. In keeping with her new work ethic, she decided that whoever was calling would simply have to wait.

Several minutes later, the phone began to ring again. As before, the party that was calling hung up as soon as the answering machine picked up. Saney could not help wondering who it was, but continued her work. She willfully blocked out any thought that it might be Julian. Hardly ten minutes went by before it rang once more. This time, Saney could no longer ignore the image of Julian desperately trying to get a hold of her. It could be something important about the welfare of Caldera, she thought, or he might have just become overwhelmed by the need to tell her how he felt about her. She knew that Julian would not have been particularly comfortable confessing either of these scenarios to an audio cassette, so she got up to answer it. She depressed the speaker button so she could hear his voice echo throughout the room.

"Hello."

When she did not get a response right away, she knew she had made a mistake picking up the phone. She thought for sure that she was about to become the target of a telemarketing sales pitch, and was about to hang up when she heard someone on the other end speak her name.

"Hello?" she said again.

"I wasn't expecting you to pick up," a male voice responded.

"Who is this?"

"This is Ron. Ron Tasker."

"How did you get my number?"

"Well, to be honest, it wasn't very difficult."

"I'm serious. How'd you get my number?"

"I do know your address."

"This number is unlisted. Now I want to know how you got it?"

"I don't see any need to be hostile here," Tasker said in a sedate tone. "The important thing is that I went through the trouble of getting it because I couldn't stop thinking about you. I was hoping you were feeling the same way and might be interested in going to dinner with me tonight. What do you say?"

Saney put a hand to her head and ran her fingers through her hair. She was so appalled, angry and spooked that she could not think of an appropriate response.

"I really don't think so, Ron," was all she could come up with.

"How about next week then?"

"Look, I have a lot going on in my life right now, and frankly I'm not interested."

"Are you seeing somebody?"

Saney could not believe the raw nerve of this guy. "No," she said flatly.

"Okay," Ron said. "I understand. I do. Really. And I appreciate your honesty."

The depth of his sincerity shocked Saney. For some reason, she was expecting a more inflammatory reaction.

"You can't blame a guy for trying," Ron continued. "Maybe I'll see you around."

There was a click on the other end of the line. Before Saney hung up, her skin had already broken out with goose bumps. She wrapped a mover's blanket around herself to help fight the chill she was feeling. One thing she did not want to do was spend too much time dwelling on Ron's phone call. She was anxious to get back to her files. But first, she felt moved to play back her recent messages, which she did. They were all from Ron. And as she listened to them, the chill she was feeling intensified with each one she heard.

While all of the messages were inherently innocuous in nature, the very idea that Ron was compelled to call that many times in such a short duration was disquieting. It did not seem likely now that he would be satisfied with the rejection she had just given him. She knew she would have to be extra careful for a while, but right now, she remained as determined as ever to continue her work despite the lingering fear. She just got up to go put on a sweater, sure that once she got into her files again she would forget all about Ron Tasker.

She was wrong.

Her progress slowed to a snail's pace. She yawned as she looked at her watch and thought that maybe she had been at it too long. But there was still so much to do, she told herself, and forced herself to keep at it.

Chris was in the middle of a double shift because Rebecca could not make it in that day. He had been on his feet since 4:00 AM, but he was not tired. He was looking forward to seeing Saney again. He had gone to her apartment on his break and had dropped her outfit off at the dry cleaners. It was ready by now, and Chris was anxious to pick it up and go take it to her. He had spoken about this to the shift manager, who told him that when things slowed down a little he could go.

Now, as the last customer inside the shop was leaving, Chris quickly removed his apron. He was about to nudge open the swinging doors that separated the back room from the front room, when he happened to glance into the dining room and saw a man walk into the bakery. Chris was instantly frozen to the spot with fear. He moved further back into the kitchen and watched his "uncle" Claybert through the glass along the back of the donut display racks. His heart skipped a beat when he saw Claybert look in his direction. Thinking he had been spotted, Chris stood motionless, unable to move. Though he had not planned on it happening so soon, he knew this day would come. He could not help but wonder what Claybert was going to do to him. Then Chris realized that Claybert was not looking at him, but at the choice of donuts available in the glass case.

Chris was relieved. The sheriff was not only big and strong, but he was mean and even more violent than Chris's foster father had been. He had seen the man beat suspects to the point where they needed to be hospitalized, and for no better reason than to see them suffer and bleed. And he had always gotten away with it by claiming he had acted in self-defense. One time, Chris had seen him kill a man, and he could still recall the incident with great detail.

Chris had been sitting in the station house with his foster father. They had been waiting for Claybert, who was not there. When he finally came in, he was pushing a handcuffed black man in front of him. The sheriff gave the man a hard shove, and because his legs were also shackled, he pitched forward and fell to the floor on his face.

"Gotta watch your step around here," Claybert said with a laugh, then walked up to the prisoner and began to kick him. "Get up. Come on, get up!" The man moaned as the sheriff tattooed his ribs with the point of his boot.

Chris saw that his foster father was smiling broadly beneath the hand he was using to cover his mouth.

"You think you can just go around looking in my windows at my girls?" the sheriff said. "Well I got news for you, boy, you ain't gonna get away with it. Just like you ain't gonna get away with what you did to little Missy Byers. You were the one who raped and killed her, ain't ya, boy?"

The man looked up at him with wide eyes. "No, sir," he said around a bleeding mouth. "I swear on my momma's soul."

"Your nigger momma ain't got no soul, boy," the sheriff said as he reached down to his side and removed his holstered gun. In the same motion he released it, letting it drop to the ground at his feet. "He's got my gun!" Claybert yelled, startling Chris. The man on the ground shrank away from the pistol as if it were a poisonous snake about ready to strike. In the next instant, Chris saw that Claybert was holding a switchblade. The prisoner screamed. Then Claybert lunged toward the black man, plunging the knife repeatedly into his cowering body.

Chris could not believe what he was seeing. His mouth dropped open but no sound came out. He thought that he might get sick to his stomach. Each time Claybert raised the blade into the air, Chris could see the man's blood dripping from its stainless steel face.

Claybert did not stop stabbing the prisoner until the man stopped screaming.

"You saw the way he grabbed my gun after I asked him about the Byers girl," the sheriff said, breathing heavily.

Claybert stared at Chris with threatening eyes. They cautioned him that he would be better off if he never spoke to anybody about what he had just seen.

And he never did.

Those were the same eyes that were now looking his way through the glass donut case. He pointed in Chris's direction, but the boy knew that it was a jelly-filled that Claybert had his eye on. After paying for the donut and a coffee, he walked out of the bakery. Chris saw him get into his unmarked cruiser, parked only two spaces from Chris's Malibu. He must not have recognized the car fixed up as it was and with a new paint job, the boy thought.

Chris waited five more minutes before he ventured out of the bakery. He sat in his car an additional five minutes and wondered what he should do.

The sheriff must have known he was in town, Chris thought. He knew he had only been lucky this time, and that such luck would not last very long. He did not want to leave Caldera, but he did not feel he had much of a choice now.

Once again, he took the tattered picture of his mother out of his wallet. Looking at it, he could not help but think of Saney. She looked so much like his mother that he almost fainted at the sight of her. Her eyes even had the same bright luster. With an index finger, he gently stroked the emulsion along her cheek as if it were her own smooth skin.

"Help me, mom," Chris said. "I don't know what to do. What's happening? Why am I here? Show me how to find the answers to these questions?"

But only his own thoughts came to him.

Chapter Thirteen

She must have fallen asleep on the couch. It was just after dusk now, and the city lights cast a steel gray pallor over everything in her apartment. She was staring at the side of the Victorian davenport in the corner of the room. She could clearly see the characteristic swirls in its walnut surface. It was not long before she began to see a human shape develop in the pattern of the wood, a distinctively male form, and she could not take her eyes away. The longer she looked, the more distinguishable its face became; narrow eyes, elongated nose, pointy ears, cavernous mouth, and razor-tipped teeth.

Finally Saney closed her eyes and did not intend on opening them again. But just then she began to hear a loud crackling and popping sound, like wood splintering, and she peeked out of one eye. What she saw was her Victorian davenport giving birth to some hideous wood creature.

Lies, she told herself. All lies, manufactured by her subconscious as a way of dealing with the trauma of her rape by her younger cousin in the woods behind her childhood home. It wanted to make sure she did not forget about it completely, so that she would not develop any irrational fears or psychosis. It was a protective response, but it was as painful now as it had been then.

As she witnessed the creature burst forth from the antique writing desk, grunting and snarling, she continued to tell herself that it was all in her mind, though as convincing as the special effects in a James Cameron film. And now there was a gaping hole in the desk, and she could see her stationery, envelopes and a roll of stamps inside. That was when Saney began to see the manifestation of the wood troll as something that was perhaps more substantial than she was willing to accept.

Then she felt something enter her body and her eyes snapped open wide. There were trees all around. She was in the woods, and she was eleven years old again. At first she thought the object was going into her bum, but it was invading her private place. At the same time, she became aware that her panties were rolled down and knotted uncomfortably just above her knees. In the gloaming of her apartment now, she looked over her shoulder and caught a glimpse of the wood troll. It was lying beside her on the couch, pressing itself tightly against her. He was putting something large inside her and it hurt. Its lower body was moving rapidly, pushing it in and out. She could feel the rough texture of its "skin" where it came in contact with the back of her legs and could hear its labored breathing.

As something inside her started to tear, she cried out, but the creature only began to pump harder and faster. The more she screamed the more violently it thrust the object, which felt like it was getting bigger.

Saney had not seen her cousin's face during the entire incident. She did not want to. Instead, she stared up at a nearby tree. She remembered staring at it for so long that she began to see a human face in the grain of the wood. So badly did she not want to accept what her cousin was doing to her that she actually began to imagine that the tree was alive, and that it was the tree that was hurting her, penetrating her with one of its knotted branches, tearing her insides apart.

When it finally stopped, the pain would not go away. She saw a tree-man with a bloody branch for a penis run off through the woods and quickly disappear among the other trees.

Now the wood troll was gone from her apartment as well. The davenport was undamaged, but the pattern in the wood was shifting, and slowly it likened itself into the face of her cousin. When Saney felt the ghostly warmth of her own blood trickle down her thighs she began to scream, immobilized by the pain radiating out from her crotch. She was afraid that if she tried to get up off the couch she would not be able to walk or run.

Saney's screams gave way to tears as she began to cry. The face slowly faded from the wood, only an arbitrary pattern remaining, and she became fully aware that it had all been a dream. She had never experienced such a vivid and horrifying nightmare, and it left her wanting only to wrap herself up into a tight ball and never open up again.

Then her door buzzer sounded and she just sat there, wishing whoever it was would just go away. However, when it sounded again, she got to her feet to answer it. She did not know who it was, but she got a strong sense that she did not have to be afraid. She crossed the room and hit the intercom button.

"Yes."

"It's Chris. From the bakery. I have your outfit from the cleaners."

"Okay, Chris. Come on up."

Saney figured she must have known that it would be him, and this reassurance gave her the intuition that she had nothing to fear. She did not think any more about it as she opened her apartment door and waited for Chris to get off the elevator. In fact, her spirits were unusually high, especially in consideration of what she had just been through. In her newfound exuberance, Saney totally forgot that she had been crying only moments before. The look on Chris's face when he first saw her was enough to break her heart.

"Are you okay?" he asked, rushing to her side.

"Oh, I'm fine, Chris. I just woke from a horrible dream. Come on inside." She turned and walked into the apartment.

Chris shut the door and followed behind her. "I'll be right out," Saney said as she crossed the room toward the bathroom. "Just put that on the couch, Chris. Thanks."

She let the water run cold, then bent over the sink to splash her face. Her eyes were still red and swollen, but she felt a lot better. Then she dried her face and came out of the bathroom.

"That must have been some dream," Chris said. "Are you sure you're all right?"

"I'm okay now. Really." She lifted the cellophane-shrouded outfit off the back of the couch and hung it up in the hall closet. "I was thinking of boiling some pasta and preparing some vegetables for dinner. You're welcome to stay. If you're hungry now, I have a spinach pie in the . . ." She stopped when she saw the pensive, distant look in the boy's eyes. He was looking at her, but Saney could tell that he had not been listening. "Is there something on your mind, Chris?"

She knew he heard her then, because he blinked.

"Did you ever want to say something but you were afraid to because of how dumb it would sound?"

"Yes," she said. "All through graduate school. But you know what I found out? There were other people who had the same exact questions I did, but it's the ones who ask the questions that get the answers."

"Well, it's not really a question." Chris paused, struggling for the right words.

Saney was sympathetic and patient, and waited for him to collect his thoughts.

"Maybe it would be better to just show you," he said, and reached into his back pocket. He took out his wallet and removed the picture of his mother, which he handed to Saney.

She stared at it, in obvious amazement at the likeness, then looked over at Chris with both curiosity and understanding.

"That's my mom who I never met," Chris said.

"It could be me," Saney said.

"I know."

Over the course of the next hour, while the two of them

shared a meal consisting of elbow pasta and steamed broccoli, Chris told her what his life was like in New Jersey and why he had come to Caldera. He told her about Claybert and how kind he had been treated by the people at the bakery. He told her all about his mother and how she had guided him this far and then suddenly deserted him. By the time he was through, Saney's eyes were beginning to tear all over again.

"Do you think that I might be your guiding force now?"

"I don't know."

"And what is it I'm supposed to be guiding you toward?"

"I don't know." Chris looked flustered. "See. I told you it would sound dumb."

"It's not dumb, Chris, if that's what you believe. Who knows, it might even be true." Saney reached out and took him by the hand.

"Do you really think so?"

"Hey, would I lie to you? I'm your guiding force now, remember?"

The funny thing was, even though Chris knew she was joking, he believed it. "What do you think I should do then?"

"About Caldera or about your uncle?"

"Both."

"I think you know that you should turn yourself in. From what I can see, you're a smart, levelheaded kid who knows that it's the right thing to do. Of course, you shouldn't surrender to your uncle if he intends to harm you. I'm sure the local police can protect you. After what your foster father did to you, there won't be a jury in this country who would convict you of his murder. The D.A. might even decide not to file charges against you. As for leaving Caldera, once the situation with your uncle is resolved, I'm not too sure what to advise. From what I've seen so far, there doesn't seem to be too much promise here."

"Really?" Chris said, hoping he did not sound too much like an awestruck babe in the woods. "It's such a big city. With so many rich people."

"Between you and me, Chris," Saney said, "the bad grossly

outweighs the good."

"Is he some kind of environmentalist, that man you were with?"

"Julian? Yes. How did you know that?"

"Didn't you tell me?"

"No. I don't think I ever did."

"Maybe he just looks like he might be an environmentalist."

"You think he has something to do with this guiding force stuff?"

"Yes."

"And you think he might be able to provide some information that would be helpful?"

Chris nodded.

Neither of them spoke any more about it. They talked about everything else, from the weather to the pets they had growing up. For Chris, it was like being in a real home, with a real mom, the way he'd always imagined it.

When Julian walked in, holding something behind his back, A.J. was watching *Judge Judy*.

"That's telling him," A.J. shouted at the TV. "Get a job."

Julian had been coming by the hospital everyday to see A.J., and this was the best he looked all week. He had responded well to the antibiotics and his condition had been upgraded several times. Now in a private room, he seemed well on his way to a complete recovery.

When A.J. finally noticed Julian standing there, he smiled and said, "Well, look who dropped in. It's Amphibian Man. Faster than a speeding newt. More powerful than a giant salamander. Able to leap taller than a bullfrog in a single bound. And he, disguised as Julian Bloom, a mild-mannered zoologist for the World Health Organization, fights a never-ending battle to find rotting logs, cool, moist places and the pursuit to live on both land and water." A.J. started to laugh, and for a while it did not seem to Julian that he was ever going to stop.

"Somebody sure is feeling a whole lot better," Julian said.

"It's going to take more than a thousand rats to ruin my day. You know that."

"And I don't work for WHO. It's a private organization called Project Earth."

"I'm just razzing you," A.J. said, then noticed the Christmas paper-wrapped box Julian was trying to hide. "What do you got there?"

Julian presented the gift to A.J. "Open it and find out."

A.J. took it with mock suspicion, shaking it and then listening to it to make sure it was not a bomb. Julian watched with a look of impatience, though he was trying hard not to smile. Then A.J. carefully peeled away the wrapping. What he eventually uncovered was a fishing tackle box. He thumbed through all the equipment inside the storage trays and compartments.

"I'll bet you don't know what half of this stuff is used for," A.J. said, looking up at Julian.

"I will, though. And you're going to teach me."

"And I didn't get you anything."

"Well, I figured I could use this more than you. You must have all of that stuff already."

"So this is a Christmas present for yourself?"

"Hey, nothing but the best for me."

"Oh, yeah. What's this?" A.J. removed a plastic frog from the box and held it up.

"That's a floating plug. And as you can see, it has a diving bill in front that will allow the plug to dive down to a certain depth when retrieved at a certain speed."

"Very good. We'll make a respectable angler out of you yet."

Julian took a few steps back toward the open door and reached out into the hallway. When he straightened up again, he held a fishing rod.

A.J. motioned to examine it more closely.

"That's boron," Julian boasted, handing it over to A.J.

"Good action," A.J. said, bending the rod slightly. "Bait-casting reel. Level-wind device. Monofilament line." His brief inspection concluded, A.J. looked at Julian as if to say, *you did good, kid.* "Very nice. But tell me, what do you expect to catch with this?"

"Oh, I don't know . . . tuna, marlin, swordfish."

A.J. laughed. "In the small freshwater lakes and rivers around here, all you're going to get are some bluegill, perch, and crappie."

"Well, I'll catch a lot of crappie, then."

"Should be easy enough. Even for you. Those fish will bite on just about anything. I've used bread dough, marshmallows, even popcorn in a pinch. A lot of anglers use live frogs as bait. Did you know that? Maybe that's what's killing off your Bufonidae family toads."

"Sure. That's it. Fishermen travel fifteen miles inland from the river banks to catch these bullfrogs, take them all the way to the Canadian River to bait them, and then go to the trouble of trekking the fifteen miles back to put their bones where they originally found them."

"I didn't say they did all *that*, especially since you can get bullfrogs at any bait shop along the river. I just said they use them, that's all."

Julian felt the mood of their conversation shift suddenly and both men fell silent. He wanted to go ahead and ask A.J. a few questions about what happened that day in the runoff pipe, but debated how to broach the subject. A.J. had never again mentioned the bodies he told Julian about seeing that first night in the hospital, and now that A.J. seemed to have taken a liking to him, Julian was hesitant to say anything that might compromise their friendship.

"A.J., do you remember telling me anything in the ICU the night of the attack. Something out of the ordinary that you saw inside the pipe."

A.J. just looked at him and shook his head. "I don't remember much of that day. I remember being down there. I saw a big pile of rat shit. And then it was lights out. I woke up here. I must have been out of it pretty good on painkillers. Was I talking about space aliens or Elvis living down there all these years?"

"Something like that."

"That must have been funny," A.J. snorted in amusement. "Too bad you didn't record it. That would have been a holler to play back now."

Just then a young nurse came in. "You boys behaving?"

"Did I ever tell you about the time I met the Rat Pack?" A.J. asked the nurse.

"No," she said, "but I can read all about it on your chart."

"No, I'm talking about Frank, Deano, Sammy . . . *the Rat Pack*."

"You never met Frank Sinatra."

"Julian, would you tell her that I'm not lying."

"He did tell me the same story the other day."

"See."

"But I didn't believe him either."

"You louse."

"A.J., I have to get going," Julian said. "I'll just leave all this stuff here and I'll see you tomorrow. I have a Christmas party to go to tonight."

"Don't worry about me. I'll be fine. You go and have a good time."

"Oh," Julian said. "I almost forgot." He pulled a cigar out of his jacket pocket.

"I hope you're not about to do a Bill Clinton impression," A.J. said.

Julian laughed and tossed the cigar to A.J.

"Look at this," A.J. said. "A genuine Tiparillo."

"Don't forget your promise. You *have to* take me fishing with you now."

A.J. removed the cellophane wrapper and stuck the cigar in his mouth. "You got it," he said. "But right now, I'm going fishing for a pretty nurse." He pretended to cast a fishing line out in the direction of the young nurse. As Julian turned to leave, he could see the nurse shaking her head and smiling.

"Hey, look!" Julian heard A.J.'s voice and his laughter coming down the hall. "I got one. I'm going to reel her in. Oh! She's too young, I gotta throw her back."

And that was the last time Julian saw A.J. alive.

Chapter Fourteen

Carl Aframe had just walked in with his wife, and Tasker instantly fixed his attention on her. She crossed the room by her husband's side, greeting everyone she was introduced to with a charitable smile. Her skin was smooth as porcelain and her medium-length chestnut brown hair perfectly framed her Kewpie doll face. She was the prettiest woman in here so far, Tasker thought, but the red head in the green dress was absolutely delectable.

Tasker always found that it was best to go to these parties stag. There were always plenty of women—every man was with one—and many of them seemed to have a roving eye for the rogue male in the group. It worked for him, anyway. There was bound to be a wife or girlfriend who was unsatisfied or insatiable and would make her carnal needs known to him with a look or a gesture. Tasker viewed these women as victims of a fuck famine, and considered himself part of the relief effort. So far this evening he had not found anyone in need, but there usually was an initial guardedness that took some time and a few drinks to erode. And then the messages of amorous longings would start to be broadcast loud and clear to Tasker.

As he looked around, sizing up the women in the room, Ron

estimated that there were at least ten he wanted to fuck, though that was probably a conservative appraisal, as more were likely to be added to the list as the night, and his alcohol intake, progressed. He liked his chances tonight, but right now the Penis Choice Award would have to go to Green Dress. Tasker made sure he kept one eye on her at all times, hoping she would be the one who would give in to her lascivious nature.

More guests were arriving, including a somewhat older woman with a very ample bosom. She was with a man Tasker had never seen before. Her rack was impressive enough that Tasker was compelled to put her on the list. He was imagining what it would feel like burying his face in her cleavage, when he felt a finger tap his shoulder.

"Ron, you look like you could use a little company."

Tasker turned around and saw one of the Project accountants, Bill Something, looking up at him. There was a cute brunette by his side, and she was smiling at Tasker. That was almost a sure-fire way to make the list, he thought, and after a brief visual examination, the brunette was easily able to secure herself a permanent spot there. She was much younger and taller than Bill. The legs that came out from under her tight red skirt seemed to go down ten feet to the floor. She was snapping cinnamon chewing gum on one side of her mouth.

Tasker could hear Bill speaking to him, but he was not listening to a word the man was saying until he heard, "Oh, how rude of me. Amy, this is Ron."

"Hi," she said, her voice husky and inviting.

"It's a *pleasure* to meet you, Amy." Tasker took her hand and held it for a long time.

Bill was oblivious, and just kept on talking. "Ron's pretty much in charge of everything here, Amy," he was saying. "The problems I mentioned to you that we're having getting a local Project Earth chapter started in Caldera, unlike most other regions we've worked in, goes far beyond financial considerations. It's not as if the city can't afford it, not by a long shot. It's just that interest is low and volunteers are scarce. Ron could probably tell you more about that. It's a very unusual situation. Ron, explain to Amy what you think will happen if this community doesn't come together to oppose its environmental foes?"

"To be perfectly honest," Tasker said, "I prefer not to mix business with pleasure." He deliberately glanced at Amy and smiled before turning to Bill. "Tomorrow we'll try to solve all that ills Caldera. Tonight, we're at a party, and the only thing we're being held accountable for is to have a good time."

"I'm with you, big guy," Bill said, gently tapping the front of Tasker's shoulder with his fist.

"Me too," Amy said, smiling. Tasker smiled back wolfishly. Tasker had not been keeping up with the progress his organization was making in Caldera the past few days, but he felt he was doing a good job of keeping everybody at Project Earth unaware of his dereliction so far. Bill certainly bought it.

Just then, some other unfortunate soul from the Project wandered close enough to Bill to get caught up in his palaver, like a fly in a spider's web. Bill did most of the talking while the other man did most of the listening. The only time the other man was able to say anything at all was when Bill stopped to catch his breath.

Tasker was not paying attention to either of them. He was totally absorbed by Amy. The only other thing he was aware of was that he was not sure if he would ever be able to focus on the business he had in Caldera. For whatever reason, he was not too worried about it, either. As he continued to stare at the alluring coquette and she stared back, Tasker felt as if something deep inside him was commandeering his body, mind . . . and soul. And it was not just that part of his anatomy in the front of his trousers that was asserting itself, but something almost alien, though surely not foreign to Tasker. When he got like this, he just could not control himself. He had tried before, but failed each time. He had seen a therapist. A psychiatrist. He had taken their medication. He had combined counseling and drugs. Changed his lifestyle. He had done everything they told him to do. He had even taken another position in the organization that would have him traveling constantly all over the world because they thought it would mitigate his condition. All he wound up doing was substituting one addiction for another. Only now, ever since he had arrived in Caldera, the other thing had started up again too. And this time it was worse. He knew this because, when he looked down at his hands, he noticed that he had once more started biting his nails. The tips of his fingers were chewed raw, and some were bleeding. And then there were the dreams that he did not even like to admit to himself that he was having. What made it even more difficult to confront was that they seemed so real. Too real. He would much rather look at Amy, Green Dress, Xenia. Anything but the mirror.

So while Bill was sidetracked, talking shop with another Project Earther, Tasker and Amy slipped away without being noticed. It was not until his one-way conversation was ending that Bill Something decided to introduce Amy and Ron. However, when he turned around, both of them were nowhere to be seen.

As Julian and Saney walked into the hotel ballroom together, they both got the same perception that everybody there was looking at them. Neither of them could understand why they would be getting so much attention, and while it made them uncomfortable, it was something that they had expected on some level. There was a sense of urgency and purpose that they now felt, both in their individual emotional lives as well as in the work they were doing in Caldera. It was not a grandiose delusion for them to believe that they were embarking on a mystery of such monumental importance than no one, including themselves, could fully understand. Julian looked at his duty somewhat differently than Saney, but they both knew that their success meant more than just clean drinking water and a night of sleep without bad dreams.

Saney saw her obligation similar to that of a Queen's, but

whose nobility had been ordained by a higher power, not by her birthright or an arranged marriage. She fell far short of believing that she had been chosen by God because, first of all, that would be a grandiose delusion, and second, she had not entertained a purely religious thought for far too long to start now. She just knew that she was the right person, if not the only person, to help Caldera recover its cognitive equilibrium.

Julian, on the other hand, viewed himself and his work the way the early existentialist philosophers had thought of themselves—as instruments of truth and knowledge. Julian was not quite presumptuous enough to think that he had been bestowed any divine knowledge, but he was confident enough in what he understood about the perils of environmental neglect to try to impress this wisdom onto others who could benefit from it.

Tonight, Julian even felt comfortable in the suit and tie he was wearing. He liked how it complimented Saney's black, hip-hugging chiffon dress, which was cut just above the knee and had a plunging neckline. Actually, he thought, it was Saney who complimented him, because with the dress she was wearing, it did not matter what Julian had on, she would make him look good.

The hall was crowded with unfamiliar faces, but with Saney at his side, Julian felt more at ease than he could ever have imagined. They proceeded across the room toward a long table crammed with fruit, appetizers, and pastry from Deluder Baker Shops.

"What do you figure," he said with a straight face, "one more time around and we're out of here?"

"Relax," Saney said. "We just got here. It'll get better."

In the middle of the table was a large punch bowl filled with a pink liquid and ice. Julian gestured toward it and Saney nodded. He poured a cup for both of them and they just stood back for a moment and took in the sights.

"It all seems so staged, doesn't it?" Julian said.

"What?"

"Christmas in Caldera. I don't know how to explain it exactly. It just doesn't have that Christmasy feeling."

"They have a Santa maitre d'," Saney pointed out. "There's paper snowflakes hanging from the ceiling. There's mistletoe everywhere."

"That's not what I mean. Even with all the commercialism, there isn't that undercurrent of good will you normally get this time of year. It's like so much window dressing."

"I think I know what you mean. There's no spirit. It's all so vulgarly pagan."

"I didn't know you were so religious."

"I'm not really," she said. "I mean, I was brought up in a Catholic home, but when I left Hungary, left my family, I guess I left my faith behind. I'm not sure what happened. Maybe I just couldn't see how God could allow so much evil to exist in the world, and disposing so many people to violence."

"Well, I suppose you're not alone there," Julian said. "There's so much information available today that people can't seem to believe anything unless they can see it or put a face to it. This is the human attribute that has succeeded in leaching the religion from Christmas."

"You sound disappointed. And you, a man of science."

"Well, I didn't have the religious upbringing you did, but it has always been a prevalent force in our society. Its tendrils are hard to escape entirely. But the things I was always interested in, and later went on to study in college, really didn't afford a place for religious faith. Atheism seemed a logical by-product of my work in the animal kingdom."

Suddenly a collective murmur arose in the room and people began to gather around the large windows that looked out at downtown Caldera. From their vantage point, Julian and Saney could see that the night sky was filled with slowly drifting snow. The light from the ballroom illuminated the flakes directly outside the window. The effect was breathtaking, provoking gasps from many.

"See that," Saney said, "maybe the pervasive spirit of the

season cannot be so easily suppressed."

As the two of them moved closer to the window to get a better look, they both spotted someone they recognized standing in front, his back to them. He was holding a snifter of cognac, and instead of regarding the snow outside the window, he was looking at the women directly around him.

Saney pulled Julian aside. "I don't like him," she whispered, hoping the man would not turn around and spot her. "Let's leave."

"Who? Why?" Julian looked around the room, confused.

"That man standing at the front of the window in the two thousand-dollar suit?"

"Ron Tasker?"

Saney continued to drag and pull Julian along, putting as much distance and as many bodies as she could between her and Tasker. "You know him?" she asked.

"Yeah. He's my boss. How do *you* know him?"

"We met last week outside my apartment building. It was early in the morning. He said he had a friend who lived in the building, so I figured it was a girlfriend. But then he gives me his card. It wasn't even a business card. It only had his name and number on it. He must have had them made up just to give to women. Naturally, I didn't call him. The next thing I know, he has *my* number and he's calling me all the time, leaving messages on my machine. Finally I spoke to him and told him that I wasn't interested. He took the rejection well, but there's something about him I don't trust."

"You really hit that one on the head," Julian said. "That guy has more pick-up lines than you've got hairs on your head."

"It's not funny, Julian. I can't believe you work for him."

"I'm sorry. It's just that he's got a reputation for being quite the ladies man."

"I can't see a woman falling for that."

"I can have a talk with him, if you like."

"No. Let's just get out of here." Suddenly Saney's eyes went wide with terror. "Oh, no," she cried out. "He's turning around.

I think he's coming this way." She took off like a shot and headed for the ladies room nearby. Julian was about to go after her when he felt a powerful hand grip his shoulder.

"I didn't expect to see you here," Tasker said.

Julian turned around and was eyeball to eyeball with Tasker.

"Ron, you're just the man I wanted to see. I haven't heard from you in a few days and was wondering what you thought of my new preliminary report."

Ron's brow furrowed.

"It included physical evidence of possible predation to an indigenous species of bullfrog."

"You mean the only evidence you've managed to collect so far have been some frog bones?"

"At the very least, I think it proves a link between the rat population and the city's expansion. That alone could establish a direct threat to the local ecosystem."

"Ah, yes, your little rat-chaser friend. I saw that on the news."

"Ron, did you even read the report?"

"Julian, now's not the time or place for this. All I can say is, you'd better come up with something more urgent than just some dead frogs. It looks like we're all going to be here for quite a while. I'll be sticking around longer than I had expected to myself. So let's take all the time we need to do this thing right." He looked up suddenly. "There's Bob Cushman. I have to go. I'll see you around."

Tasker walked off, leaving Julian alone and confused. All the lab tests had not come back yet, but Julian was sure he had collected more than enough data to show that Project Earth needed to intervene, and soon. It seemed to be an open and shut case. Dead frogs or no dead frogs, there was more than sufficient evidence to warrant the calling in of the environmental National Guard—Project Earth—to Caldera.

Julian got a sick feeling in his stomach. Something was not right, and he had a sense that it had to do with more than just the environment.

He caught up with Saney near the ladies room and they left the party together. It was a quiet, tense ride home for both of them.

Chapter Fifteen

Chris knew that he had to get out of Caldera. With his uncle hot on his trail, he had little choice. It was only because of Saney that he felt any reluctance at all about leaving. Saney wanted him to surrender, but if he did that, Chris knew that he would be trapped, and with nowhere to run, he would be a sitting duck in a shooting gallery when Claybert found him.

He had given his mother one last chance to offer her advice, staring at her picture all that night, but it was no use. Maybe this place had clouded the ability he'd once had to receive communications from her, he thought. Perhaps it would even be restored once he got away.

Chris was considering just up and leaving without saying good-bye or telling anybody where he was going. But as he was preparing to depart, he was suddenly seized by a pang of guilt. He had pretty much been given free run of the estate since his arrival, and now he was planning on sneaking out. It did not seem right. He did not want to seem ungrateful to his host, who had been so good to him. But the urge to leave was just as strong as his guilt, and he zipped up everything that he had come there with into his backpack.

Chris had some cash that he wanted to leave in repayment

for the work that was done on his car, plus a little extra for the room and board. It probably was not enough, but it was all he had, and he wanted to show his appreciation somehow. Also, it made Chris feel better about himself and more responsible for his own life.

Just before he left the room for the last time, he paused, realizing that he could not just leave the money on the bureau like a chamber maid's gratuity and not say anything to the man who had given him so much. Chris thought the man deserved to be told just how much his hospitality was appreciated. It was the very least Chris could do. The money, after all, meant nothing to Deluder. Its only purpose was to leave Chris with a clear conscience.

He checked the entire second floor, but there was no sign of Deluder. He then proceeded to the lower portion of the house. The first place he looked was the garage, which was actually more like a hangar. The first set of lights he flipped on revealed only a small fraction of Deluder's Smithsonian-like car collection. He had everything from the modern day elitist luxury imports to a classic Model-T.

Deluder was not in there either, but Chris made his way further inside just to get one last look at the black 1949 Mercury club coupe. It was Chris's dream car, one he'd always imagined himself driving. He could have gotten in it and indulged the fantasy that much more, but thought better of it and decided to move along. He paused suddenly as he was looking out across the garage at all the cars, struck by the peculiar state they were in. None of them seemed to have been reconditioned. They were all clearly used. And filthy. Many had badly worn tires, rust stains, dings and dents, and sun-scorched interiors. It was as if Deluder had recently taken the cars out on the road himself. Chris supposed he could afford to do just that, but it was odd to see them this way. It was like stepping back in time to when these cars were actually maneuvering along unpaved dirt roads all over the world, vehicular dinosaurs.

Chris continued on, stepping through a door that he thought

would lead him into another portion of the garage. Instead, he discovered several smaller rooms that he had not known existed. One of the rooms was filled entirely with games that, like the cars, represented a history of the industry. The museum of games and toys in this collection went back much further in time than the automobiles. Some of the relics looked like they had been salvaged, not only from other countries, but from bygone civilizations.

This guy seemed to collect everything, Chris thought as he walked into a factory of some kind. The saccharine smell instantly gave away what commodities came out of this room. Production was at a standstill now, but the contents of machines that turned out gumballs, chocolate bars, jelly beans and just about every kind of candy imaginable were spilled across the countertops.

There was always another layer to peel away from the mysteries of the Deluder mansion, and Chris did not know what he would find behind the next door. He got some indication when he heard a swift impact sound that was very familiar, but which he could not immediately identify. It came again a short time later. Then again, and at regular intervals thereafter. Chris looked around. Ahead, he spotted a doorless archway. He passed through it and then followed the hallway to the left. Further along, white light was filtering in through an aperture of some kind on the right. It was another doorless archway, and as Chris neared the threshold, he had to shield his eyes from the brilliance. At first he thought he had stepped out into the sunshine. He could even distinguish the outline of trees in the distance and grass in the foreground. But when his eyes adjusted to the light, he realized that what he was staring into was actually a cavernous roofed interior, as big as the great outdoors. Upon closer inspection, Chris came to see that the room was an artificial single-hole golf course, built to scale and complete in every detail, including a water hazard and sand traps. But the trees were not real. The grass was fake. The walls were one big panoramic mural of a hilly outdoor landscape and the sky was blue paint. The lighting, so many sodium arc bulbs, gave the illusion of sunshine.

A man was standing ten feet from Chris. He was holding a golf club, about ready to swing. He did not take his eyes off the ball. Then, in one fluid motion, he pulled the club back, brought it forward again and made contact with the ball on the tee in front of him. He lifted his head to follow the tiny white dot as it sailed two hundred plus yards into the middle of the false fairway. The man-made green was still a couple hundred yards away.

"Got a little underneath that one," the man said, then turned to Chris and smiled. "You must be Chris. Do you golf?" He did not wait for Chris to reply as he bent down to pick up some kind of remote control unit. "We could shorten up the course for you, if you like," he said, and touched one of the buttons. Chris immediately heard the drone of a powerful motor and felt the entire room begin to vibrate. A moment later, the floor and the walls began to move while the distant green was hydraulically relocated closer to the tee. "Or, we could complicate things and have a dog leg to the left." He pressed a second button and the walls and floor began to shift again to accommodate the new specifications. "Or maybe you want to oblige your hook and have a dog leg right." Another button put the room into motion in the opposite direction.

Finally the man looked up at Chris, who was at a loss for words.

"I know, a bit extravagant," the man said, "But you've seen the rest of the place. It's my style, I'm afraid."

The man was young. Not all that much older than he was, Chris guessed. He had dark hair and prominent facial features. His eyes, nose, lips, and ears all seemed to be too large for his stature. But he was well dressed and groomed, and by anyone's account good-looking.

"I'm Alex Deluder," he said, offering his hand.

Chris shook his hand and said, "*You're* Deluder?"

"Let me guess, I seem too young to have acquired all this

and you're wondering how a few bakeries could sustain such a lifestyle. Well, to be honest, it can't. If you're thinking old money, you are correct. But in my own defense, let me say that I have added to my birthright where others may have squandered their own. I've made some good investments. Now, I have some new money to go along with the old money. I may look like a twenty-something fortunate son, but I have traveled the world extensively and I have seen more suffering than you can imagine. I also like to think that I give back to the world, rather than simply taking from it, as a means of increasing my assets."

"Wait a minute, if you're Deluder, who's that man in the suit who brought me here?"

"Ah, that's Emeril. He runs my everyday affairs. What you might call a personal assistant. He has been with me all along. He oversees a number of charitable foundations within the community. I've given him the freedom to extend good will upon those in need in the name of Deluder Bake Shops."

"That reminds me," Chris said. "I want to thank you for everything you've done for me. My car. The room and board. And I wanted to give you this, as fair payment for all you've done." Chris reached into his pocket, pulled out a wad of cash, and presented it to Deluder. "It's not nearly enough, but it's all I have."

Deluder shook his head and waved his hand in refusal.

"Please, take it," Chris said. "It will make me feel better."

Deluder hesitated, but finally took it when he saw the conviction in Chris's eyes.

"I see you have your bag packed. Are you leaving Caldera?"

"There's nothing here for me."

"Where will you go?"

"I don't know," Chris said.

"Well, remember, the doors here are always open." Deluder held up the money Chris had given him and then looked thoughtfully at the boy. "For you to offer me this, it shows the kind of character you have." After a deliberate pause, he said, "You know, I usually travel during the holidays, but for some reason, I decided at the last minute to stay home this year. I've already given my staff the time off, and I was thinking, since we both have no immediate plans, what do say we use this money to go out and buy ourselves a big, fancy holiday feast. Just the two of us. None of that bakery food, but something to really sink our teeth into. Some steak. Veal. Lamb. A final meal before you leave Caldera. How about it, Chris? Surely, you could not protest how I decide to spend my money."

Chris wavered slightly, but that was all Deluder needed.

"It's a deal, then," Deluder said. "How's tomorrow night." Even though he worded it like a question, it was spoken as a statement.

Deluder led Chris back inside through the vast garage. "I'll even let you drive," he told Chris. "Pick out any one you want." Chris was stunned. "Are you serious?"

Deluder flipped on a bank of lights, illuminating the entire garage.

There had to be a hundred cars in front of Chris, but his eyes were immediately drawn to the black 1949 club coupe, and he did not need to look any further. Chris pointed and they went over to it together.

"The James Dean Mercury," Deluder said, opening the driver's side door. "Just like the one he drove in 1955 in *Rebel Without a Cause*. Excellent choice. This one was rebuilt using Jahns racing pistons and an Isky three-quarter race cam. The engine was blueprinted and statically and dynamically balanced. It's got Edelbrock finned aluminum heads, Edelbrock four-barrel intake manifold, Carter four-barrel Carburetor and dual exhausts with 40-inch glasspacks. The original 110 now has close to 150 horses. Get in, Chris. Take it out for a test run. The keys are inside."

Chris did not have to be told twice. He sank into the calfskin seat and took everything in. The headliner was black. The pleated seat inserts were black with wine red bolsters and the door panels matched. It had an ivory custom steering wheel and matching knobs for the gearshift lever and turn signal. The overdrive had been wired into a toggle switch that allowed the driver to engage, disengage or lock the gear. Chris looked expectantly at Deluder, who smiled and nodded, giving Chris the okay to start the automobile. It turned over smoothly the first time he tried it and the engine hummed to life, its bridled power now at Chris's fingertips.

Deluder matched Chris's exuberant smile.

Soon after the boy drove the car out of the garage, Deluder was joined by Emeril.

"He isn't going anywhere," Deluder said.

"No, sir."

They languished in silent contentment for a moment, before Deluder turned to Emeril and said, "How about a round of golf? Best of nine holes."

"As you wish?"

They turned together and headed for the indoor golf range.

Chapter Sixteen

Because it was so early, Saney had asked Julian to come up to her apartment. What was to follow was not something she had planned, though the dim lights and the fragrant candles might have suggested otherwise. They were sitting on the couch watching Jimmy Stewart in *Magic Town*. Not halfway into the movie, Saney turned to look at Julian. He looked back at her, and after a moment he whispered, "I have to kiss you." Saney could barely hear him over the sudden pounding of blood in her ears. Then Julian pressed his lips tentatively against hers. Saney closed her eyes and kissed him back so he would not pull away.

They stayed locked to each other that way for what seemed to Saney like both an eternity and a millisecond. In reality, it was much closer to the latter, and because she had forgotten to breathe, after about a minute she started to feel lightheaded. Saney exhaled deeply. She could feel Julian's desire as he wrapped his arms even more tightly around her, one hand on her back and the other cradling her head. The pressure he applied was tender, but firm, as if he were trying to pull her through his body.

Saney could feel the muscles in his back straining. She pressed herself tightly against him and felt her breasts compact almost painfully against his chest. She imagined that her nipples were making small indentations in Julian's flesh.

Then, in an action that was quite bold for Julian, he pulled his right hand back and reached down the front of her dress and under her bra. Saney started panting with excitement into his mouth as he found a nipple and began to rub it between his fingers.

They were chewing on each other's lips, their mouths opening and closing hungrily over one another. Somewhere in this frenzy of activity, Saney was able to slip out of her dress. When he pulled his tongue out of her mouth and held her at arm's length to look at her, his passion and longing was evident on his face.

Overwhelmed by desire, Julian pressed his lips hard against hers. When he began to lick them, Saney removed her bra. All she had on now were her pantyhose. Julian then guided his tongue to her chin and down her neck. As he nuzzled her breasts, he ran both his hands down her back to her ass. Saney raised her pelvis off the couch, allowing Julian to roll the stockings down over her hips. As Julian's probing digits began to explore the mysteries of her inner body, Saney placed her hand on his crotch and he responded instantly to her touch.

Maybe it was the high levels of stress they had experienced over the course of the week that incited such passion in them. Whatever it was, they made love multiple times despite better judgment that would normally tell Saney to hold off for a while. But she had no regrets afterward. In fact, she never thought a sexual encounter could be so satisfying. She had so few experiences, and they had all been so long ago. Each of those previous times she had forced herself to have sex because she did not want to develop a fear of physical intimacy as the result of the rape. That was what made this experience with Julian so different; she did not think about the incident all evening.

Julian, on the other hand, was exhausted. He felt like he had just competed in some major athletic event, like a triathlon. His inner thighs and the muscles on the sides of his butt were tight and already starting to ache. He knew he was in really bad sex shape, and he wondered if it was noticeable to Saney. He was holding her gently now as she lay beside him sleeping. He wanted to stay just like this, and fall asleep next to her. But as much as he would have liked to spend the night, he knew the decent thing to do was to go home. Unless she *invited* him to stay, he thought.

Julian decided to get up and take a shower.

Tana sat alone on her velvet love seat, empty wine glass in hand. On the coffee table in front of her was a half empty bottle of Australian shiraz. A Yanni CD, playing softly in the background, clicked off as the last track concluded.

She was smiling as she carefully placed her glass down beside the bottle. She was not happy, but the wine had tempered her mood. She was glad for that at least, because she did not want to be reminded of what a fool she had been. She had known all along that Ron was not the kind of guy a girl should get involved with, so she had no one to blame but herself for being stood up tonight. What she could not understand was why Ron would go to the trouble of calling her to ask if she was going to be home tonight if he had no intention of coming by.

Tana got up on unsteady feet and kicked off her pumps as she walked toward the bedroom. She was wearing a clingy black dress that was now hiked up to the top of her thighs. It had become the outfit to wear when she wanted to impress a man. Now, she was feeling anything but sexy. Rejection was something she simply could not accept. She had to fight an impulse to call Ron on his cell phone. He could easily have gotten tied up at work, she thought, or had become delayed by any number of minor emergencies, such as a flat tire.

Tana told herself it did not matter as she grabbed the cigarettes box off the bedside table and then flopped down onto her bed. She moaned softly as her head was momentarily flushed of blood and the bedroom seemed to darken. She lit up and inhaled deeply. As she withdrew the smoke from her lungs, she closed her eyes and stretched out on the mattress. She felt herself instantly relax, blocking out all thoughts of Ron and her feelings of rejection. Her left arm dropped over the side of the bed, the cigarette dangling between two fingers.

Tana heard a noise coming from somewhere in the apartment and forced her eyes open. She was in such a restful state, however, that she thought she might have been dreaming when she saw the silhouetted figure in the doorway, back lit by the bright light from the living room. She imagined that it was Ron. He had come after all, she thought.

Tana smiled playfully. "How'd you get in," she said in mock fright. "That's breaking and entering." She opened her legs wide enough to reveal that she was not wearing panties. "Promise not to break me," she said.

The figure approached the bed.

Tana opened her legs and closed her eyes. They would never open again.

When Julian returned to bed a short time later, Saney awoke and looked at him with wide, adoring eyes. She was about to speak, but hesitated, deciding at the last minute to change how she was going to word her thought.

"Don't look at me like that," Julian warned her. "That's how this whole thing got started in the first place. I don't have enough strength left to pump gas."

Saney allowed herself to smile, despite the weight of her thoughts. "Do you get the feeling that we just passed a point where things will never be the same again?" she said finally. She was going to say, *Julian, do you have a feeling we're not in Kansas anymore*, but she thought the reference to her all-time favorite movie would have seemed flippant.

"I've had that feeling for a long time. Ever since I arrived in Caldera. Ever since we first met. But that's just foolishness, right?"

"I'm not so sure. I feel the same way. There's something about you. About us. And now with Chris, too. He was drawn to me because of my resemblance to his mother, but I'm not so sure it's all coincidence. He even mentioned you."

Julian gave it some thought, but the longer he did, the more questions he had. "Do you suppose the environmental problems and the psychological instabilities of the people here are related somehow?"

"I don't believe that one is directly causing the other, no. But I do think they are connected in some non-interdependent way. And that some unnatural force may be responsible."

"Are you saying that you believe something supernatural is corrupting the environment *and* people's states of mind?"

"I don't see how else all of this can be explained."

"Well, it really hasn't been explained yet, although obviously there's got to be some sort of reason for what's going on here. From my end, I know how environmental toxins can have profound affects on human behavior."

"Julian, I can appreciate the basic tenet in what you're saying, but the tenfold incidence rate of psychoses and other chronic disabling mental disorders per capita in Caldera cannot be wholly precipitated by the affects of CFC's and contaminated drinking water."

"Wait a minute now. I am willing to concede that I'm at a disadvantage in debating whether mental illness has inherently biological or environmental roots, but I refuse to consider that the dynamics of Caldera's woes are the consequence of supernatural rather than natural influences. Stress and viral infection, both of which are categorically environmental in nature, can play a major role in triggering psychoses. The disruption of clear thinking and rational behavior could just as well be the direct result of the introduction of some unknown chemical agent, an oxitoxin into the environment."

"True. And so-called 'normal' people, when deprived of sleep or certain stimuli, can also experience symptoms of psychosis. These people are often distanced from their families.

They shut themselves in. There are people all around, yet they are all alone. They don't know who their neighbors are. This is how people in big cities, like Caldera, tend to live. But, the problem with all the scenarios we both just described is that there are very few people, if any, who fit into them. I know. I've been studying their case histories. In other words, people are acting nutso for no good reason. And unless you can identify a virus that is responsible, then we have little choice but to consider the preternatural."

"Saney, I think you're being a bit impulsive and forsaking your scientific training. The natural world is more than capable of nurturing the kind of problems you've described?"

"What I'm describing goes beyond physical and mental illness. I sense a growing evil in this city, Julian, and I know you feel it too, so don't deny it. As a psychiatrist, I've always thought of evil as something innate, part of our human genetic make-up, and that some people were just more inherently evil than others. Recently, I've come to notice that the one thing that all of my patients are suffering from is blind, overwhelming fear. And I believe that something evil is responsible for their fear."

"Do you mean to suggest that people have no control over their own behavior? That they are somehow excused for their actions because their genes have predetermined their conduct, or the Devil made them do it?"

"No," Saney said in protest. "That's not what I meant. We all have the capacity to change, to differentiate right from wrong and alter our behavior. However, where that capacity to change happens to come from is seated deep within the human brain and in the mysterious chemicals and hormones to which our bodies are slaves. When there is an inability to produce certain chemicals, or when hormones are defective in some way, bad decisions can become more commonplace for some people. Just to give one example, studies have indicated that the ratio of maximum security inmates diagnosed with schizophrenia is at least six hundred percentage points higher than the outside population. That's not an excuse for criminal behavior, Julian, that's scientific fact. Fear is something every bit as tangible as schizophrenia, and when it gets a foothold on a person, the affects can be detrimental. This is what I think is going on in Caldera. What is triggering this fear is what we have to find out."

What she said actually made a lot of sense to Julian. And he could not disregard the fact that the rumination had come from a well-educated, highly intelligent, and sensitive woman. "All right," he said, "maybe this thing is more complex than I first thought. But now that we're in the 21st century, can we really continue to equate what we don't understand to ancient fears and superstition?"

Their discussion did not go any further, because just then a fire alarm sounded. It was so loud as to pull the breath and whatever words they may have spoken right out of their mouths. They hurriedly dressed, while outside in the hall they heard the sounds of opening doors, shuffling feet and loud, nervous voices.

Chris opened the club coupe up on a long stretch of highway just outside of Caldera. The road seemed to jump out of the way of the sizzling tires. The speedometer needle was pegged as far as it could go, and the car was still accelerating. The boy did not just imagine himself to be James Dean, at that moment in time he *was* Dean. It was a feeling of exhilaration Chris only dared to imagine.

Lost in another place and time, Chris did not hear the sirens far behind him. But when a State Police cruiser pulled out onto the highway from the right shoulder just ahead of him, lights flashing, Chris was suddenly splashed in the face by the cold water of reality. He gradually slowed and pulled the dream machine into the break down lane. It seemed like he was waiting a long time before the police finally arrived.

A.J. was almost asleep when he heard the door to his room open and then close softly. He waited for the light to come on and to hear a nurse's voice. Neither of these things occurred.

"Is there somebody here?"

He wrinkled his nose and sniffed the air as a foul odor suddenly permeated the room. Though unpleasant, it was one that he knew very well. He also understood that he would have to get awfully close to a wet rat for the smell to become as intense as this one.

With the curtain drawn around his bed, A.J. fell silent and just listened. There was no sound now. Then he looked down at the floor near the foot of his bed and noticed that his tackle box was gone. As the rancid smell intensified, A.J. reached over and repeatedly pressed the button on the side of his bed to ring the nurse's station.

He felt like a sitting duck just waiting there, so he swung his legs over the side of the bed and tried to stand. The initial pain was crippling, but much of it quickly subsided and he endured what remained as he pushed himself forward. He used the wall for support, but after just a few steps he became winded. The door was just on the other side of the curtain now. A.J. paused and took a deep breath in preparation for his final attempt to make it to the door and then out into the hall.

All of a sudden the curtain started coming down on him as the thin, plastic rings stretched and broke under the stress of some unknown force. He became instantly tangled in the curtain and fell to the ground. Unable to move because someone was on top of him, he screamed out loud. The hand pressed against his face, however, muffled his call for help. A.J. made a futile attempt to bite the hand over his mouth, but only managed to get his teeth around a wad of curtain.

At that moment, A.J. felt a warm wetness begin to spread across his midsection. He stopped struggling, and all at once his pain left him. His final thought was of his beloved Jeanie. She was with him on the deck of his Hyde Drift Boat. He was fly-fishing, and the brown trout were biting like crazy as the shore receded further and further from view.

Chapter Seventeen

Julian opened the front door for Saney and the young man from the bakery. "Hi, Chris," he said. "Come on in, you guys."

Chris just smiled in acknowledgment and followed Saney inside. He stuck close to her side, practically mimicking her every move. When she removed her coat and gave it to Julian, he did the same.

"So, how did it go?" Julian asked after he closeted the coats.

Saney sat down heavily on the sofa and Chris took a seat beside her.

"The police picked Chris up last night," Saney said, glancing sidelong at the boy, "driving like the Devil in one of Deluder's antique cars." She looked back at Julian. "Chris was asked a few questions and then he was let go."

"The local police didn't detain him in connection with the death of his foster father?"

"No," Saney said. "They didn't even give him a speeding ticket."

"Maybe they didn't know about it," Julian said.

"No, I told them," Chris said. "The policeman didn't sound very interested in it, though."

"Was this policeman wearing a gray suit?" Julian asked.

"Yeah."

"Fiftyish. Salt and pepper hair, thinning. A sty in the corner of his right eye?"

"That's him."

"The same guy interviewed me," Saney said. "Come to think of it, he was the only one in the room." She looked at Chris and he nodded in concurrence.

"His name is Bubin," Julian said. "What happened to Tana?"

Saney said, "Apparently, she fell asleep with a cigarette. But it's suspicious because the extent of the damage was minimal and she was hardly touched by the flames. She succumbed to smoke inhalation. They're checking to see if there were any drugs or alcohol in her system that might have incapacitated her. Also, an elderly woman who lives across from her told the police she saw a man outside Tana's apartment shortly before the fire broke out. But the only description she was able to give was that he was 'not short.'"

"A cop wouldn't just volunteer that kind of information in a possible homicide investigation," Julian said. "Why did he want to talk to you in the first place?"

"Well, I had been talking to her professionally. We had become friends, and she lived two floors above me. He wanted to know if she had spoken with me about any of the guys she had been seeing lately. I told him she had never mentioned anybody to me. And then he let me go. How about you? How was your interview?"

Julian took a deep breath before he began. "A.J. was found in his hospital bed . . . disemboweled. A knife used for gutting fish was taken from the tackle box I'd given him and identified as the murder weapon. Whoever did that to him left him with a fishing hook and a dead rat stuck in his mouth. I'm probably the prime suspect. I had been the last visitor to see him." Julian leaned backward, and he would have fallen if the wall had not been there to catch him. "He was still alive when one of the nurses found him."

Saney got up and stood beside Julian, putting an arm around him in support.

"It seems," Julian continued, "that this detective did his homework and found out about all the strange deaths and unsolved murder cases I'd been around my whole life."

"You're going to need a lawyer."

"I suppose," Julian said. As he stared off absently, it was clear to Saney that he wanted to distance himself from her, and everything else. His arms were folded and he had turned away from her. But Saney would not allow him to escape that easily. She got right in his face and stayed there, even as he tried to pull away.

"What's wrong, Julian?"

Julian swiveled his head around suddenly and looked her in the eye. "What if I did it? Huh? What if I killed A.J.? What if I killed all of them? Sometimes I think that I have. I mean, I don't remember it, but it is possible isn't it? I could be blocking it all out. I could have one of those split personalities. It all can't be coincidental that everybody I come in contact with ends up in a cemetery. And since imaginary friends are not capable of homicide, then I must be responsible. And the cops know it. This one cop does, anyway. Maybe he's got some evidence to prove it this time."

"No, Julian," Saney said. "I don't believe that."

"Why not, because you know me so well?" he yelled. "Or because you're likely to be next on the hit parade?"

Saney looked at him and did not know what to say.

"I'm sorry," he said. "I don't want anything to happen to you, Saney. I don't know what to think anymore. It's been going on for so long, that seeing people die has become a way of life for me. Some people have bunions, some have halitosis, others astigmatism. Me, I have this." He paused, then gently cupped Saney's face in his hands. He looked directly into her eyes and, with controlled anger, begged her, "Tell me that I didn't do it."

"All I know," Saney began, "is that you've never been able to love anybody because of your fear of them being taken away

151

from you. How those people died is a matter for the police. I'm more concerned with finding a way to stop you from blaming yourself for their deaths and give you the confidence to love somebody again without apprehension. But I need your help. You seem ready for a change."

"Do you really think it's all in my mind?"

Saney stared at him for a long moment. "I don't for one second think that I'm going to be murdered, by you or anybody else. But I do think you're trying to push me out of your life because you're afraid I'm going to abandon you like your parents did. Their death was an accident. And I'm not going anywhere, Julian. Do you believe me?"

Julian appeared preoccupied. He did not respond right away. "I was told not to leave town," he finally said.

"Chris and I were told the same thing," Saney said, though Julian did not seem to hear her.

"The detective didn't believe that I got an e-mail from my imaginary friend," he said. "What a surprise."

"Julian, where's your computer?"

He looked across the room.

Saney followed his eyes to the laptop sitting on a pile of boxes. "I'm going to show you that you're not crazy."

"Knock yourself out," he said.

As she got on-line, Julian looked around for Chris, who was nowhere in sight. He walked to the kitchen. Not there. He was not in the bathroom or the bedroom either. Julian knew that the boy had to be in the house somewhere. Then he saw the cellar door partially opened and feeble rays of light crawling up out of the cold, dank hole like wounded soldiers.

Julian descended the basement stairs, trying to be as quiet as he could. He spotted Chris standing in front of an empty work bench. He was holding the small black box which Julian had stubbed his toe on a few days earlier.

"What's this?" Chris asked without looking up.

Julian had been so quiet that he thought Chris might have been talking to himself. But before he had a chance to respond, the boy began to unfasten the bloated and rusted clasps that held the box together. Julian knew what was inside, but he found himself watching Chris with anticipation just the same.

Even unclasped, the case would not open. Chris struggled to separate the two halves. Finally there was a little popping sound. A cloud of rust and mildew shot up into the air around the lid as it came free. The boy just stared down at the various lengths and thickness of the needles and pins inside the case.

Julian stepped closer and Chris finally looked up at him.

"What are they?" the boy asked.

"A family heirloom," Julian said. "To be honest, I don't know why I still have them. They look like they belong in a museum. What do you make of them, Chris?"

Chris looked down at the sharp, pointy instruments and just shook his head unknowingly.

"Julian," Saney called from upstairs. "Come here. Look at this."

Julian was about to leave, when something on the work bench caught his eye. It was the Christmas present that he found on his doorstep the same day he nearly tripped over the mysterious black box. He suddenly reached for the small wrapped gift and started to open it as he went back upstairs.

He did not know what to expect, but when he finally tore all the paper and tape away, he stopped dead in his tracks halfway across the living room. It was only an *Uno* deck, but the cards meant something more to Julian. It was a game he had played continually as a young boy. He would entertain himself for hours on end, dealing one hand for himself, one for Nicholas and then playing them both out.

"Do you want to know where that e-mail came from, Julian?" Saney asked.

"Huh?" Julian said, hearing the sound of her voice and looking up.

"Whoever sent you that e-mail did it through a local phone line," she said, then read the number out loud.

Julian just stared blankly at her.

"Pretty awesome, huh?" she said. "Aren't you going to ask me how I did it?"

Julian continued to stare through her as if she was not there, his complexion ashen.

"Julian, what is it?" Saney said, her voice trembling slightly.

"That number. It's one of the company lines at Project Earth." He looked down then at the package of colorful cards in his hand.

"Julian, you didn't send that e-mail to yourself. That detective is wrong."

"What difference does it make?" He flung the *Uno* deck across the room, the cards exploding from the pack when it struck the far wall. "You're going to die next anyway. It can't be stopped."

"Julian, don't talk like that. You're not being rational. You've got to listen to me." Chris had returned from the basement and was standing beside Saney.

"No. I want you to leave here and never come back."

"Are you serious?"

"Yes. It's the only way."

"What about Caldera? What about what we wanted to do here? What about us?"

"I don't care."

"You don't mean that."

Julian retrieved their coats and then rushed over to the front door. "Just leave," he said, and threw open the door. "And don't come back. Either of you. It's for your own good."

"No, Julian . . ."

Julian made a threatening move toward Saney with genuine malice in his eyes, but stopped just short of putting his hands on her. "I fucking mean it!" he screamed. "GET OUT!" He slammed his fist against the wall beside her head for emphasis.

Saney looked at him in disbelief and horror for a moment, then said, "Come on, Chris." She turned and walked out ahead of the boy, who followed sheepishly behind her.

Julian slammed the door shut behind them, instantly

regretting what he had done. Even if it was in their best interest, he could not believe he had raised his hands to Saney. He did not know what had come over him. Saney's car drove off, but Julian could not hear it because his ears were ringing and his head was throbbing.

Out of physical discomfort and mental fatigue, Julian collapsed onto the couch. While waiting for the pain to subside, he fought to keep himself from drifting off to sleep. He did not want to see the visions that were waiting to show themselves behind his closed eyes. He also wanted to start making the necessary preparations so he could leave Caldera as soon as possible. He did not care about the police, Project Earth, or Caldera. All Julian wanted to do was make sure that no one else got hurt. If he stayed, he knew that he would be responsible for whatever happened. And the lives of a few people were worth a whole lot more than the existence of some aboriginal species of frog. At least that's how he would justify his actions to himself at times, like now, when he felt any remorse whatsoever about leaving a city that needed him and a woman that he needed.

Chapter Eighteen

The man who walked into the Caldera Police Station made the hairs on the back of Thomas Bubin's neck stand straight up. His purposeful gait and dour facial expression told Bubin that this man was going to be trouble. He watched from a distance as the man stopped and spoke in a loud, commanding voice to the desk sergeant, but began to move closer so that he would be in a better position in case anything happened.

When the man reached into his pocket and removed something metallic, Bubin had seen enough. He walked over to the desk and stood beside Sergeant McGuirl. "What seems to be the problem here?" he asked.

The man looked around at him like he was an annoying insect, and one he had never seen before.

"Well, you look like somebody in charge around here," the man spat. "As I was telling this desk jockey, I'm Sheriff Claybert Crowley, Winston County, New Jersey." He displayed his badge in front of him as if he were King Arthur brandishing the magical Excalibur. "I need to find a fugitive wanted for murder who I happen to know is somewhere in this hell hole of a city of yours. I'm going to need full cooperation from your department to find this fucker. I asked nicely once, now I'm going to have to get a little ornery to get my point across."

"Sheriff," Bubin began, even-toned, trying not to provoke the man, "I'm a special agent with the FBI and I'm sure I can be of assistance to you. Our National Crime Information Center has a countrywide database . . ."

"I don't give a flyin' fuck about the FBI and your databases. I want this kid's ass in my custody within twenty-four hours or I'm going to turn this city upside down looking for him myself." He slammed a photograph of the boy down on the desk and took a step backward, placing his hands defiantly on his hips. In the process, his right hand swept back the front of his coat to reveal his holstered revolver.

Bubin may have flinched inwardly, but his response was cool and deliberate, and he was steady enough to draw his own side arm if it came to that.

"Sheriff, if you're going to continue this display of bravado here in the station, then I'm going to have to lock you up until you calm down. If, instead, you want to come with me into a private office and calmly talk to me about this case, that might be to everyone's advantage, especially your own."

Claybert's eyes were hate-filled as he stood there glaring at Bubin.

Bubin knew instinctively that he had to act first. If he waited any longer, somebody was going to get hurt. A split second before Claybert reached for his gun, Bubin lunged at the man. They both fell to floor, wrestling for position.

Despite the New Jersey lawman's significant size advantage, Bubin was ultimately able to subdue Claybert with the help of other officers in the station. After locking a set of handcuffs around the bigger man's wrists, Bubin removed Claybert's gun while a couple of uniforms manhandled the unruly sheriff, dragging him toward a holding cell.

"I know he's here," Claybert yelled after Bubin. "And you're protecting him. Well, it's not going to do any good. You're going to pay for this. You hear me? EVERY LAST ONE OF YOU!"

"Are you okay?" McGuirl asked Bubin.

"I'm fine," he said, as he dusted himself off.

"Jesus, what the hell got into that guy?"

"I don't know, sergeant, but I've got enough to do here without worrying about some troublemaker from New Jersey tying me up. Why don't you have Hackley and Kopeci sit down with that hothead after he cools off and see what they can get out of him." Bubin was about to walk away when he realized he had the sheriff's revolver in his hand. Glancing down at the gun, he noticed all the scuffs and scars and the way the nose of the barrel was warped and discolored. Bubin realized right away that the sheriff's weapon had seen some heavy use.

"Why don't you run a check on this while you're at it."

McGuirl took the gun from Bubin, who turned and left the station.

Chris was still looking at his menu. Deluder had his folded in front of him. "I always order the surf and turf," he said with a smile. "I can never decide which I like best. So I choose both. Maybe I do that because our ancestors once swam the oceans before they adapted to life on land. Do you think man evolved from the sea, Chris? Or are you from the Adam and Eve old school?"

"I don't know," Chris answered earnestly.

Their waiter arrived then and took their order. It was no surprise what Deluder would be having, but when Chris asked for the vegetarian lasagna, Deluder raised an eyebrow.

"Are you a vegetarian, Chris?" Deluder asked when they were alone again.

Chris just shook his head.

"Because I've often wondered if we're not all cannibals, in a sense. Vegetarians think they can get around it, but even the plant kingdom cannot be so far removed from us if we *were* all minced on the same cutting board. How do you feel about that, Chris?"

The boy just shrugged noncommittally, then he turned and looked around the dark and elegant dining room. Colorful bulbs inside the numerous fish tanks effectively showcased a variety of exotic species and provided most of the interior lighting. The sound of air bubbles competed with the hushed conversational tones of the restaurant's more evolved patrons. Chris had noticed that there were no prices listed in the menu, but he knew that the money he had given to Deluder would not be nearly enough to pay for their dinner.

"I don't want you to spend all the money I gave you on a meal for me," Chris said, suddenly looking back at Deluder.

"If that's what you're worried about, Chris, forget it. We're here to both grieve your leaving Caldera and celebrate your moving on to someplace better. Money is not an issue. So get anything and everything you want."

Deluder smiled expansively and Chris smiled back.

Just then the wine steward approached. He introduced himself and presented Deluder with an elegant, leather-bound folder inscribed with gold lettering. As he carefully began to peruse its contents, Chris watched him. He could see Deluder's lips moving slightly as he read several listings quietly to himself in consideration. His eyes appeared aqua. Maybe it was a trick of the aquarium lighting, but Chris could have sworn they had been brown previously. There were a lot of things about this man that required you to look twice, the boy realized. For instance, he knew Deluder was young, but he could easily have been mistaken for one of Chris's schoolmates. The skin on his face was smooth and without a hint of stubble. Even his hands were soft and white, like porcelain. Chris would not have been surprised at all if the wine steward asked Deluder for his ID.

Chris was able to glance over the top of the menu. He could not read French if it was right side up, but the prices were listed in dollars, and even upside down he could not believe how expensive many of the bottles were.

"There it is," Deluder suddenly said. He snapped the leather booklet closed and handed it back to the steward. "Bring us the

1975 Chateauneuf-du-Pape from Chateau de Beaucasel, please."

"Splendid choice, sir."

When the man left, Deluder leaned close to Chris and said, "You're about to drink a wine whose grapes were harvested before you were even born. How does that make you feel?"

"I don't know."

"The vast majority of all wines do not improve with age. The one I selected for us is of that minority that does. It's still the same wine that it was when it was first put in the bottle, but somehow it just tastes better now. It's like something that you once despised in youth and later grow to appreciate."

"Like spinach?"

"Good example." Deluder seemed to have the boy's full attention now and he knew it. He stared deeply into Chris's eyes and held them. "But there are also some things that you can never like, under any circumstances, no matter how accustomed to them you get."

"Like what?" Chris asked.

"Well, using the wine example again, we know that not all of them age well. It depends on the vintage, the blend of the grapes, as well as a host of other factors. The Pape improves. But, a merlot, forget it; after so many years, it just becomes rancid, undrinkable."

Chris looked at him with a lost expression.

"All right then, let's take a different approach. Maybe there's someone in your life that has done you wrong and you can never forgive them. No matter what else they ever do or say. No matter how much time goes by. Do you have someone like that in your life, Chris?"

He hesitated. "I suppose."

"Who?"

"My foster father treated me badly."

"Well, doesn't that just eat you up inside? Doesn't it just motivate you to spend the rest of your existence trying to get back at him?"

"My foster father treated everybody badly."

"Are you making excuses for him?"

"No," Chris said evenly. "He wasn't a nice man. I don't know why. But I don't hate him. And I forgive him for the things he did and how he was."

"Tell me, what were some of the things he did to you?"

Chris faltered, feeling a strong sense of mounting guilt and the need to confess. "I killed him, okay," Chris said bluntly.

Deluder continued to look at the boy, unmoved, as if he had already known.

"It was an accident," Chris went on. "He was going to kill me. I tried to stop him and he fell out of a window."

Just then, the wine steward reappeared. He popped the cork, and as he was pouring a small amount into their glasses, the waiter brought their food.

When both had left, Deluder raised his glass to his lips, closed his eyes and took a very deliberate sip of wine, which he seemed to hold in his mouth for a long time before swallowing. Then he opened his eyes and smiled. He held his glass in the air and goaded Chris to do the same. The boy, however, picked up his water instead. They touched crystal and drank.

Chris then watched Deluder as he cut and skewered a piece of rare meat. It left a thin trail of blood across the white table cloth as he placed it on his tongue and moaned in delight.

"So Chris," Deluder said, his lips red with meat juice and wine, "tell me why you came to Caldera."

Chris thought about it, then said, "I was hoping to find out something about myself. Who I am. Where I came from."

"Yes, but why Caldera, in particular?"

He did not hesitate removing his mother's photograph and handing it to Deluder.

"She's very beautiful. Who is she?"

"It's my mom. She put me up for adoption when I was a baby and I haven't seen her since. I don't know where she is, if she's alive or dead. But I intend to find out."

"I can understand if that's why you want to leave Caldera. But maybe there's another reason." He paused to break a lobster tail with his hands. Pulling out the white meat, he said, "I can make your problems go away. Would you like that?"

Chris was slow to respond.

"Don't answer now. We'll talk more later. Please, eat before your meal gets cold."

They did not speak another word as they ate, and Chris's thoughts immediately turned to Saney. She had been on the verge of tears when he left her that afternoon. He did not like to see her that way. He wished he could do something about it, but he did not know what. Just then, something told him that Saney needed him. He was not sure if the thought had come from his mother, or if it was his own conception, but he knew he had to leave at that moment.

Saney's tears had long since dried, but she was still anguished over Julian's harsh words and severe actions. She empathized with what he was going through, but she was hurt because he did not trust her enough to open up and share his feelings. She had gone for a late-night walk to clear her head and had just returned. Getting her blood circulating a little, combined with the cool night air, seemed to do the trick.

When she saw the blinking light on her answering machine telling her she had three messages, she immediately hit PLAY, hoping one, or all of them were from Julian, calling to apologize. Saney held her breath and listened intently. There was some static, but nobody spoke. The other two calls were hang-ups as well, the last one coming only five moments before. *Maybe they had been from Julian*, she could not resist thinking. While she silently debated whether or not she should take the first step and call him, the phone rang, startling her. She instantly picked it up, but before she could say anything, whoever was on the other end hung up.

The dead air sent a shiver up her spine. She did not bother to put the phone back in its cradle.

As soon as Tasker heard her voice, he hung up. He knew that he had her right where he wanted her. With no time to waste, he began preparing himself. As usual, he took a quick shower and carefully removed all the stubble on and around his cock and balls. He thought that there was no better feeling in the world than pushing his cleanly shaven manmeat all the way inside a woman.

When he was done, he splashed on some cologne and put on his best suit. Then he grabbed the little Beretta 950OBS, which he called, The Persuader, and left the condo. When his looks, his charm, and his shaved goods were not enough, The Persuader would be used to help convince the unwilling. It fit inconspicuously in his waistband at the base of his spine, and under his overcoat it was all but undetectable. He had not needed to persuade anybody yet, but as he proceeded in anxious anticipation toward Xenia's, he thought this might be the night.

Chapter Nineteen

"Hello!" Claybert yelled, holding onto the bars of the cell. "Is there anybody here beside these lowlifes you threw me in here with?"

Three men were asleep on the long bench that was attached to a concrete wall of the cell. Another man was sleeping on the floor.

"This is unlawful detention," Claybert continued. "I'm a police officer, and I demand to be released this minute! DO YOU HEAR ME OUT THERE?"

"We can hear you," officer Hackley said as he approached the cell. "Unfortunately, there's nothing I can do for you. Since you're not willing to talk, you're just going to have to wait until Agent Bubin's ready to deal with you."

"You don't understand. I want out of this monkey cage RIGHT NOW!"

It was all the uniformed officer could do to keep from laughing. "I hate to be the one to break this to you, but you're not going anywhere." He held up Claybert's Colt .45 automatic and said, "Seems you've been a busy little beaver. Shooting up a bar in Texas, killing at least one person, and maiming two others." Hackley moved closer to the cell, shaking his head. "I don't know how they do things in Cow Flop, New Jersey, or wherever the fuck you're from, but around here cold-blooded killers are put away. And they don't come out no matter how big they talk."

Claybert's eyes were blazing. "You little pissant beat-pounder. You better get used to it, because you'll never get out of that uniform."

"And you'll never get out of that cell. Except when you get transferred to a state prison, in protective custody, of course, so the general population won't have a chance to make a bitch out of a killer cop."

"I'm tracking a killer!" Claybert shrieked, jamming his body up against the bars. He reached between them to try to grab a hold of Hackley, who just laughed as he danced out of the range of the grasping hands.

All of a sudden Claybert quieted down and a smile stained his face.

"What's your problem?"

"That's not my gun," Claybert said.

"Yes it is."

Claybert shook his head. "No. It's not."

Hackley stared at it for a moment, then looked back up at Claybert, who stuck his head face between the bars to get a better look.

"Let me see it," Claybert said.

As Hackley held the gun out for Claybert's inspection, the prisoner swiftly reached out and pulled the weapon from the officer's hand. Claybert stepped back into the cell with it and grinned.

"It's empty," Hackley said, untroubled.

Claybert turned the gun over in his hand and removed the wood panel from one side of the grip. From inside the gun, he withdrew something, and Hackley instantly became concerned. It was a bullet, which Claybert promptly slipped into the chamber, pulling the slide and barrel back as he did so, and cocked the hammer. Then he took two quick steps forward as the cop managed only one back. With his arms sticking between the bars of the cell and the barrel of the gun trained on Hackley, he fired. The explosion of noise and fire woke three of the drunks from their slumber. The bullet struck Hackley's left temple at a speed of nearly 700 feet per second and exited the back of his skull at a significantly lower velocity. Pieces of bone and gray matter spattered the wall behind the officer. Before the body hit the ground, Claybert could hear several sets of feet rushing toward the cell from the outer room. He immediately dropped to the floor, face down. He closed his eyes and positioned the gun out of view, beneath his torso, as the doors burst open.

Three uniformed officers rushed in, guns drawn, followed by a fourth and then finally a fifth. Several attended to the downed officer while the others approached the cell with some hesitation, seeing another man lying prone on the floor, possibly injured. There was a lot of confusion. One of the officers was yelling at the drunks to try to get them to explain what had happened. Another, a rookie, not sensing any immediate danger, holstered his weapon and removed a set of keys from his belt. He proceeded to unlock the cell door, intending to check on the prisoner.

"Don't go into the cell with your gun," the officer who was contending with the drunks yelled. But it was too late. The rookie was bent over Claybert, who raised himself up suddenly and, with surprising quickness and dexterity, withdrew the officer's revolver. In the same motion, before the stunned cop could react, Claybert got a shot off. The slug tore into the cop's chest and he pitched backward through the open cell door.

Hoping to capitalize on the element of surprise, Claybert stood up and fired a single round at each of the police officers in the room. He hit his mark every time, inflicting just enough damage to create an escape route for himself.

Before any further backup could arrive, Claybert made a hasty retreat toward the emergency door at the back of the room. He stopped only to remove a fully loaded firearm from one of the wounded officers.

As Claybert approached the door, he reached out to touch the metal handle, expecting an alarm to sound. Instead, what he heard was a loud reverberating boom that rattled his eardrum. He stopped, but it was not intentional. When he tried to push off on his right leg, he found that the limb would not respond to his brain's request. He simultaneously felt a numbing warmth on the back of his thigh, and only then did Claybert realize that he had been shot. With no time to waste, he wheeled around with his gun out in front of him. He saw a single uniformed officer standing and aiming his weapon at him from across the room.

"FREEZE!" the cop yelled.

Claybert aimed and fired the instant the command was spoken. The cop discharged his own weapon just as he was struck in the hand. The bullet obliterated two of his fingers and caused him to pull his shot into the wall far to the right of his target.

Claybert turned back around and pushed himself through the door. The alarm went off and he left the building dragging the useless leg behind him. His patrol car was right where he had left it, with the keys still in the ignition. He jumped into the battered Grand Marquis and started her up. He had to slide way over some toward the passenger side so that he could work the gas and brakes with his left foot. He drove off erratically as he barreled into the street.

Claybert drove hard, his heart pounding, but gradually he caught his breath and he began to ease up on the pedal. He held his wounded leg tightly with his right hand, trying to stem the flow of blood, which was pooling up on the seat under him and dripping down onto the floorboards.

Julian sat on his rented couch, in his rented house, just staring out of the living room window at the shadowy Caldera suburbs. It had taken only a short time to get his belongings together. Much of his things were still in boxes from the day he'd arrived in Caldera.

Ready to go, but unsure if it was the right thing to do, he wondered why he had said the things he had to Saney. It bothered Julian tremendously to know how little influence he seemed to have over his actions at times. It also frightened him. If he was not holding the reins of his own life tight enough, it only stood to reason that it would be that much easier for someone to come along and snatch them from him. He really wanted to be with Saney, but for some reason, he was sitting alone with his things packed, prepared to walk out of her life forever. If not himself, he pondered, then who had control of those reins and where was he being guided?

Julian could not help recalling what he and Saney had talked about previously. While it was not hard for him to acknowledge the advances in the psychiatric field, Julian still maintained that environmental, more so than genetic influences, were likely to be humanity's puppeteer. What troubled him about his own philosophy, however, was that he did not know how he could have become so inclined to behave in ways that were not favorable to him.

Julian considered the different influences that might have motivated such diametrically opposing individuals as Mother Teresa and Jeffrey Dahmer. Besides the obvious fact that one person was driven toward good and the other toward evil, he questioned where their individual forces of inspiration were derived from. From within? From without? From a will or force stronger than their own, perhaps? To be fair, and not use the example of two extreme personalities, any individual in society can be shown to act humanely one moment and then grossly inhuman the next. Julian had proven that himself. Such a riddle, he knew, might never be resolved to everyone's satisfaction. The only thing he was sure about was that he would be a fool if he left Caldera and Saney now. So Julian got up, determined to ask Saney for her forgiveness and commit to cleaning up Caldera at all costs. He thought to phone her before he left, and as he was dialing her number, he could not help wondering if perhaps he was being directed, in even this minor action, by some unknowable force. Julian knew it was a fatalistic notion. It even smacked of theism. And that was not his style at all.

When Julian got a busy signal, he thought it odd that Saney would be on the phone at this hour, but he was just glad she was home and awake.

"SHIT," Claybert screamed in frustration. He thought about his brother and how he had failed to bring his murderer to justice. To make matters worse, he could no longer feel his right leg. He knew he had lost a lot of blood, but he continued to apply pressure to the wound, which he was able to keep partially closed and facilitate some clotting. He had been driving aimlessly for a half hour now, having no idea where he was going, or even where he was. He was starting to feel dizzy and he struggled to stay awake. He could no longer think straight, and he knew his body could go into shock at any moment. With every last bit of strength he had, Claybert fought to keep from losing consciousness. Just then, he saw something that made him think that he really was beginning to hallucinate.

Driving right in front of him was a car he might not have recognized but for the New Jersey tags. It was the kid's Chevy Malibu, all right, although it looked slightly different than what he remembered.

Another stroke of luck, Claybert thought, and all at once his fatigue dissipated and he was once again filled with a sense or urgency and purpose. And hate.

Claybert concentrated on staying far enough back so that he would not alert Chris to his presence. All the while, he had to keep reminding himself that the kid had murdered his brother. He did this so he would not forget why he wanted so badly to kill the boy, because for long stretches of time, he could not remember.

Chapter Twenty

Tasker stood behind a broad cypress tree near the side of the Xenia's apartment building, biding his time and biting his fingernails. From his position, he could see the entire parking lot. It was well lit, though he was concealed in deep shadow. He had been waiting over an hour for somebody to return home so that he could follow them inside. He was confident that most people would not even bother to turn around to look at him, let alone ask if he lived there. He wanted to make sure he was not seen by too many potential eyewitnesses. It would just be a lot easier and a lot less messy if The Persuader was not needed.

So far, he had only seen a couple of people leave. One was a young man whose date must have ended early and without intercourse. Perhaps a little heavy petting, Tasker thought, a brush of a nipple if the kid was quick-fingered enough. But after a half hour or forty-five minutes of the young woman resisting his advances—the poor fellow's hard-on aching to be paroled from trouser prison, but getting an extended sentence instead— he finally decided to call it quits and go home to jack off instead. Tasker remembered having similar experiences, but that was before he gained THE KNOWLEDGE, after which he had never been plagued by blue balls again.

THE KNOWLEDGE came to him from a gynecologist. Tasker had made an appointment to see him so that he could learn all about the genital sensitivities of the gentler sex; what she liked, what she did not like, how hard, how often, why and how she responds to various stimuli, and so much more. He put to practice right away all these new insights and the results turned out better than he dared to hope. It seemed that women talked about him to each other, and as more found out about THE KNOWLEDGE he had, the more opportunity he was afforded to practice and become better at satisfying even the most fickle female libido. Now he used THE KNOWLEDGE to pleasure woman the world over.

The only other person Tasker had seen leave the building was an old man. He was wearing a sweat suit that looked like it had just been thrown on so he could go to the local convenient store to pick up a pack of cigarettes. Tasker was hoping he would return soon. Not only was it getting colder outside, but the old man was exactly what he was looking for. He probably could not see worth a lick, and unreliable eyes were just as good as dead eyes.

Then a pair of headlights turned into the lot from the street. The car pulled into a handicap space near the front of the building. When the brake lights were released, Tasker saw that it was the old man's Buick Regal and he sprang into action.

He walked at a casually brisk pace, tucking his chin down to his chest and raising his shoulders in case there were any security cameras.

The old man was slow getting from his car into the building's security lobby. Tasker had to hesitate outside momentarily while the old man found his keys to the interior door and slipped them into the lock. As he pushed the door open, the man noticed someone entering behind him. He stopped and turned his scared, wrinkled face up at Tasker.

"Cold night tonight," Tasker said disarmingly. He smiled as he squeezed through the doorway past the old man.

Tasker bypassed the elevator and found the staircase. While

he was not particularly looking forward to the prospect of walking up ten flights of stairs, he knew there would be less risk of being seen that way. And it was a small price to pay for what he would be getting on the other end, he thought, feeling three inches of steel pressing against his back and seven inches of steel in the front.

As soon as Julian stepped inside the security lobby of Saney's apartment building, he thought about turning around and leaving. At one time he might have done just that, but now he buzzed her unit, and when he did she invited him up. She sounded surprised that it was him, and maybe even a little glad, though Julian knew that might only have been wishful thinking on his part. Once he was let inside, he made a dash for the elevator. The doors were closing, and just before they shut completely, he stuck his arm inside and forced them to reopen, much to the surprise and ire of an old man standing in the back of the car.

"Cold out there," was all Julian could think to say as he stepped into the elevator, smiled and looked away. Up seven flights, Julian felt the weight of scrutinizing eyes upon him. When the old man got out, he stopped abruptly and slowly turned around. He peered unabashedly at Julian until the doors finally drew closed like a peep show window.

Julian was preoccupied, rehearsing in his mind what he was going to say to Saney. But as soon as he was let out on the tenth floor, he simply forgot everything that he had prepared to tell her. Then her apartment door opened as he was approaching and Saney was standing in the doorway. She had no expression on her face as she stepped aside to allow him to enter.

"First of all," Julian began, before she could even close the door behind him, "I just want to tell you that I'm sorry for all those things I said. I don't know where it came from, but I didn't mean any of it. I take full responsibility, but I think it has something to do with this city, whether it's environmental, psychological, or something else. I also think we can help this place and I know you can help me."

"Do you really mean that?"

"I do," Julian said. "My way of thinking hasn't done me much good. I want to take a more proactive stance to try to live the way I want . . . Will you help me?"

"Of course."

Julian was relieved, then as an afterthought he said, "I'm not turning to your profession out of default. I'm really not. Even if I can't change anything about the way I am, I want to at least try, because I can't stand how things are now. I've been running away from people my whole life. I have avoided forming lasting connections. And I'm just not willing to accept that anymore. Especially now that I met you. As a matter of fact, there's something I've been wanting to tell you. I'm crazy about you. That's why I'm here. I've been afraid to admit it to myself all this time, let alone tell you how I felt. How's that for a first step?"

Julian's confession took Saney by surprise, and she hesitated before saying, "Since you were brave enough to come over here and confide in me, there's something I've been putting off telling you because I was afraid of how it might look. Ever since I arrived in Caldera, I too have been haunted by recurring nightmares. I hadn't had them in years, then they recently started again. They have to do with an incident that happened to me when I was a girl. A younger cousin of mine raped me in the woods near my house. He was 9, I was 11. We were playing doctor. I never told anybody about it. I didn't know what he was doing, and when I was old enough to understand it didn't seem like a big deal. I mean, it never really seemed to bother me all that much, aside from the occasional nightmare. Anyway, the nightmares I'm having now seem more real and frightening than I ever remember them being. I just thought you should know that we're all in the same boat on this."

"You got that right. All aboard the S.S. Ty-D-Bol. And bring your own paddle."

There was a long silence, but it was not ponderous or clumsy. In fact, it was just the opposite. They both felt relieved, purged of secret burdens.

"What do we do now?" Julian asked.

"I'm not sure, but I don't think we can afford to lose any more time. As for you personally, the most difficult part of the whole psychoanalytical process are the changes that you have to make within yourself—your way of thinking, your very approach to life. All your experiences and how you've learned to deal with them will have to be relearned. It's not going to be easy. But you're already showing signs of progress and your willingness to initiate change is a promising indication of success."

"You mean there isn't some hypnotic suggestion you can use on me or a pill you can prescribe that will cure me instantly?"

"Actually, there is one thing you can try," Saney said. "It's an old trick, and rather simplistic, but I've found it to be very effective."

"I'm listening."

"Elephant shoes," she said.

"Elephant shoes?"

"That's right. When you say the words 'elephant shoes,' you position your tongue and lips the same as you do when you say, 'I love you' . . . I told you it was simplistic, not to mention corny, but it can help a person to get slowly accustomed to expressing their feelings, without actually saying those big three words."

"Elephant shoes, huh," Julian repeated.

When Chris turned into the parking lot of the downtown apartment building, Claybert pulled into a No Parking Zone on the street and killed the lights. From there, he had a clear view of the Chevy. He watched Chris step out of the car. It was the first time he had seen the kid since his brother was killed, which now seemed like it had been a year ago, rather than a week. He felt his anger bubble up at the mere sight of him, but he forced himself to wait for the right moment before making his move. He wanted to make sure he was not overly excited when the time came; he did not want to make the mistake of killing the boy too quickly. He was going to suffer for what he did. And Claybert was going to do everything he could to make certain of that.

As the boy approached the apartment, Claybert got out of his cruiser, gun in hand, and made his way along the shadows of the building. Ahead of him, Chris entered the lobby that served as a security check point for visitors. Chris would have to wait there while he dialed the resident's number and was given access to the building's interior.

That was the moment Claybert's leg began to throb like nobody's business. He could feel a wave of cascading blackness invade his brain, and as his consciousness waned, he thought, *just a little bit longer.*

But it was not to be, and the next thing Claybert knew, he was looking up at the sodium arc lamp of a light post high above him as semi-awareness momentarily returned. The sheriff found himself lying on the ground near the entrance of the apartment and Chris was long gone. The fury he felt when he came to realize that he had passed out for some unknown length of time actually energized him. It was the worst possible time for his luck to change, but he was determined not to let a little misfortune deter him from his quest. He had come too damn far. He staggered to his feet and threw himself through the door, into the vestibule. The menu of names on the wall before him only confused him further. He raised his gun and trained it on the interior door, then pumped out three successive shots. The locking mechanism shattered and the door opened easily. Claybert advanced sluggishly along the narrow corridor inside. After a few paces, he came across a single elevator. With nowhere to go but up, he jabbed the button. At that same moment he saw an arrow begin to move across a crescent dial above the elevator. It had started on 10 before coming down to the first floor. When the doors opened, Claybert knew precisely where to go. Maybe he had not been out that long after all, he thought.

He was too exhausted to hold his head up, so he stared down at the floor and the bloody footprints his saturated shoes had made.

When he got off the elevator, he was faced with a choice. To his right and his left were long corridors with identically closed doors on both sides. Both halls were well lit, but the apartments behind the doors were all dark—except for one just ahead on the right. Light escaped from the narrow slit along the bottom of the door. Claybert walked toward it on unsteady feet, then stopped and looked up. Number 1013. He did not hesitate raising his weapon and shooting out the lock with a single bullet. The door arced slowly inward without any assistance.

Through the dissipating smoke of the revolver's discharge, the sheriff saw three people look up at him, their faces white as sheets. He recognized only Chris.

"Uncle Clay!" Chris said in shock.

"Don't act surprised to see me, boy," Claybert said. "You think you were just going to kill my brother and get away with it?" He brought his gun up one final time, looking through the sight to make sure the barrel was locked on Chris. "This is for what you did to Terrence," he said. His entire body tensed in the instant before he pulled the trigger.

There was a loud report, but it did not come from Claybert's gun. A spray of blood rose up from the top of the sheriff's head as he pitched forward. The .25-caliber slug was still spinning around inside his skull like a roulette ball on the rim of the wheel even as his body hit the floor.

No one noticed the man standing in the doorway holding a smoking gun in his hand. They were staring in shock at the lifeless body of the crazy man who, only seconds before, had burst into the apartment with homicidal intentions of his own.

"No one will ever hurt you again," a voice whispered softly.

Julian looked up, but by then the person who had spoken these words was gone.

PART III.

The Apostate

Apostates and runaways,
such as have Christ's forsaken
Of whom the devil, with seven more evil,
hath fresh possession taken:
Sinners ingrain, reserved to pain
and torments most severe:
Because 'gainst light they sinned with spite,
are also placed there

-Michael Wigglesworth, *The Day of Doom*

When an unclean spirit has gone out of a man, it wanders
through arid wastes searching for a resting-place; failing to find
one it says, "I will go back to where I came from."

-LUKE 11:24

Chapter Twenty-One

When Tasker got back to his condominium, he was shaking uncontrollably. He dropped The Persuader on the couch and continued straight to the bathroom. He began to undress as he drew himself a hot bath. Even as he sank into the steaming water, he could not stop shaking. Tasker knew that something was not right. He did not know what, but it had all started after he had come to Caldera. He would often become confused, sometimes not even sure where he was. This was not the same as the travel lag he had experienced last year after staying in a dozen different hotels in a dozen different cities within a month's time. One thing was certain, he no longer felt in control of his own life, but more like an attendant, who was being told things he did not want to hear and taken to places he did not want to go. And whatever it was that had drawn him to Caldera, it seemed to have something more permanent in mind for him. He had just bought this condo, had arranged to have all his stuff brought here, and he had no idea why he had done that.

But he did not want to think about any of that right now. He was too tired. He was tired almost all the time. Now, the instant he closed his eyes, Tasker's mind was once again transported somewhere else. He no longer bothered to fight it.

179

The memories and feelings were jumbled together, and overwhelming: the childhood sexual abuse by his mother, the confusion, his mother's accident, the further confusion that followed, and the anger. Mostly, it was anger. In the beginning, it was directionless, random. Then after his mother died, he was sent to a boarding house and met a small boy who was much younger than him, a boy who changed everything. This event laid down the tracks for the runaway train that was young Ronnie Tasker's anger.

He had been looking out of the window at the other children playing in the summer sunshine when Miss McNeil walked into the room with a small boy in tow.

"Ronnie, why aren't you outside playing with the other children?"

"I don't feel like it," Ronnie said.

"Are you sick?"

"No."

"Well then, why don't you say hello to Julian. He's going to be staying with us for awhile. He'll be staying in here with you, Joey, and Nicky. Dominic is going upstairs with the older boys. Julian will be taking his bunk, below you."

Ronnie approached Julian and leaned over so that they were eye to eye. "Hi, Julian." he said.

The new boy did not say anything. He was only three years old, but something about him instantly drew Ronnie in. Looking at Julian, Ronnie was reminded of himself at that age, just before the onslaught of all that pain and anger that he did not understand. Before the corrosive events that took place early in his life and changed him forever from the innocent, curious boy he was, to the confused, angry child he had become. Ronnie saw Julian as a young boy who possessed something Ronnie would never have himself—the chance to be adopted into a normal family and grow up to be someone important. At nine, Ronnie already knew that he would always have to fend for himself, and that the responsibility that the state assumed for his well-being would just stop one day, and then he would be turned loose on society. What was truly remarkable about Ronnie's reaction toward Julian was that he did not harbor any contempt or jealous rage for the boy. Instead, he made a promise to himself right then and there that he would never let anyone hurt this child. While Ronnie himself had been left unprotected from his mother's abuse, and then made vulnerable to the shortcomings of the current child welfare system, he vowed to ensure that no such harm would ever come to Julian.

"Julian is a bit shy," Miss McNeil said. "Why don't you two get acquainted. The other children will be in shortly." She touched Julian's neck lightly and Ronnie reacted, pulling the boy to him and out of Miss McNeil's reach.

She looked at Ronnie with surprise, then smiled and looked at Julian.

"See," she said, "you've made a friend already. I'll see you boys later."

"Bye, Miss M.," Ronnie said.

When she was gone, Ronnie took the small bag Julian was carrying and placed it on one of the lower bunk beds. "This is where you'll be sleeping," he said. "You're going to like it here. Miss M. makes the best bread you ever had. And sometimes brownies."

Still, Julian remained silent.

"What happened to your parents, Julian? Did they die? Did they abandon you? Neglect you? Abuse you? Do you know?"

Julian just looked at him.

"That's OK. I can find out. I know how to get into the office at night and where to look up stuff like that."

As Ronnie smiled at the boy, the confusion in his head slowly abated. He now had somewhere to direct his rage, and if anybody ever did anything to hurt Julian, they would feel the full brunt of his inner fury. As far as Ronnie was concerned, anyone who interacted with Julian had the potential to harm him. No one was to be trusted. Not even Miss M. Not your own mother. No one. Whether it was being physically and sexually abused, or not being given any brownies for dessert as a punishment for fighting, it all hurt the same. And if there was one thing Ronnie understood, it was pain. So whenever Julian might be faced with pain of any kind, someone would pay the price. And it would be Ronnie who would exact that price.

Ronnie reached under his bed and pulled out a game with red and blue plastic robots in a small square boxing ring.

"You want to play Rock 'Em Sock 'Em Robots with me, Julian?"

The boy shrugged.

"Come on."

Ronnie jumped on Julian's bed with the game and the younger boy joined him.

That's when Tasker's memory began to fade. All at once he was returned from the haunted regions of his mindscape and found himself sitting in a tub of cool water. He emerged disoriented, and at first he did not know that he was in Caldera, New Mexico, in his new condominium unit, for which he had grossly overpaid.

The chill of the water took his breath away. He jumped out of the tub and wrapped a heavy cotton towel around himself. As he stood there shivering, unable to get warm, he perceived a new directive. He did not know where it came from, but it was clear and strong. It was even more imperative than his all-consuming will to protect Julian. It had to be, because it was telling him to *Kill* Julian. And Xenia. And the boy with them. The force was so powerful, he knew that even if he had the strength to fight it, it would kill him instead.

With an all-out war of confusion and pain in his head, Tasker would have been willing to do anything to make it stop. Then he was shown what it would be like if he did what he had been instructed. The pain just disappeared, and he was promised that it would go away forever. And that was all the incentive Tasker needed.

Chapter Twenty-Two

Julian was seated in a large conference room on the third floor of the Caldera police station. He was alone. He had been sitting there for twenty minutes already, wondering if he was being watched. With every passing second, he became more nervous, and he knew that he had every right to be. There had been another death, and he was right in the middle of it. Again. He would be asked about this latest bloodshed, and then he would be asked about the circumstances surrounding the deaths of all the other people in the past. He was sure of it. And he no answers to give. None that would help his case, anyway.

Julian did not smoke, but if he did, he thought this would be the perfect situation for it.

Suddenly, like receiving Morse code, an inner directive told him, *YOU MUST RUN*stop. Julian responded, *NO*stop. He tried to put a halt to this internal dialogue, but was unsuccessful.

*THEY'RE ON TO YOU*stop

*I DIDN'T DO ANYTHING*stop

*BUT WHAT IF THEY FIND OUT YOU DID DO SOMETHING*stop

*THEY JUST WANT TO ASK ME A FEW QUESTIONS*stop

WHAT IF YOU FIND OUT THAT YOU DID

SOMETHINGstop

*I DIDN'T DO ANYTHING AND I DON'T KNOW WHO DID I AM NOT GOING TO BE AFRAID ANY MORE SANEY BELIEVES IN ME I BELIEVE HER*stop

Suddenly a door hinge squeaked and Julian looked up. The detective he had spoken to after A.J. was killed walked into the room. Somehow, this man seemed very familiar to Julian. And it had nothing to do with their first encounter. Julian remembered thinking the same thing last time. Even with that distinctive growth below his right eye, and the odd way that the corners of his mouth were naturally upturned, making it appear as if he were smiling all the time, Julian could not place him.

"Care for some coffee?" Bubin asked, raising the mug he was holding. "It's fresh."

Julian shook his head and Bubin took a seat at the conference table across from him. Bubin stared at him for a long moment, then asked, "Do you have any questions?"

Julian looked back at him dubiously. "What questions should I have?"

Bubin just shrugged.

"All right, I got one," Julian said. "Where is everybody? A big city like this and you're the only homicide detective on the force?"

"I'm not with the Caldera Police. I'm a special investigator with the FBI."

"OK. Next question. Are you going to tell me what you have on me?"

"Is that what you would like?"

"Hey, I want to know what's going on just as much as you. I can only tell you what I remember. There's a lot of things I don't know myself. So if you have some evidence against me, I'd like to know what it is."

"Mr. Bloom, first of all, I'm not accusing you of anything. I don't think you're responsible for any of the deaths in Caldera, or any other one, for that matter. But I do think you can help me find out who is."

"What do you want me to do?"

"There's only one thing to do," Bubin said. "Set a trap for this guy."

Julian sat back in his chair and looked at Bubin with great interest. "Who do you think is responsible, then?"

"Someone," Bubin said.

"Well, do you have some kind of plan?"

"Yup."

"Are you going to tell me what it is?"

"Nope."

At first, Julian did not know what to make of this guy, and had been naturally intrigued. But now, he was starting to become visibly agitated by Bubin's curt responses.

"I'm sorry," Bubin said, "but the less you know, the better off you are. At least for now. It's going to be dangerous enough as it is for all of you."

"You're not thinking of using Saney and Chris as part of this trap, are you? Because I won't let that happen."

"I thought you wanted to find out who was responsible?"

Julian hesitated. "I do. But what do they have to do with it?"

"It's this way or no way. Those are the choices. I only brought you in here tell you that. I can't make you do anything. Just understand, that otherwise, we might never find out who the villain is."

"I don't want to risk the lives of any more people."

"Neither do I. But I mean it when I tell you that it's not going to resolve itself any other way. It's as simple as that. Things will just keep going on like they are. Only they will get worse. Much, much worse. And if you can live with that, then you're free to walk out of here right now."

"That's not fair," Julian protested. "You bring me over here and tell me virtually nothing, except that you want me to jeopardize the lives of people I care about. And then you put me over a barrel by deliberately playing on my weakness."

"This isn't personal, Mr. Bloom. I'm on your side. In fact, with everything I know about you from your file, I like you and

I respect what you do. Aside from that, I'm just a God-fearing, ex-Marine from Manchester, New Hampshire trying to do his job the best way he knows how."

Now this guy was really confusing Julian. He seemed genuine enough, but something told Julian that Bubin was not completely on the level.

JUST GET UP GO TO THE DOOR AND RUN DON'T EVEN LOOK BACKstop

SHUT UPstop

"Why haven't you asked *me* any questions? Maybe you know everything about me, but what if there's something you've missed?"

"There isn't."

"How do you know?"

"Faith."

"Don't you mean intuition; a hunch, a cop's sixth sense?"

"No," Bubin said definitively. "Faith."

Just then Julian made an interesting observation about Bubin. He seemed more deeply religious than anybody he had ever met, *especially* since he had arrived in Caldera.

"Mr. Bloom," Bubin began, "if you knew in your heart that something was right, you wouldn't question it. You would just do it. Wouldn't you?"

After what Julian was experiencing with Saney, he could not disagree with him on that. "I suppose so."

"Then, you are somewhat religious."

"Now, that's just what I mean," Julian said. "You don't know anything about me. You don't know that I'm an atheist. I'm not sure what it has to do with anything, but I can't even remember the last time I stepped foot in a church. Or isn't any of that information in my file?"

Bubin just looked at him and deliberately avoided responding to Julian's inquiry in any way.

"Aren't you going to ask me about the imaginary friend I had as a child that's now sending me e-mail and threatening to kill everybody I get close to?"

"You can save that for your shrink."

"Oh, yeah, well maybe *I'm* the killer. . . . That's right. I could be a homicidal nutcase. Did you ever think of that?"

"No."

Julian, who had been becoming increasingly frustrated with the whole dialogue, was suddenly buoyed up emotionally, and perhaps spiritually. Whatever secrets this man was hiding, Julian felt he could be trusted. Then he just put himself in Bubin's hands by saying, "I'm not sure what I'm getting myself into, but I'll do what you want. Is there anything I should know?"

Bubin shook his head.

"But what do I do?"

"Just be yourself. Go on as if we never had this conversation. Live your life as you always have."

Julian wanted to laugh, but the guy was dead serious. "Are you going to contact me? How will I know if what I'm doing is right?"

"You'll just know," Bubin said. Then he stood up abruptly, moved out from behind the table and headed toward the door.

"I guess we're all here to catch the same man," Julian said.

Bubin had one hand on the doorknob, and just as he started to pull it open, he closed it again. He turned around to face Julian. "We're here to catch a mythical monster, not a man." Then he pulled the door open and left Julian alone again.

Julian remained seated, and took a moment to quietly consider the words Bubin had just used and the look he had in his eyes when he spoke them.

We're here to catch a mythical monster, not a man.

To call a serial killer a monster, even a mythical monster, was not too far of a stretch for a metaphor in this case. But the way Bubin cast his eyes at Julian at that moment made it seem like more than just a statement that reflected his personal outrage. The level of intensity and determination in his eyes and his voice was such that he really did mean to find somebody that was more than just a man, more than just a serial killer, but an actual mythical monster.

But, Julian rationalized, since there were no such things as monsters, at least not mythical ones, it meant that, despite Bubin's histrionics, his intention was to bring a notorious multi-state serial killer to justice. Case closed.

Still, all the way home, Julian could not get Bubin's words out of his mind.

We're here to catch a mythical monster, not a man.

He tiptoed into the house. Saney and Chris had stayed the night. The two of them had fallen asleep on the couch. He did not want to wake them. They must have been exhausted, he thought. They had been through an awful lot the past few days. They all had. And whatever Bubin was planning for them, it was almost a certainty that the worst was yet to come. They would need their rest, now that Julian had involved them both. He could only hope that he was doing the right thing.

The TV was still on. The volume was low, but Julian recognized the black and white images of the old movie. He was no film buff, but he knew Bogie and Bacall. It looked like, *The Big Sleep*. It was one of the few Bogart movies that Julian had seen.

Watching the light from the television flicker on their sleeping faces, Julian could not help smiling. They looked so much like mother and son. Saney was reclined against the arm of the couch. She had one arm protectively draped across the top of Chris's shoulder, while the boy's head was nestled against the side of Saney's hip.

Julian went to his room and got ready for bed as quietly as possible. Out of the corner of his eye, he saw a light flashing on his computer atop the bureau. He hesitated, but then walked over to the terminal. The familiar blinking icon on his desktop told him that he had mail. He did not want to open it. He was afraid it would be from . . . *a mythical monster* . . .

Nicholas.

Spooked, Julian turned off the computer. Then he pulled the electrical cord out of the wall and removed the battery pack, just to be on the safe side.

He had trouble falling asleep, and the whole night Bubin's words replayed over and over in his mind, like an old record album skipping on the same spot.

He tried to block it out.

Elephant shoes, he thought.

But every time he closed his eyes, the image he saw was of some hybrid creature, half elephant, half mythical monster, wearing a pair of wing tips and sitting in front of a computer typing I LOVE YOU over and over onto the screen with the tips of its razor-sharp claws. Blood and broken fingernails lay all around the computer and on the keyboard.

Julian did not fall asleep that night.

Chapter Twenty-Three

Julian heard somebody in the kitchen and got out of bed. Chris was still asleep on the couch and Saney was buttering some toast while eggs were frying on the stove and coffee simmered in the pot. She was startled by Julian's appearance.

"I wanted to surprise you with breakfast in bed," she said, sounding disappointed. "Did I wake you?"

"No, I haven't been able to sleep."

"I'm sorry I wasn't awake when you got back," Saney said. "How did it go last night?"

Julian poured himself a cup of coffee and they both sat down at the small kitchen table. "Well," he began, "I had a rather interesting conversation with that Bubin character. As it turns out, he's not a police detective. He's an FBI agent. You're not going to believe this, but he didn't ask me about any of the deaths from my past. Or about Nicholas. Like with Chris, he didn't want to know anything."

"None of this makes sense," Saney said. "What's going on here?"

"I don't know. But Bubin knows more than he's letting on."

"You don't trust him?"

"No," Julian said. "In fact, just the opposite. That's what's so strange. He told me I had nothing to do with any of it, and I believed him. He also told me I could help him catch whoever is responsible, and I agreed. He managed to ease my mind in a way I never thought possible. But he was very vague about the whole thing. There's a lot he's not willing, or able, to reveal for some reason."

"Do you have any kind of feeling at all as to what it might be that he's being less than honest with you about?"

Julian considered it, then shook his head. "No."

"There must be something," Saney insisted. "Think. If your gut feelings are this strong, there must be a basis to it somehow. It doesn't matter how unusual it may sound, you mustn't be afraid to say what's on your mind."

Looking at Saney's face, Julian knew she was right. "This is going to sound ridiculous," he said haltingly.

"It's okay, Julian. Just say it"

"I don't know where I got this from, and Bubin was being very disingenuous about who he was looking for, but I got the impression that he might be trying to track down . . ." He was about to say it, then stopped himself momentarily. Finally he just forced the word out of his mouth. ". . . Satan. There. I said it. Go ahead and laugh now."

"I'm not going to laugh," Saney said. "That was how you felt when you were talking with this man and your feelings are valid."

"But Satan?" Julian said. He stood up and turned away from her, shamed. "I don't believe in Satan. I don't think I even believe in God. I can't believe what I just said."

Saney got up and stood beside him. "Julian," she said, forcing him to look at her, "are you embarrassed because your perception might be thought of as outlandish by some, or are you embarrassed because you don't have faith?"

Julian's eyes widened suddenly. "What?"

"Well, previously you've said you were an atheist, now I just heard you say you don't *think* you even believe in God."

Julian shook his head. "I don't know what to believe

anymore."

"It's okay, Julian. There's nothing wrong with having doubt. But what was it that the FBI agent said to lead you to believe he might be tracking Satan?"

"Well," Julian said, "he did make several references to religion and faith. But, I guess it was when he used the term 'mythical monster,' to describe whoever it is he wants me to help him find, that really got me thinking. Oh, well, so much for my gut feelings. Though, as far as scientific evidence goes, I suppose it's every bit as substantial as the frog bones I've collected."

"Julian, the feelings you're expressing can be very overpowering. It's quite a leap you've taken, from not being able to communicate your feelings at all to articulating such a strong intuitive emotion."

"I don't need to be patronized right now, Saney."

"I'm totally serious, Julian," she said solemnly, but for some reason, the look on his face made her want to laugh, and she did everything she could to contain it.

Julian, however, observed her effort. It seemed for a moment that he might take offense, but then his face brightened and it was all he could do to keep from laughing himself. "Satan," he snorted derisively.

They both managed to hold back what amounted to nervous laughter and just smiled at each other. Then Julian held up a finger on each side of his head to simulate horns. "Look," he said. "It's Satan."

That did it. Suddenly they both erupted in a fit of uncontrollable laughter.

It was Saney who first noticed Chris standing in the kitchen doorway. When she stopped laughing, so did Julian. But when he looked around at the boy, whose hair was mussed and sticking straight up on either side of his head, like horns, he started laughing again, and that got Saney going as well.

"What's so funny?" Chris said self-consciously.

"Nothing," Saney said in a dismissive tone, then got up and

poured Chris a glass of orange juice. "Do you want something to eat, Chris?"

"No, thanks. I'm not really hungry."

"Can I ask you a question, Chris?" said Julian.

"Sure."

"Why do you think you haven't been arrested in the death of your foster father?"

Chris thought about it for a moment, then said, "Because they know it was an accident. And that he was a wicked man, who abused all the kids on the farm."

"That's what a sympathetic jury probably would have decided, but that kind of judgment isn't exactly the function of the police. Or the FBI."

"What are you suggesting, Julian?" Saney asked.

"I'm just stating what's obvious; maybe Bubin isn't exactly who he claims to be."

"But you said you trusted him."

"I do. But he might have a good reason to be lying. Maybe he needs Chris and can't afford to have him arrested. The same thing for me."

"But what does he need Chris and *you* for?"

"That's what we need to find out."

"I don't understand," Chris said. "What's the big deal? Whatever the reason the cops have, even if they screwed up and overlooked something, who cares. Maybe we should all be thankful, take it as a blessing and just get out of here."

"That was my first instinct, too," Julian said. "Unfortunately, that's not something we can do."

"Why not?" Chris asked. "What do we have to stick around here for?"

Saney looked at Julian. "Tell him," she said.

"Tell me what?"

Julian looked Chris in the eyes and pointedly said, "There is reason to believe that this FBI agent is in Caldera, not to look for you or me, but to find a mythical villain from the bible—the Devil. I know it sounds stupid, but that's what we were laughing about when you came in."

Chris was quiet for a moment, then said, "Then we're all involved in this together?"

Saney nodded. "As strange as it may sound, the more thought I give it, the more believable it all seems. I don't think us being together like this is a coincidence. I came here and found that people were suffering grave mental harm. Julian discovered that the environment can't take much more abuse."

"Then you came along, Chris," Julian added, "with your foster father's brother chasing you across the country. Now, we have to ask ourselves why a New Jersey lawman would come all this way to catch a fugitive from justice, and then wind up going on a killing spree."

"You think this city is somehow the cause of everything you described?" Chris asked.

Julian did not say anything. He just looked back at Chris with as close to a blank expression as possible, hoping the boy would come to his own conclusion.

"If you could look at this place from our perspective," Saney said to Chris, "you'd notice that there are a lot of bad people here and a lot of bad things are happening that are difficult to explain."

"Yes," Chris said, "but how much worse can Caldera be than any other big city?"

"All I can say is that Caldera is New York City gone completely to hell."

"So you both think that the people here are under the influence of some malevolent force?"

"Like I said, the problems here don't seem to be wholly attributed to either human factors or environmental influences. Anything else is purely speculation. For all we know, there could be a simple, rational explanation for everything."

"You know what I just realized?" Julian said. He had moved over to the large picture window at the front of the house. The curtains were pulled aside and he was just staring out through the glass. "No matter what direction you look—toward the city, away from the city, wherever—you won't see one steeple reaching up toward the heavens. You want to know why? Because there are no churches here, that's why." Julian turned around to look at them. "Have either of you seen one? A half million people in Caldera and not a single Roman Catholic cathedral. Not one Protestant church. Not a solitary Jewish synagogue, Buddhist temple, or Muslim mosque. Not even a local chapter of the Jehovah's Witnesses."

Chris and Saney looked at each other. They both were trying to think of a location where they had seen a church, but neither could come up with one.

Nobody spoke for a span of several minutes. They were all trying to digest the provocative theories that had been tossed around the small, Spanish-style adobe house that morning.

Suddenly Saney's eyes lit up and she said, "I had a patient last week who was suffering from tardive dyskinesia, a neuromuscular affliction caused by drugs used to treat mental illness. He shot himself in a Texas bar. The same bar, Chris, where your uncle Claybert thought he was Wyatt Earp at the O.K. Corral. Anyway, this patient came to me who was despondent because he believed that Christ had walked into his motel looking for a room. He described a teen-age boy with fair hair." She looked at Chris and did not say anything more. As Julian looked at the two of them, especially the expression on Chris's face, he too understood what Saney was getting at.

Nobody, however, could bring themselves to say what they were all thinking.

Perhaps, it was a simple case of denial, Julian thought, because it was such an unreal concept to accept. But sooner or later, he knew they would have to confront the notion to which Saney had just alluded—Chris was the Son of God, at least an adopted one.

If he was so willing to accept the existence of the Devil, Julian wondered how much of a stretch it would actually be to acknowledge the presence of Christ in Caldera? But this ecclesiastical debate proved too much for Julian—in fact, for all of them—to think about at that moment. The rest of the day, the three of them hardly spoke at all. Each went about their business as if none of it had ever been discussed. Saney kept herself busy straightening up the mess around Julian's house. Chris spent most of his time outside detailing his Malibu, while Julian did some work on the computer. Saney did not even have to announce when lunch was ready. Julian and Chris smelled the food and just went into the kitchen.

As they were eating, Julian suddenly looked up. A strange expression washed over his face. Then he got up from the table, grabbed his coat, and said he would be right back. He returned a short time later carrying several large bags with the Deluder Bake Shops logo on the front. Saney watched as he nonchalantly dumped the entire contents of bagels onto the coffee table and the floor around it. Then he went into the kitchen and came out with a box of sandwich bags. As if completely unaware of Saney's presence, he began to break off a little piece from each variety of bagel and put them into individual baggies, which he labeled with a Sharpie.

By the time Julian got through the entire inventory, there were various-sized chunks of bagels, in every flavor imaginable, scattered in a five foot radius around him. Finally, he looked up at Saney.

"Ergot," was all he said, as if it were the answer to the mystery of life itself.

"What?"

"Saney, what is the one thing that the people of Caldera all have in common?"

She shook her head. "I give up."

"Deluder Bake Shops. Most people seem to visit one of the area bakeries, at least occasionally. And what kind of foods are they consuming there? Foods made from grains which might be tainted with ergot, that's what kind."

"What exactly is this Ergot?" Saney asked.

"It's a fungus that infects rye. If ingested, it can be poisonous. But, it can also act as a hallucinogen. LSD is made from ergot. In 16th century Europe, people who ate rye bread tainted with ergot believed that they could be transformed into wolves. That's how the werewolf legend started."

Out of courtesy, Saney took a moment to try to decipher some meaning from his rhetoric, then scratched her head and said, "So?"

"So, what if these bagels are infected with ergot?"

"Then people will think that they're werewolves?"

"Not necessarily. You see, lycanthropy was a rampant fear of most people, for various reasons, at *that* particular period in time. Today, if there is a universal fear that society suffers from as a whole, then that's what they will hallucinate about. But, you of all people should know that there is no universal fear anymore. Our society has as many phobias as the ancient Greeks had gods."

"Are these bagels even made of rye?"

"Perhaps," Julian said. "But if not, there might be some other toxin involved. And it could have a similar effect on a person's brain chemistry, exaggerating their particular fear. And don't forget that rye is widely used as livestock feed for animals whose meat and milk everyone consumes. I'm going to take these samples to a lab for analysis."

Saney was shaking her head. "What about all the things we discussed earlier?"

Julian looked as if he did not understand what she was talking about, then said, "Look, I'm just trying to keep an open mind about this, that's all. I need to look at all the evidence before drawing any conclusions. I'm a scientist. You can understand that."

"I do," she said, and gave him a hug. Through the window now, they looked out at Chris waxing his car. It was a mild day, the sun was shining, and the boy had his sleeves rolled up. For whatever reason that they were thrown together, they seemed to have become an instant family. And to all of them, it just felt right.

Chapter Twenty-Four

"Thank you, Mr. Bubin," said the attendant who was checking boarding passes at the gate. "Enjoy your flight."

Bubin just smiled. He was still catching his breath after his run through the Caldera's grossly undersized airport, for which Bubin was now thankful because he would not have made his flight if there had been more than one terminal building. While everything else in the city was expanding, the airport remained unchanged. It was as if people were allowed to filter into the city unchecked, but once situated, their movements were restricted, confining them to the city limits.

Bubin breathed a sigh of relief as he entered the boarding bridge. The electric sign above the gate that read Boston, Massachusetts winked out as he boarded the three-engine McDonnell Douglas DC-10.

Everyone else was seated. The drinking glasses of the other first-class passengers were half-empty when Bubin sat down. He ordered a scotch, and while the plane was being prepared for takeoff, he sipped it slowly as he listened to the safety demonstration. For the first time since this little odyssey began, Bubin had a chance to relax.

After a brief layover and a plane change in Boston, Bubin

would arrive at Bradley International Airport, where he would be just a short drive away from Ronald Gary Tasker's permanent home address at 70 Alexander Street in the small Connecticut town of Middletown. He did not know what he expected to find there, but he knew that whatever it was, it was sure to be eye-opening. He had a good six hours to think about it, but for now he was content to just sit back and enjoy all the pampering that the airline had to offer.

As soon as the jet was airborne, however, Bubin began to feel a general sense of unease. Quickly, his apprehension became more specific. First, he began to worry about the safety of the aircraft. Flying and Thomas Bubin had always been a marriage of convenience. His work obligated him to fly regularly, but it always made him nervous. And while he was not completely comfortable in an airplane, he had never felt such a foreboding sense of dread and impending disaster as he did now.

He found himself questioning whether or not the man, the woman, and the boy back in Caldera would be able to do what was needed for this mission to succeed, or, if indeed, it was even possible to defeat this foe. When he started to wonder if it was all worth it, Bubin knew the Devil was hard at work. The dirty scoundrel would scratch and claw until he found a chink in the spiritual armor of even the most devout individual, and then he would exploit that weakness for all it was worth. And then, before you knew it, he had your soul.

Bubin literally *was* chasing the Devil, and he knew that the Devil was looking at him in the rear-view mirror. Any fear that Bubin showed would only serve to increase *His* power and make Bubin more susceptible to *His* will.

All this worrying must have taken its toll on Bubin, who suddenly became very tired. But just as his head dropped back and he was about to nod off, the captain's voice intruded over the cabin's loudspeakers to announce that they were starting initial descent.

The cabin was hot, the air was stale, and the landing was

worse than any Bubin could recall. However, when he got off the plane on the first leg of his trip, perspiring and feeling a bit nauseous, the subfreezing New England weather had an immediate affect on him, alleviating much of his discomfort and uneasiness.

Even so, what consequence all this conscious thought about the Devil would have on his subconscious mind would not be fully determined, Bubin knew, until he arrived at Tasker's house.

He had planned on going right to his hotel to get some rest after a quick bite to eat, and then start the investigation the following morning. For some reason, however, he decided to go to Tasker's directly from the airport.

It was dusk by the time he rented a car and arrived at the house. The darkness only made Bubin's weariness and hunger that much more poignant, and now he fully regretted coming out here this late.

A cold wind buffeted him as he left the heat of the car behind and approached the ranch-style home. All the other residences on the street were decorated for the holidays. But there was no glittering Christmas tree in the window or icicle lights hanging from the gutters of number 70. It was dark and deserted.

Bubin walked up the stone steps and onto the small porch. He rang the bell, though he did not expect anybody to be there, least of all Tasker. Finding the front door locked, he peered through the adjacent window, certain there had to be something inside that would be useful. Bubin pried open the screen and pushed up the unlocked window. Reaching around inside, he found the door's dead bolt and threw it back.

"Hello," he called out as he entered the house. "Is there anybody here?"

He flipped a bunch of light switches on a panel, but the interior remained in near total darkness. Proceeding slowly along a pantry, he encountered a stairway on his right. To his left was a small living room. He moved past them both. Ahead was the kitchen. It was separated from the pantry by a set of swinging doors. He could see the outline of a porcelain sink between the slats.

Suddenly the smell of freshly baked apples and cinnamon spice hit Bubin hard and jogged his memory. The aroma reminded him of the house he had grown up in. And as he looked around more closely, he came to realize that not only did the scent of the house come back to him, but so did the house itself. The layout was exactly the same as he remembered it: The pantry, the living room on the left, the stairs on the right which led up to the bedrooms and the swinging kitchen doors that he used to push open and pretend he was Clint Eastwood going into a saloon to look for bad guys.

Then he looked down and saw the lighthouse nightlight in the electrical outlet on the pantry wall. It was a souvenir his family had picked up on a trip to Hampton Beach one summer. The bulb was blown out.

He had grown up a couple hundred miles from here, so Bubin knew that it could not be real. It was a trick. Then it occurred to him, if he could not go to his childhood home, then his childhood home would come to him somehow, in a dream or hallucination.

Bubin continued to shuffle forward, but before he reached the swinging doors he stopped and peered over the top, not feeling a bit like Clint Eastwood now. He caught a glimpse of a cooling apple pie on the counter near the refrigerator. His mother would make one every Christmas that was positively bursting with the sweetest apples. Steam was coming off this one. He could feel the heat still escaping the oven, which was not on, but the door was open and the bake rack was sticking out of it like a lazy tongue.

Looking further around the room, he recognized all the appliances and fixtures, as well as the linoleum floor pattern. Even the magnets on the refrigerator were the same, including the one in the shape of Florida, which Uncle Billy had given him after returning from a family vacation at Disney World. In fact, there was no discernible difference between what Bubin was seeing now and the last Christmas he spent in the house as a boy, when he had tiptoed downstairs in the middle of the night to see if Santa Claus had come yet. When he saw that there were no presents in the living room, he thought it was because they had not put up a tree that year. Later that Christmas morning, his father would tell him that Santa did not have enough time to go to all the houses that year, and that he was going to leave twice as many presents in those houses the following Christmas. It would be several more years before Tommy Bubin came to understand that there was no tree and no presents because his father had lost his job that summer and had been out of work for several months.

Presently, with the ghostly smell of cooling apples still clinging in the air like powdered sugar on a doughnut, Bubin looked down and saw Alphie. The frail cocker spaniel was lying on her side next to the kitchen table. She was perfectly still, except for the slight respiration that expanded her chest. But she was not sleeping. Something was wrong. Her eyes were open, but glossy. They shifted only slightly to look at Bubin, and when she tried to wag her tail it only quivered.

Bubin's eyes filled with tears as he was forced to relive that painful Christmas morning and watch a beloved pet, who he had spent the first nine years of his life with, die all over again.

Bubin stepped through the swinging doors into the kitchen and bent down beside the dying dog. Alphie attempted to move her head, perhaps wanting to lick his face one last time, but could not. He cradled her in his arms and could feel the old girl's heart laboring. With tears streaming down his face, he tried to comfort his dog, hoping that he would be able to do something for her this time. He stroked her head from the end of her nose back behind her long, floppy ears.

"No, Alphie," he cried. "Don't die again."

But even as he spoke these words, her condition deteriorated. Her chest expanded and contrasted at a noticeably slower rate, and a thin white film had formed over her eyes.

"No, please. I love you, Alphie."

Suddenly the dog's eyes opened wide and her legs began to spasm, kicking out involuntarily. Then her little body went limp. Her head lolled lifelessly to one side and her little pink tongue slipped out of the side of her mouth. Her chest was still. Alphie was dead.

Bubin continued to stroke her head as he cried helplessly, just as he had done that Christmas morning when he was nine. As his tears fell onto her tan coat, he tried to keep his sobbing to a barely audible level so as not to wake his father, who did not like to have his sleep interrupted these days. He would be particularly harsh if he had been awakened for a "no good" reason, such as Alphie dying. Only a few days before, his father had said they were going to give Alphie away to some people on a farm because it was costing too much to feed and take care of her. Bubin remembered begging his father not to give her away, volunteering to take care of the dog himself and pay for her food, even though he had not gotten an allowance for months. During that time, his family had stopped using most electrical appliances. They were not allowed to watch television and he had gone to school wearing the same clothes everyday. But he did not care about any of that, or what the kids said about him at school. He just wanted to keep Alphie.

Bubin wondered what he was going to do with Alphie now. He stood up, holding the dead animal in his arms. He knew he had to bury her, but he did not want to put her in the cold ground. He glanced around then and happened to notice something on top of the refrigerator that looked out of place. It was a small blue box. It was open. When he was a boy it had been too high for him to reach. But now he was easily able to grasp it and take it down. Through tear-blurred eyes, he read the label: TRISODIUM PHOSPHATE.

There was white powder inside. Bubin held his nose over the box, but had to quickly turn away from the noxious fumes. All these years later, Bubin finally learned that Alphie had been poisoned and he had been lied to and deceived. There had been no farm, and all he got for Christmas that year was a dead dog.

Nothing more had ever been mentioned about Alphie after that day, but on those occasions when he missed her the most, Bubin could recall visiting the spot in the backyard where the dog had been buried. When his father started working again, they were forced to move two towns over. After that, he began to think about Alphie less and less.

For Bubin now, it had been years since the little cocker spaniel had even entered his mind, and it made him sad to think that he had nearly forgotten about her.

Presently, he let the box of poison slip from his grasp and drop to the floor. As a cloud of white dust swirled around his feet, Bubin suddenly turned to leave the room, to flee the house altogether, knowing that it was all an illusion, though not a product of his imagination. He wanted to get as far away from the house as possible, and once he jumped into his rented Cavalier and started driving, he began to feel the spell slowly breaking. Bubin understood that he had been chasing his own tail, and that he had been at the mercy of the Devil, who had gotten him good this time. Bubin conceded the battle, but the war was far from over. He acknowledged that there was still a lot of work ahead. The disciples of the new millennium would first have to be convinced that the kind of evil that had invaded Caldera was not harbored inside each of them, as Xenia believed, nor was it the result of an opportunistic bacteriform or some other pathogen, as Julian was more apt to suspect. Instead, they would find out that it was a completely extrinsic and unnatural force that had a conscious and very concrete goal in mind—to destroy the creatures that God loved so much and that *He*, Satan, eternally despised. He was certainly well on *His* way to accomplishing His diabolical end. He had successfully recruited the apostates of the new millennium to a remote New Mexican town, where He could exploit them and hold them at sway with their own fears. A man's fear was, after all, the Devil's sustenance. It made Him stronger, and strength was what He would need when He mounted His final assault on humanity. In all of history, never had Satan's power been so formidable. God had to intervene. And He did.

But was it too late?

That's what Bubin feared.

God's power was limitless, but the survival of humankind now depended upon the ingenuity and resolve of a taciturn environmentalist, a female psychiatrist, and a sixteen-year old boy, none of whom would ever fully understand the consequential and prophetic roles they would play in history. That was just the way it had to be. There had been too much bloodshed in the past. Too much treachery and betrayal. This time, everything rested in the hands of three ordinary people, though what they needed to accomplish together was extraordinary.

Chapter Twenty-Five

Saney was seated in front of Julian's computer when he came bursting into the house. He had a sheet of paper in his hand that he was waving around like a celebrant with a flag at a Fourth of July parade.

"Here they are," he said, a bit too loudly.

"What?" Saney asked.

"The results from the lab." He placed the two-page report on the computer keyboard in front of Saney. "It's all right there," he continued. "The bagels I brought in for testing were baked with a grain called *triticale*, which is produced by crossbreeding wheat and rye. Very high in protein. And, as it turns out, ergot. I also found out that to produce triticale, the plants are treated with a chemical agent that is extracted from a poisonous plant called colchicum. In small quantities, the drug yielded from this plant has some medicinal uses for humans. But the lab found very high concentration levels of this chemical in many of the bagels sampled. This in itself could prove detrimental to the health and well being of the consumer. Go ahead, read it for yourself if you don't believe me."

"I believe you, Julian," Saney said, giving the report only a cursory glance.

"You think it's a coincidence that all those bagels show signs of contamination, while everyone in town is acting so strange?"

"I didn't say anything?"

"My question now is this: was the contamination accidental or was it put there intentionally?" Julian noticed the look of indifference on Saney's face, which interrupted his train of thought. "All right. What is it? There's obviously something you're not telling me. What is it?"

"Well," she began, "before you get any more excited, I wanted to tell you that I've been doing some research of my own. I think you'll find this every bit as interesting as your fungus among us theory."

Saney put aside Julian's lab report and touched a button on the keyboard. Instantly, the computer screen began to scroll through a list of names that went by too fast for Julian to read.

"What's all this?" he asked.

"That's a list of all the agents registered with the FBI."

Julian looked at her, astonished. "Where did you get that?"

"This is the entire bureau's payroll."

"You hacked into the Justice Department's database?"

"And look at this," Saney said, then typed in the name BUBIN, THOMAS and pressed another button that stopped the scroll at once. A profile page with a picture and bio of the agent appeared. It was obvious that this was not the same man they knew. "According to this," Saney continued, "Special Agent Thomas Bubin was thirty-five years old when he was killed 'in the line of duty' in Kuwait on February 24, 1991."

"If Bubin's dead," said Julian, "then who is this guy claiming to be him? And why?"

Suddenly he noticed that Saney was peering peculiarly at the computer screen, transfixed by something she saw.

"What is it, Saney?"

"You don't see it?"

"See what?"

"On the computer. Look closely and tell me what you see."

Julian put his face right in front of the screen and began to read from it. "Bubin, Thomas, born May 15, 1955, Omaha, Nebraska. Graduated Georgetown University . . ."

"No," Saney protested. "Stand back a little. Try to look beyond the printed words. Deep-focus your eyes."

Julian shook his head in frustration. "I don't see anything . . . Wait . . . Yes." Suddenly an image crystallized before him. His jaw dropped. At first he thought it was Saney's reflection on the screen, but while there was a striking resemblance, the face was clearly not hers.

They both knew it was Chris's mother.

"Oh my God!"

"Well, close enough," Saney said.

In the virtual background between the written text, her image was visible. However, it was smoky and distant, as if it was not so much *on* the screen as *in* it. She was posed in a similar manner as the picture Chris had of her. She stared back at them with eyes that revealed the woman's great depth and strength.

Julian held his head at different angles and distances to be sure it was not a trick of the light. "Try going to another site," he said. "Change the screen. See what happens."

Saney clicked onto several different web pages, but still the image remained. She even tried turning the computer off, but the face did not disappear. In fact, against the darker field, it just became more defined and unmistakable. They could see it now without having to try.

It was obviously Chris's mother, but what else it was supposed to represent remained unclear. They only knew that it had been revealed to them for *some* reason.

"Is this the sign we've been waiting for?" Julian asked.

Saney turned to Julian, countenancing a similar look of amazement. "You know, an atheist or agnostic person wouldn't even believe they were seeing this. They wouldn't accept it on *any* terms, whether it was motivated by a fungus, a bad childhood, or anything else."

"What are you trying to say?"

She paused, then said, "Maybe we were chosen, Julian."

"Come on, Saney," he said incredulously, though he had been thinking the exact same thing. "Why us? Why not the pope, Billy Graham, Jesse Jackson, or somebody like that?"

"If all the people in this city are atheists, faithless, spiritually apathetic, or however else you want to describe them, then that makes us different. While we may be far from pious, we're not like them either. We're just displaced, somewhere in between the pope and the people of Caldera."

"I don't know, Saney." He looked from her to the screen. "You think anyone else can see this?"

"I know *somebody* who would be awfully happy to see it"

"But it doesn't help us any," Julian said. "We still don't know what we're supposed to do."

Saney thought for a moment, then said, "Well, we're in a town where nobody believes in anything and their personal fears control their entire lives. Now, I know for a fact that people who lack spiritual faith have been clinically shown to harbor more fears and phobias than people with strong religious beliefs. Maybe we're supposed to help Chris stamp out the root cause of it all."

"But Chris doesn't know what *he's* supposed to do either. How can we help him?"

"Bubin," Saney said. "Or whoever he is. He knows something. I think it's time we go down to the police station and have a talk with *him*."

"I'm not so sure Bubin knows all that we're giving him credit for. He's probably trying to find the answers himself. But you're right. He's all we got."

They embraced each other for a long moment as they struggled to understand their role in what was taking place in Caldera. They knew that whatever they were about to undertake was going to be draining, both physically and emotionally, and they tried to garner strength from one another, as well as from the image of Chris's mother on the computer screen. They would take it wherever they could get it. This was no time to be choosy.

"All right," Julian said, separating from her. "Let's go. We'll take that with us."

Saney gently closed the notebook computer and they left the house together.

On the drive downtown, Saney sat with the laptop balanced on her knees, staring at the face of the woman who could have been her sister. If only Chris were here to see this, she thought. It had not been easy convincing him to stick around Caldera a little longer, but this celestial download will certainly go a long way to assure him that he had made the right decision. He was back at the bake shop now, working extra hours just to pass the time. They all tried to keep busy while they waited . . . for a sign, perhaps, or just until they could figure out what to do next. This image of Chris's mother could very well be what they needed to help get them moving in the right direction.

Julian carefully observed the surroundings as he drove. "It's almost Christmas," he said, "and among all the decorated trees, colored bulbs, lawn Santas and reindeer, there's not one nativity scene."

Saney looked out the window herself, then back down at the computer screen and thought, this truly was the electronic age.

Chapter Twenty-Six

When they arrived at the police station, Saney insisted on carrying the computer herself. She felt a strange bond with the woman whose image was still on the screen, and not just because they looked so much alike. This woman may have been Chris's real mother, but Saney had begun to develop a strong maternal love all her own for the boy.

Once inside, they were greeted by a sergeant seated behind a desk on one side of the entryway. The nameplate in front of him read: SERGEANT DAVID McGUIRL.

"Can I help you folks," McGuirl said with an undertone of impatience. There was a lot of activity inside. A large number of criminals were being processed. The holding cells were all full. People were yelling and screaming. Maybe they had come at a bad time, Julian thought, but he was determined not to leave the precinct until Bubin told them everything he knew.

"Yes," Julian said. He had to speak loudly to be heard over the shouting. "We're looking for an agent who goes by the name, Thomas Bubin. He's supposed to be with the FBI."

"What is it exactly that you nice people want to speak with the FBI about?"

"It's more of a personal matter, actually. We know he's

working through this department, investigating a case we're involved in. So if you could just tell us where he is, we won't waste any more of your time."

"I'm sorry," McGuirl said, "Agent Bubin is not available right now."

"That's all right, we'll wait. Does he have an office he's using here?"

"Look, I don't have time for this. Bubin's not in. Why don't you try back later."

"When is he due to return?"

"Listen up, because I'm only going to tell you one more time. After that I'm going to have to . . ."

Saney impulsively flipped up the top half of the laptop and revealed the mysterious image to the sergeant. Instantly, McGuirl's demeanor changed, his expression softened.

Julian looked at Saney quizzically, as if to say, *How did you know he'd react that way?*

Saney shrugged, as if to tell him, *I just had a hunch.*

The cop continued to stare at the computer with a contented smile. Saney had to close the laptop to divert McGuirl's attention back to them.

"I recognize you now," McGuirl said suddenly. "You're Julian Bloom." Then he turned to Saney. "And you look very familiar, too."

"Xenia Wieland. But please, call me Saney."

"Saney, I'm Sergeant McGuirl. Delighted to meet you."

"Okay," Julian said, "now that the introductions are done, could you please tell us where we can find Agent Bubin?"

McGuirl looked briefly around the police station before leaning in close to them. "I'm probably not supposed to tell you this," he said in a hushed tone. "But I like you guys. This Agent Bubin you want to talk to, I don't know who he really is, but he's not a fed. We called the feds when we found out that kid who killed his foster father in New Jersey was here, but as soon as they found out that this Bubin guy was involved, they backed right off. Whoever he is, he's in charge. He went back east for a little while. Something to do with the investigation, I'm sure. He's supposed to be back some time today. That's all I know." Then the cop leaned back in his chair, asserting an air of professional detachment.

"Thank you, sergeant," Julian said. "You've been very helpful."

McGuirl nodded impartially, but just as Julian and Saney were about to turn around and leave, the accommodating cop winked at them.

They had no sooner left the building, when Bubin stepped out of a cab directly in front of them. It seemed as if he might walk right past them without any acknowledgment.

"We have to talk," Bubin said as he came upon them and stopped at the last moment.

"Damn right we do," Julian said. "You can start by telling us who you really are. We know you're not Bubin and we know you don't work for the FBI."

"You're right on both counts. But this is not the appropriate place to discuss such matters. I work for a highly clandestine organization, and I can tell you that my superiors would not appreciate me divulging such sensitive information on the street this way."

"Oh, *clandestine* is it," Julian taunted. "Why didn't you say so?" Julian glanced down at Bubin's shoes momentarily. "I should have known by the Shoe-Phone. Tell me, do you get unlimited local calling on those things?"

"Why don't we all go inside and talk about this. Under the Cone of Silence, of course." Bubin walked into the police station ahead of Julian and Saney.

He led them through the back of the station house, where a bearded man in handcuffs had just broken free from the arresting officers who had been detaining him. He was headed straight for the exit, and the three of them, when a cop in street clothes intercepted the man right in front of Saney. As backup converged to assist the detective, the bearded man's struggle for freedom became more violent. He was hissing and shouting obscenities, spittle shooting out of his mouth.

Thinking quickly, Saney pulled open the laptop and held the screen directly in front of the belligerent prisoner. Miraculously, he quieted down at once and was escorted to a holding cell without any further difficulty.

Bubin seemed entirely unimpressed by what had just taken place. He took them to a small room on the uppermost floor, away from all the commotion.

When they were all seated comfortably, Bubin began by saying, "As you so aptly have discovered, my real name is not Thomas Bubin. Bubin is actually a code name used by all the American agents in my field of expertise. The Bubin before me was killed on assignment, during the Gulf War."

"How was he killed?" Julian wanted to know.

"First, I think I should explain what I do."

"That sounds fair," Saney said before Julian could object. She was hoping to diffuse his hostility, and considered flashing him the image on the computer.

"Thank you," Bubin said to Saney. Then, addressing both of them, he said, "I'm actually not even employed by the U.S. government, per se. I'm paid through the Justice Department, but that's only because I'm an American citizen. The organization that I work for doesn't have a payroll department. Much like you, Julian, my focus encompasses the entire globe. Essentially, I work for all the nations of the world. This 'organization' might best be described as a covert multi-national task force, sort of like the UN meets *The X-Files*."

"What exactly do you do for this global organization?" Julian asked.

"Instead of investigating UFO sightings and alien abductions on the world stage, it is my job to examine what is referred to as 'theological phenomenon.' I look into things such as sightings of the Virgin Mary, signs of the Apocalypse, the Second Coming, manifestations of Lucifer, things like that."

Julian reached across the table in front of Saney and set the PC up for Bubin's inspection. "So something like this is nothing new to you?" Julian said. "You probably see faces on a computer that's been turned off all the time."

Bubin folded the screen back down without even looking at it. "What I'm most concerned about," he said, "is when many of these things all come together at the same time, as they seem to have here in Caldera."

"You mean Armageddon?" Saney asked.

"In a manner of speaking, yes. But don't make the mistake of confusing what you're seeing with either those big-budget Hollywood interpretations or the strict biblical translation of the event. People who interpret the Scriptures too literally take up the majority of my time, as I'm forced to sift through the bogus accounts of fanatical and delusional people. Contrary to the endorsements of popular culture, there is no laundry list of signs to let us know that the Apocalypse is near. That's my job. I pretty much learn as I go, rooting through the tangled misconceptions and myths about the Devil, who by the way doesn't *bargain* for anybody's soul. He just takes it. There are scholars who believe that Satan can wrest the soul out of your body without you even knowing it, and then replace you with a soulless body that looks exactly like you, so nobody else knows either."

"What happens to the old bodies?" Julian asked.

"I don't know. It's really just a myth; the Loch Ness Monster of my profession. I shouldn't even have mentioned it."

Julian and Saney could both sense Bubin's discomfort talking about this, but he quickly picked up with his doomsday discourse again.

"Now, we know that history is on our side. The Power of Good has always been able to thwart the Devil's insurrections in the past, but the tables seemed to have turned and now the playing field is level. Some even think it might be in Satan's favor. We're in a time where less and less people in the world have faith. And that makes us all vulnerable."

"Is that why there are no churches in Caldera?" Julian asked.

Bubin nodded. "This is only the beginning. Satan is the

Great Apostate. He's brought together the faithless and keeps them under His power by exploiting their fears. Since faithlessness is the breeding ground for fear, and fear is what empowers Satan, then as this city expands, so does Satan's influence. That's what the problem is here in Caldera."

"I don't understand," Julian said.

"There are no places of worship in this city, you've noticed that. But with all the construction going on around here, have you ever once seen a construction worker, an architect, anyone with a hard hat or a set of blueprints?"

Julian still looked puzzled.

"What about sanitation workers, plumbers, electricians, politicians, the people responsible for keeping a city of any size functioning and habitable?"

"Are you saying Caldera doesn't really exist?"

"No. But it was built by Satan. And that's what the people who are flocking here are attracted to. He's bringing them all together."

A lengthy silence stretched out as Julian and Saney grappled with this concept.

"What exactly is our role in all this?" Saney finally asked.

Bubin shook his head. "I told you everything I can. The rest will hopefully become apparent before it's too late. You've got to have faith."

"But Saney and I aren't any different from the other people here. We don't have a lot of faith. We were just talking about this. We came here as non-believers ourselves."

"I honestly do not care what you believe or do not believe. What's happening here is real. Both of you are involved. You have been chosen. Accept it and let's move forward. The Devil is somewhere in Caldera and we do not have a lot of time."

"What do we have to go on right now?" Saney asked.

"Well, I just got back from Middletown, Connecticut. And I think I found what we're looking for."

"In Middletown?" Julian said. "That's where I was born."

"It's also the town where Ron Tasker was born."

Julian exchanged a brief look of disbelief with Saney. "I don't get it. What's the parallel here?"

"Well, there's more to it than just that. You see, I left the abandoned house, which was listed as Tasker's permanent residence, thinking only about getting on the next plane back to Caldera. But as I was driving to the airport, I started to realize that the Devil had to be chasing me out of there for a reason. So I decided to stick around and find out what that reason was. I did some research, and then I realized that you, Julian, had been born there. Literally, you were *born* in that house. It was the same house where you lived with your parents before they were killed in the car accident."

"Wait a minute," Julian said, almost coming out of his seat. "Why would Tasker list my parents' house as his permanent address."

"As it turns out, the home is legitimately his. Apparently the property had changed hands a number of times before Tasker purchased it some years ago. He obviously spent very little time there because of all the traveling he does. He's apparently moved, for good now, having recently purchased a condo in western Caldera."

Julian was dumbstruck and unable to formulate any questions, so Bubin went on.

"Lastly," he said, "I went to visit Saint Mary's Devotional Boarding House, the facility where you spent the earliest part of your life, before you went into the foster home. You were probably too young to remember any of it, but all your records were still there and I took the liberty of looking through them. Nothing particularly noteworthy. But while I had the time, I absently thumbed through some of the other files, and surprise, Ron Tasker's name popped up. He was in the same boarding house, at the same time as you."

"I don't believe it," Julian said.

"Did Ron's file include a psychological profile?" Saney asked.

"*Did it ever.*"

"What was the diagnosis?"

"Transference neurosis with a narcissistic personality. But the final piece of the puzzle was a name that kept popping up in Ron's file. The name was that of a much younger boy that Tasker had befriended—a three year old by the name of Julian Bloom."

Julian looked at Saney and frowned. "What does all this mean?"

"It means Ron was fixated on you in a very unnatural way. The fact that he has been living in the house where you once lived is a good indication of that. As is the fact that you two are working for the same organization now."

Suddenly Saney paused, her eyes opening wide. "You know, he could be the one who's been writing you all those years, and more recently sending you those e-mails. He might even be responsible for the deaths of all those other people. He could have been trying to protect you from anybody that might one day hurt or betray you. By eliminating them, they would never pose a threat to you . . . *Ron Tasker is your imaginary friend.*"

Julian laughed. "That's preposterous."

"No, it's not," Saney said. "When did Nicholas first appear to you?"

"I don't know. Shortly after my parents were killed. I think."

"So your imaginary friend was there with you at the boarding house. You could have told Ron about Nicholas. Or he could have overheard you talking to him."

"Look, even if what you're saying is true, how does that make Ron the Devil?"

"The Devil doesn't usually make public appearances. He dwells in others. He's the King Of Lies. Who better to send than Ron to get to you three—God's chosen ones?"

"That's enough," Julian shouted. "This is becoming more ridiculous by the second. I don't want to hear any more." He stood up, ready to walk out of the room.

"Julian," Saney said, "we're not ganging up on you, but these things do make more sense than what we've been able to come up with—a personality-altering fungus and mass psychosis.

"I don't know. It's just too much."

"I know," Saney said, taking him by the hand. She looked him directly in the eyes, and said, "Try to remember why you decided to come to me after you thought you wanted to leave Caldera. Remember what your intuition told you when you heard 'mythical monster' for the first time. Remember how you were the one who pointed out that there weren't any churches on the street corners. Remember how the image of Chris's mother remained on the screen after the computer was shut off? . . . And most of all, remember elephant shoes."

Julian was silent, and by the look in his eyes, she knew she had gotten through to him.

"All right," he finally said. "Let's suppose you're right. Tell me, why had he left me alone for so long, and then all of a sudden start doing it again?"

"He could have been substituting his sexual conquests for his fixation with you, until something brought back his old impulses."

"So he killed A.J. and that New Jersey sheriff?"

"Tana, as well."

"Why Tana?"

"He must have thought you and her had something going on."

"Why would he think that?"

"He could have been following you the day you went to her office looking for me. He probably hadn't known about our relationship. If he had, I might have been the one dead."

"So, let me get this straight. Tasker has been stalking me since our days at the boarding house together, killing everybody who got close to me because, what, he wanted to protect me from the feelings of abandonment and loss I showed as a result of my parents' death. Then, maybe he gets some help, some medication and loses interest in me. But, when he comes to Caldera he finds that he has not quite kicked his old sociopathic habit. He'd have to be pretty fucked up to pull something like that off. But you're the shrink here, Saney. What's your professional opinion on this guy?"

She paused, then said, "I'd say he's pretty much fucked up."

"You know, one of the first instances I remember was when I was about seven. I was living in a foster home with another boy. His name was Ermond. We were playing soccer in the basement with a rubber ball. I went upstairs to get us something to drink. When I came back down, Ermond's head had been split open. He was lying next to a structural steel support beam, bleeding to death. Sometime after the funeral, I went into the basement closet to get something. On the floor, I noticed fingernail clippings. I could tell that they had been chewed. I didn't know what was going on then, but now it's terrifying to think that he had been in that closet all that time, just biting his nails and waiting."

Saney embraced him tightly. No one spoke for several moments.

Finally Julian turned to Bubin and said, "What do we do now?"

"Only one thing *to* do," Bubin said. "Surprise Tasker at his new condo here in Caldera. He won't be expecting us."

Julian was not sure if he was up to the task. "Hold on," he said, suddenly. "You still haven't told us how Agent Bubin was involved in this before he was killed in *Desert Storm*."

Bubin hesitated, deliberating whether or not he should tell them. "I'll say this," he began, "Thomas Bubin was the actual name of a man who in late seventeenth century colonial America was known as a "pricker." He wandered through the settlement with a collection of sharp instruments piercing the moles, freckles, or other skin abnormalities of people, women mostly, that he suspected of witchcraft. If this pricking did not cause pain or draw blood, it was considered proof positive that the woman was in league with the Devil. Invariably, these women would be charged, tried and sentenced to death as heretics based on this evidence alone."

Noticing that the two of them were staring at his sty, he paused momentarily, feeling the need to explain it.

"I know," he said self-consciously, gently touching the swollen eyelash follicle. "What can I do? I've always been prone to infection. Anyway, as the witch hysteria in Salem began to wane, and the last case against an accused witch was dismissed, this "pricker," Thomas Bubin, prophesied before the court of the eventual return of Satan. He warned that increasing public skepticism would become a tool of the Devil. Then he placed the case containing his pins and needles on the desk of the magistrate and was never seen again."

"Let me guess," Saney said. "These instruments are the only things that can destroy Satan. And Chris is the only one who can use them to any effect, right?" Seeing in Bubin's face that this was correct, she asked, "So where are we supposed to get a three hundred year old bag of pins and needles?"

"I have them," Julian spoke up suddenly. Saney looked at him, but he just stared straight ahead.

"I thought you might." Bubin was smiling. "Come. We don't have much time. I'll drive."

"What about Chris?" Saney asked. "He's still at work."

"We'll pick him up on the way," Bubin said. "And don't tell him what's on the computer until I say so." He walked out of the room taking long strides. Julian and Saney followed as best they could.

Chapter Twenty-Seven

"I'll get him," Saney said as Bubin pulled into the bake shop parking lot. She sprung out of the car when it stopped. "I'll be right out."

During the silence that followed between the two men, Julian looked over at Bubin and said, "How is it you know so much about Saney, Chris, and myself? How did you know that all three of us were involved in this? And how'd you know where to find us, or that we'd all be here together?"

Bubin just smiled. "Like I said before, Julian, some things require a little faith."

After a brief pause, Julian turned back to Bubin and said, "I know there are things you can't tell me, and I'm sure there's a good reason, so I'm not going to press it. But I was hoping maybe you could tell me how you can believe in something that you've never seen. How you can be so devoted to something unconditionally, all the while never being entirely sure if it even exists?"

A solemn smile dominated Bubin's face. "Faith is just one of those things that you have to experience for yourself. Then you will understand. It's like love. When you feel it, you won't question its existence. You won't need to see it or touch it to know it's there. And you can't force someone to have faith, just like you can't force someone to love."

As Julian considered the logic behind Bubin's words, Saney came back to the car with Chris by her side and they got into the back seat together.

But Bubin did not put the car into gear right away. Instead, he shifted in his seat to face the boy.

"Hi, Chris," Bubin said. "I just want to let you know we've all been doing a lot of talking recently. But now the time has come for us to take action. Unlike *The Rolling Stones*, time is not on our side. Though, I suppose, time is not on their side anymore either. Anyway, here." He lifted the case Julian had retrieved from his house and held it out for Chris. The boy accepted it reluctantly. Then Bubin faced forward and drove out of the parking lot, heading west, toward Tasker's condominium. Chris did not have to open the case because he knew what was inside. What he did not know was what he was supposed to do with it. He looked to Saney, who told him everything that had been discussed, and several things that were not. Throughout the recapitulation, Chris just looked at her without expression. When she was finished, he did not ask any questions. She concluded just as they arrived at the condominium.

Bubin pulled into a guest parking space and turned off the engine. He looked around at Chris one more time and said, "Remember, he's no different than any other man."

Finally Chris spoke. "How do I know he's *not* just a man?" he said. "Just because you say he's the Devil, that doesn't mean he is."

Bubin looked at Julian, as if to elicit his support for this divinely-authorized murder conspiracy. But Julian, who was still dealing with doubts of his own, wondered what it might be like for the boy, being told that he could very possibly be the son of God, and then being called upon to kill someone who may or may not be the common enemy of all mankind.

"I'm not a killer," Chris continued. "You think it'll be like pushing my foster father out of that window? That was an accident. He was trying to kill me."

He was clearly upset, and as Saney tried to console him. Bubin only looked impatient and irritable.

"There is something very peculiar about this city and its inhabitants, Chris," Saney said. "I've been finding it increasingly difficult to rely on any of the usual psychological dictates I'm familiar with to explain what's going on here. That's not to say that none exist, but there is some serious compelling evidence that something supernatural, if not diabolical, is at work in Caldera. The bottom line is you have to decide for yourself. Follow your heart. That's all any of us can do."

"Let me just take a moment to clear up a few things," Bubin interjected, garnering all his diplomatic skills and powers of influence. "He is in a human guise and cannot change form. As Saney said, the instruments in your hands are the only things that can kill Him. And you are the only one who can use them effectively. Please keep that in mind. And even if Tasker is just a mortal man, those pins won't harm him, as long as he's had a tetanus booster. Maybe knowing this will make it easier for you."

Chris remained silent, still not wholly convinced. Bubin responded by procuring the notebook computer from Saney and opening it in front of the boy.

Chris flinched. A vein stood out on his forehead as his eyes bore down at the image of his mother.

"Her name is Sister Helen Rubio," Bubin said. "She's a missionary nun in a small town in Spain."

"A nun?" Saney said. After a pause, she concluded, "Oh, she must have had Chris before she took her final vows."

No," Bubin said. "She's been at the same mission for twenty years. She gave birth to Chris sixteen years ago and was immediately forced to give him up for adoption. She didn't want him to suffer the same stigma that she would have to endure for the rest of her life, so she saw to it that he was taken to America."

Chris was staring intently at Bubin. His face was flushed a deep red as his heart violently tattooed the inside of his chest. Saney put a hand on his shoulder.

"I've been there myself, Chris," Bubin continued. "I've spoken with your mother and I've seen the official documents in which she's on record as claiming that she had never been intimate with a man in the nine months prior to your birth, or any time previous. She would have been 'excused from her religious obligations' if not for the medical testimony from numerous doctors who examined her during the pregnancy. They jointly determined that conception could not have occurred from normal coitus because her hymen was still intact. However, since it was never conclusively established how the impregnation *had* been accomplished, church officials were more than happy to send Chris to the U.S. so that the entire matter would be forgotten that much sooner."

Chris's eyes fell back onto the computer.

"Go with your feelings," Saney told him. "What is your heart telling you?"

His eyes remained riveted to the computer screen.

"There is precious little time," Bubin said. "You must decide now."

Chris touched the screen lightly with a finger, and then the image of his mother slowly began to fade away. When her face had disappeared completely, he looked up.

"Okay," the boy said. "I'm ready."

Bubin stepped out of the car first and the others followed. Chris carried the case of needles close by his side. Like a lynch mob, they approached Tasker's residence.

"It's this unit here," Bubin said, approaching the front door. Julian was closest to him, and he saw Bubin take something out of his pocket. He used the object to jimmy the lock. An instant later the door was swinging open. He took a couple of steps inside, then stopped and motioned to the others. They proceeded cautiously, not knowing for certain whether Tasker was home or not.

It suddenly occurred to Julian that they had no other weapons with them beside those archaic needles, and he felt naked and vulnerable. They might be able to vanquish the Prince of Darkness, but what about Princess, the Doberman pinscher.

Several paces behind the two men, Saney took a hold of Chris's free hand, which was damp with nervous perspiration. She made a vow to herself to stay right by his side no matter what happened. She could not help thinking how they must have looked like the four characters from *The Wizard of Oz* entering the Wicked Witch's castle.

Instead of a castle, however, they made their way through the L-shaped lower floor of a modern condominium. It was not long before they came upon two sets of stairs. One went up, the other down. Both led to an unknowable blackness, and they paused before the divergence.

"Which way?" Julian asked.

Bubin gave an immediate and silent nod toward the descending staircase. Chris released Saney's hand and he opened the cracked leather case. He selected one of the sharp-pointed instruments, then moved up beside Bubin. Saney remained close by him, followed by Julian. Together, they started down into the lower portion of the apartment house.

At the bottom, Bubin stopped to flip a switch. Instantly, the room illuminated with cool fluorescent light.

They all stood there on the landing staring in silent wonder at the unusual tableau before them. Like a Pentagon war room, one entire wall was comprised of a large map of the world. Most of the countries were shaded red, but a few remained white. Filing cabinets lined the other three walls, almost to the ceiling. In the center of the room was a large oval conference table. Papers were scattered across its surface.

"Incredible," Bubin whispered to himself as the others dispersed.

Saney and Chris began opening filing cabinet drawers while Julian examined the contents on the table in the middle of the room.

"These cabinets are alphabetized," Saney said. "*By country.* There are individual folders inside . . . Some have pictures . . . ID's . . . birth certificates . . . They're all women, and all native to the country their files are in . . . Each folder has a date handwritten on the inside (under the heading, DATE FUCKED, which she did not feel the need to mention) and several pages describing an explicit sexual encounter."

"Satan does like the ladies," Bubin said from across the room.

"What's this?" Chris asked, pulling a pair of panties out of the folder he was riffling through.

"A souvenir," Bubin said, looking up from the compact disc player that he had come across atop one of the shorter stacks of filing cabinets. It was powered up. An LED was glowing. He hit the PLAY button and a digitally remastered CD of Ricky Nelson's *Travelin' Man* came blaring through the wall speakers in each corner of the room.

At that time, Saney noticed a particular filing cabinet which caught her attention. It was labeled VATICAN CITY. She pulled it open and found a single folder inside.

"Well, how about this," Saney said. "He even did it in the Vatican."

Bubin said, "The holiest of holy places. Not the easiest place to get laid. Less than two-tenths of a square mile and only a thousand residents."

"How many countries are there in he world?" Chris wanted to know.

"Independent countries," Bubin said, "somewhere in the neighborhood of two-hundred. Very nearly, anyway."

"Bubin," Julian said softly, wanting to get only his attention. "Look at this."

Bubin went over to the conference table where Julian showed him a file that was obviously still in progress. On the cover, in large red letters, was written COUNTRY; HUNGARY. There were numerous Polaroids of Saney inside, like surveillance photos, along with volumes of information about her. They both realized that the date Tasker had written on the inside was the same night that he shot and killed the New Jersey sheriff in Saney's apartment.

What occurred next happened so fast that none of them would have been able to recount the events with any degree of unanimity.

Shots suddenly rang out. Two bullets whizzed by Julian's head. "EVERYBODY GET DOWN!" Bubin yelled. Saney screamed. Chris made a move forward, but Bubin grabbed him and pushed him to the ground. Three rounds that were intended for Chris entered Bubin's chest instead. The needle that the boy was carrying fell from his grasp and disappeared somewhere in the thick shag carpeting. With Bubin down, they were all but defenseless.

Then someone stepped out of the shadows of the stairway, a hulking madman, his face twisted in a sour grimace. It was Ron Tasker.

Saney and Chris drew closer to one another, huddling together. Julian positioned himself between them and Tasker, using his body as a shield.

Tasker slowly raised his weapon and trained it on Julian.

"NO!" Chris shouted.

Tasker suddenly hesitated, and then his hand began to shake. Soon, his entire arm, as if warring with an unseen force, began to rise and shift slowly away from Julian. It did not stop, but continued upward, until the Beretta 950OBS was pointed at the ceiling. Tasker was perspiring from the contrasting will of his muscles. Then the arm started to flex, the gun leveling at Tasker's own temple. He was breathing heavily, his teeth gritted together and the strain showing on his face. The barrel came within an inch of his head. "I told you, Julian," Tasker said as his twitching finger tensed on the trigger, "no one will ever hurt . . ."

Then the gun went off. Before Ron's body even struck the floor, Julian leaped over to where Bubin was lying and found that he was still alive. Blood was seeping out of multiple wounds, too many for Julian to stem with pressure. When Saney and Chris joined Julian's effort to save the life of their fallen friend, Bubin's eyes widened to look at them all. He shook his head slowly, as if telling them not to bother. He tried to speak, but his words were faint and barely audible.

"You'll know what to do from here. Have faith in yourself. . . . Now go kill this bastard." And then he made a hollow sound deep in his throat and his last breath went out of him. The bleeding stopped almost instantly.

Julian felt profoundly sad and lost as he looked at Saney, who was cradling Chris in her arms and sobbing uncontrollably. The man lying on the ground in his own blood had spared them the same fate, Julian realized, trading his life for theirs.

Julian turned back to Bubin and rolled his eyelids down.

Chapter Twenty-Eight

They sat silently in Julian's kitchen, individually trying to figure out what had happened. So far, none of them had been able to get a solid grasp on it yet. There were too many questions that were still unanswered. What puzzled Julian most was how the police managed to arrive only seconds after Tasker's body (sans a good portion of his head) hit the floor. Maybe it was a little longer, Julian thought, but they were all taken into custody by silent, tight-jawed men in dark suits and then released without even being questioned. It was highly unusual and very frustrating. Julian could not help feeling that they had been used.

"Where do we go from here?" Julian asked.

Saney shook her head. They were all at a loss.

"The needles," Chris said suddenly from the other side of the room. His voice was subdued, but resolute. He was turning one of them over slowly in his hands. "How exactly did you come across them?"

Julian looked up to meet the boy's thoughtful eyes.

"After my parents were killed, that case was the one item that wasn't confiscated by creditors. If it had any value, nobody recognized it. A social worker came across it and gave it to me.

I've had it ever since."

"Do you have any idea what its origin might be?"

Julian looked uncomfortable, and he glanced at Saney briefly before turning back to Chris.

"In high school," Julian began, "we all had to trace our family trees. Amazingly, I found that mine went all the way back to the Mayflower. One of my ancestors was a judge who sat on the bench during the witch trials in Salem. I read a book somewhere that he was one of the last magistrates to hear a case of witchcraft. A year after it was all over, he supposedly had become so despondent over the court-sanctioned murder of so many innocent women that he took his own life, piercing his brain by inserting one of the needles into his eye. Somehow the needles survived in my family through the centuries. And now I have them. I didn't think much of them until Bubin pointed out their significance."

Saney said, "Bubin mentioned a 'pricker' in Salem who prophesied Satan's return. The judge who he gave his needles to could have been your ancestor."

"Maybe," Julian said. "But how does that help us?"

"Well, during that time, as people started to question some of the harsher aspects of their religion, which had allowed so many innocent women to be persecuted and killed, maybe that disillusionment was a turning point for Satan. It could have started the erosion of society's religious faith, which conversely empowers Satan, just like Bubin said. After three hundred years, maybe there is enough anti-religious sentiment now for Satan to make His power play. And that's what we're witnessing in Caldera today. Nobody believes in anything anymore. Maybe Satan even planned the whole witch hunt backlash as a means to an end. Maybe it was inevitable that this day would come, and you just wound up *holding the bag*, so to speak, when it did."

"All that may be true, Saney, but my original question remains; where do we go from here? If Tasker isn't Satan, then tell me who is?"

His challenge was met with further silence.

Finally, it was Chris who spoke up again. "The more I think about it," he said, "the more it seems to me that we're supposed to figure it out for ourselves. I think that's the same reason my mom stopped communicating with me."

"That's elementary now that the one person who had any clue of what was going on around here is dead. We have no choice but to figure it out for ourselves."

"But I think Mr. Bubin sacrificed himself."

Julian and Saney both looked at the boy crossways. Julian saw Saney's expression and thought they both might have looked like the Gary Coleman character on that old TV show just before he said, *Whatchu you talkin' 'bout, Willis*?

"You think he wanted to die?" Saney asked.

"I think he *had* to die," Chris said. "I think he knew Tasker wasn't the one. I think he knows who Satan is. And I think his entire purpose was to show us that in order to destroy Satan, we must first figure out who He is for ourselves."

"I believe you're right," Saney said. "We were all non-believers who were drawn here by our fears, like the others, but Bubin showed us who we are. He showed us what we're capable of."

The collective sorrow they felt over the loss of their unlikely friend was evident on their faces as they talked about him. But Julian also looked troubled. "I don't understand," he said, shaking his head. "What difference does it make *who* figures it out?"

"Maybe that's just how it has to be done," Chris said. "In order for Satan to be destroyed, the destroyers must do it completely on their own."

"Yeah," Saney added, "maybe every time the Devil tries to take over the world, a Bubin is commissioned to sacrifice himself for the sake of everyone. Like our Bubin did, and the one before him, all the way back to the Salem."

"So last time the Devil was in Kuwait?"

"Or Iraq," Saney pointed out.

"None of this information is very useful to us since we still don't know what we have to do."

"We have to kill Satan." Chris said.

"Well, if either of you can tell me who He is, let me know. Maybe we should do what the people did in Salem. Just start sticking those pins into everyone until we find Him?"

"But Bubin's not the only one who knows," Saney insisted. "Don't you see that? We know who He is. Deep down, instinctively, we all know. We just have to think. Concentrate. Have faith in ourselves, like Bubin said. No matter how ridiculous we think it sounds . . . Now, does anybody have a feeling about who Satan might be? Come on. We're all thinking of only one person. Somebody say it. Chris. Who are you thinking of?"

Chris opened his mouth to speak, then took an extra moment to look back and forth from Saney to Julian before he said, "Deluder." The name rolled off his tongue like a lead weight, and the regretful way he hung his head belied the sense of relief he felt upon speaking it.

"That's who I was thinking of," Julian said. "Ergot or not."

"Me too. I was taught that Satan was an intimate enemy, not a distant one."

"I guess we know what we have to do now," Chris said.

"Let's get going then," Julian said.

They left Julian's house then, sure about who they had to confront and why. But the one question none of them wanted to ask was what it was going to be like. Could it be as easy as knocking on Deluder's door and sticking him with a needle? GAME OVER.

They would find out soon enough.

It had found its way into the old pipe. The smell instantly whipped its primitive brain into a covetous hunger. It was the smell of this blood, stale and old, but still powerful, which innerved the small brown rat. It knew instinctively that this was not the blood of anything that slithered between rocks or soared in the sky or hopped about in the tall grass. It was none of those, or any other animal it was used to eating. This odor came from the sweetest blood known to the rat kingdom—the blood of those upright creatures, who thankfully made so much waste out of what was still useful. It knew that one of these uprights would occasionally fall into the pipe and get trapped there, so the rat was determined to make sure that the waste-maker did not go to waste. Its rudimentary ability to reason also told it that the large pack of brown rats, like himself, which occupied the pipe, had probably already gotten to the trapped upright creature. But it continued onward anyway, spurred by the promise that there might be some scraps left behind.

The blood-lusting rat wove its way cautiously and silently through the pipe. It was dark, but the rodent saw all. So far, there was no sign of the large pack that harbored there. It was an outcast, a rogue vermin that chose to be alone. It did not enjoy the tribal way of life that so many of its kind did. It was out for itself. It slept where and when it wanted, scavenged or preyed at its own discretion, and only moved when it chose, which was frequently. It decided where to urinate, defecate, and with whom to copulate. As a result of its way of life, it was much smaller than many of its brethren and had to be extra careful.

Now the smell of human blood was overpowering. There was lots of it, and the rat was aware that it was getting closer to the source. It was easy to become exuberant, but then it got the sense that there were many more brown bodies in the pipe than it had anticipated, and the small rat stopped right where it was, fearful to take another step.

Suddenly, it discovered a breach in the cement floor and it began to dig into the soft earth below. Its scavenger mentality instructed it to burrow down and then tunnel its way underground until it reached the place where the savory blood was located. Then it would come back up to get a taste of what was saturating the entire pipe with its intoxicating perfume.

It made sure it went down extra deep so as not to alert the other rats to its own smell. Before too long, however, it began to get tired. The little muscles of its forelegs were burning, while the inside of the channel it was boring got very warm. It wanted to rest, to drink, but the intensity of its desire for human blood kept it moving relentlessly. Further and further down it went.

All of a sudden the ground beneath it gave way. For an instant, the creature felt the sensation of free falling. It felt something else too—a searing heat, so intense that the ends of its whiskers curled. Then it landed hard on a sloped gravel surface, whose angle was too great for it to stop its descent completely. As the scared rat continued to accelerate down the incline, it dug its claws furiously into the ground for purchase. There was none to be had, but it did manage to slow its speed significantly. Finally it came to a rest, but its hindquarters were teetering over the edge of a steep overhang as it desperately kicked its legs out to keep itself from falling.

The temperature there was hotter than anything it had ever known before. It could smell the hair on its body smoldering. After only a couple of seconds, its flesh blackened and the fat of its body started to sizzle. It was being burned alive.

Terrified, it swiveled its head behind its back to survey the source of the heat. As soon as it did, all the moisture in its beady little eyes was dried instantly by the superheated air. Near blind, it could see only traces of a slowly churning river of red and orange glowing far below.

Its back legs were now useless, the flesh charred and desiccated muscle exposed. It began to squeak in terror and pain. But the heat from the inferno quickly constricted its throat and silenced the animal.

The rat was dead long before its front claws finally relinquished their hold on the mineral-rich soil and it began to fall downward toward the streaming lava flow. The little brown body was vaporized before it came in contact with the surface of the molten rock.

As if the rat had been offered as a sacrifice, the lava tunnel responded with a mild tremor, its appetite only whetted.

Chapter Twenty-Nine

As Julian drove, Chris navigated them through the wide, tree-lined boulevards of affluent western Caldera toward Deluder's mansion. The rows of houses not only became bigger and more expensive the further west they drove, but they also were getting further apart from one another and more set back from the street. Eventually, large flowering trees and shrubs, positioned all along perimeters of all the properties, made it impossible to view the homes in the predawn light. Many were enclosed with wrought iron gates that sealed off the driveway from intruders.

"This is it," Chris suddenly said.

Julian turned into an unusual downward sloping drive. There was no guard present in the guard shack and they continued on uninterrupted. Chris had clued them in on the extravagance of Deluder's lifestyle, but somehow his description did not seem to do justice to the opulence of the bakery mogul's living arrangements.

Julian and Saney gasped as they surveyed the grounds. On the vast acreage, which featured miles of paved jogging trails, a lighted tennis court, a stocked manmade pond and a gunite swimming pool/spa with a fully functional octagonal summer house, stood a monolithic 18th century-inspired brickwork dwelling that easily contained twenty thousand square feet of living space. Separating the circular driveway from the mansion's grand entrance was an elegant courtyard, highlighted by an exquisite three-tiered fountain and a statuary garden.

Julian pulled the car to a stop and turned off the engine. "Everyone ready for this?" he asked.

"I want you both to know something," Chris began, looking at each of them as he spoke. "I'm really glad it was you two. I just wanted to tell you that in case . . . you know . . . something happens to me."

"There's no need to talk like that, Chris" Saney said.

"No, it's okay," he said. "Maybe I'm supposed to die, too. Like Bubin. I'm ready."

"We feel the same way about you, and about what we're doing. Whether it was coincidence or something else, we somehow ended up finding each other. Logic tells me that we wouldn't even have gotten this far if we were doomed to fail."

"And rest assured," Julian asserted, "I'm going to do everything in my power to see to it that we all get out of this safely. We know what we have to do, now let's go do it. Before I change my mind again and convince myself that we're about to make a big mistake."

With that, they all got out of the car together.

As they walked through the courtyard, Julian paused before one of the statues, recalling it from an art class he had taken in college. It was a medieval Bohemian sculpture of Mary holding Baby Jesus, called the *Sternberk Madonna*. If it was a reproduction, Julian thought, it was an awfully good one. He saw Chris, who was clutching the black leather case tightly in front of him, take notice of it as well.

The front door was invitingly left unlocked, and Julian felt like a rat entering a baited trap. He went in first and was greeted by a magnificent crystal chandelier, which graced a dramatic dual staircase. The impressive two story, marble-floored foyer anchored two wings. Awestruck, Julian and Saney wandered off in different directions.

Off one wing was an elegant formal sunken living room that was introduced by architectural columns of pure white marble. Saney peeked into the great room with its two-sided fireplace and window wall, marveling at the quality and quantity of the antique furnishings inside. Though she knew this was not the time for a sightseeing tour, she strolled through the room anyway.

Off the other wing was a gourmet chef's kitchen and butler's pantry, featuring a massive walk-in refrigerator, which captured Julian's attention.

"Up here," Chris called out from the stairs.

Julian and Saney quickly joined him on the staircase and followed him up to the second floor. The boy paused at the top. There was light coming from the bathroom at the end of the hall. The door was open and steam was escaping. Chris opened the case, and after a moment's thought he selected the smallest and least conspicuous needle from inside. He concealed it easily in the palm of his hand. Then he handed the case to Saney, took a deep breath, and proceeded down the hall with Saney and Julian behind him.

As Chris approached the door, he could feel his palm becoming slick, either from the steam or his own perspiration, and the needle was in danger of slipping out of his grasp. He paused only to get a better grip on the two-inch needle, then stepped through the doorway to confront the man inside, flanked by Saney and Julian.

The steam was not very thick, but the bathroom was large and Deluder was barely visible at the far end. There were two separate dressing areas. They were divided by a block glass wall with bench seating on both sides. There were clerestory stained glass windows, an immense sunken Roman tub, and a separate marble Jacuzzi, not to mention the largest and most ornate toilet that could ever have been imagined. It was obscene in scale and as grand as the papal throne. The bowl itself was yellow-tan, which led Julian to suspect that it was made of ivory rather than porcelain, and the entire fixture was inlaid with gold.

Deluder must have seen movement in one of the room's many mirrors, because he turned suddenly to face them. Shaving cream covered half of his face and he was holding a straight razor in his left hand. He squinted through the steam and the distance, trying to determine who was in the bathroom doorway. He began to take slow and deliberate steps forward. He used a small hand towel to wipe off the remaining cream from his cheeks and neck.

"Chris?" Deluder said. "Is that you?" He continued to advance, and when he saw that it was the boy, a smile stretched across his face.

Deluder had only a towel wrapped around his waist, and Julian found himself surprised, and more than a little amused, by this sight. Could this be the Devil incarnate, he wondered as he looked at this appreciably young man, whose wet hair revealed places where it had already begun to thin. Additionally, his arms and legs were bony and his stomach was soft and puffy, love handles spilling out over the top of the towel. If Deluder was Satan, and they could not defeat him, then the meek (and flabby) would, indeed, inherit the earth, Julian thought.

Deluder stopped just a few feet in front of Chris. Still smiling, he said, "I'm glad you didn't leave town, Chris. I see you have some friends with you. Aren't you going to introduce me to them?"

But Chris was quiet. Deluder looked at him, bewildered. Then he turned his eyes on Saney and Julian for help.

"Big day planned?" Julian asked.

Deluder could only frown at the obscurity of the question. Then he noticed the needle Chris was clenching tightly in his hand. He looked into Chris's eyes for an explanation.

"What's going on here, Chris?"

Still, Chris did not say anything. This time it was Saney who spoke.

"We know who you are," she said. "You're Satan."

Deluder just stood there looking at each of them, then he

suddenly threw his head back and began to laugh hysterically.

Deluder's laughter stopped just as suddenly as it started when he realized that nobody else was laughing. "Wait," he said. "You're serious?"

Now Chris raised his arm and steadied himself, the small needle barely visible in his hand.

Deluder looked directly at the boy. "You've got to be kidding, Chris. You came over here to kill me . . . with *that*?" He began to laugh again, and this time it did not seem as if he was going to stop.

Julian certainly understood the levity of the situation. All he could think about was that the battle between the supreme powers of good and evil was about to be settled with a sewing needle.

Between cycles of laughter, Deluder asked, "What would lead you to believe that I'm the Devil, of all things?"

"Did you know your dough is infected with a fungus that can make people sick or cause them to hallucinate?"

"No, but that might explain your behavior. Maybe it's making *you* hallucinate that an honest business man is the Devil."

"You can't fool us," Saney said.

Deluder threw his hands up whimsically, still chortling. "You caught me. I guess the jig is up." Then he looked at Chris more seriously and said, "Surely you don't believe any of this nonsense." But the boy was still holding the needle out in front of him as if it were a crucifix before a vampire. "Let's talk about this logically. Let me get dressed. We'll go down into my study, have some coffee, and try to sort this whole thing out. Okay?"

"No, Chris," Saney advised.

"Chris, put the weapon down."

"Don't listen to him."

The boy seemed to hesitate, unsure what to do.

"Chris, it's me. What about all the things I've done for you? I helped you get your car fixed, got you a job, took you in. I wouldn't do anything to hurt you. Now put that thing away before somebody gets hurt."

"Trust your instincts, Chris," Saney said. "What's your heart telling you?"

"Think about what you're doing for a second. Do you expect to stab me with a little pin and—poof—make me disappear like an over-inflated balloon? Are you people on drugs? Listen to what you're saying. Do I look like *Satan* to you?"

The boy was either getting tired or losing his resolve, because his arm had dropped slightly.

"That's right, Chris. You can't kill an ant with that thing."

"Maybe," Saney began, "we're not supposed to kill you. Maybe the needle is just a symbol, and its true strength lies in the person who sticks you with it. So few people even believe in the Devil anymore, maybe the needle can only harm you if the person doing the sticking *believes* it can harm you."

"And," Julian added, "if skepticism is the source of your own power, we're about to pull the plug on it. Perhaps you thought that you could succeed with anonymity, just sneak in when nobody was thinking about you. But we see you, don't we? And we can stop you. You know it, too."

"That's just pure insanity. You can't believe that."

Suddenly Julian extended the index finger of his right hand. "Prick it," he told Chris, who hesitated. "Go head, Chris, prick my finger."

Slowly Chris pressed the sharp tip against Julian's finger, easily piercing the delicate skin. A droplet of blood gathered on the end of the finger and the needle.

"Now do the same to Saney. And then to yourself."

The idea had only just occurred to him that having all their blood commingled on the tip of the needle would make it that much more potent when it came time to pierce Deluder.

Chris did what he had been instructed, and when each of them had been pricked, Julian looked at Deluder and said, "Now it's your turn."

Chris raised the bloodstained needle and extended it toward

Deluder, who moved back several paces in response.

"What are you so afraid of?" Julian said. "The panic shows on your face."

"Look, I'm not going to stand by passively while you try to skewer me. I have a right to defend myself. That doesn't prove anything. Besides, it's just not sanitary."

Chris stepped forward in pursuit.

"You've been misled," Deluder said, backpedaling at the same pace.

Julian and Saney followed Chris into the bathroom. Deluder continued to retreat.

"If I really were the Devil, don't you think I would have turned you into toads, or something, by now." He tried to sound jaunty and wry, but his voice began to rise. "You think the real Devil would be this helpless?"

Chris backed Deluder all the way up to the sink at the far end of the cavernous bathroom.

"If it's money you want, I have plenty," Deluder said, but by then it was already too late. Chris jabbed his arm forward, quick as a piston. Deluder made a soft sound in his throat and grabbed the top of his right hand where he had been pricked. He remained quiet and still for a moment while they all looked on. When he lifted his head next, he was smirking.

"You see," Deluder said in a smug and clearly triumphant tone. "Nothing happened." He slowly edged away from them and headed out of the room wearing nothing but a towel. He stopped suddenly in the doorway and turned to face them. "If you think I'm the Devil," Deluder said, "wait until my lawyers get a hold of you. You'll pay for this."

They all knew Deluder was lying. His hand was not even bleeding. Then he stepped out of the bathroom and disappeared down the hall. And just like that, it was all over. All the tension left the room at once. A Gordian knot if ever there was one, Julian thought.

The three of them stood in Deluder's bathroom, just staring at each other in disbelief. Until the tremor struck. As soon as the floor they were standing on began to rock violently, Julian grabbed Saney and Chris. He rushed them into the hallway and down the stairs toward the front door. The ground that held the foundation rose and fell for several frightening seconds. Small objects and large fixtures alike were shaken loose from the fracturing walls and ceiling as they made their escape.

Chapter Thirty

The quake had subsided by the time they made it out of the house. And since everybody seemed okay, Julian packed them right back into the rental car and drove off. None of them asked about Deluder. In fact, no one said a single word until they were safely away from the mansion. While they did not know where Deluder was, they were sure that they would not be seeing him any more. They also knew that while Satan may have failed in achieving his nefarious plan this time, He would be back some day to try again. Hopefully that would not be for a long, long time. But if there was one thing that the Devil had plenty of— besides an infinite contempt for man—it was time.

What most concerned all of them at that time was what their own futures held, because almost immediately after pricking Deluder, each of them became very much aware that their memory of the events of the past few days was quickly fading. With Bubin no longer there to explain things, all they had was each other, and an increasingly foggy perception of what came before.

Julian turned on the car radio, hoping to hear some kind of news about the tremor they felt. He had been in more violent quakes, and ones that had a much longer duration. He had been doing field work in the San Gabriel Mountains when the Northridge earthquake rocked the San Fernando Valley in 1994. By comparison, this latest tremor was relatively minor. Finally, one station did make mention that a 4-second jolt that registered 3.7 on the Richter scale was confirmed, with the epicenter determined to be somewhere in Western Caldera. Julian got the impression that such a small seismic event was not much of a news item around here, but he was just relieved that they had not been feeling the effect of a larger quake that was centered further away, in Albuquerque or Santa Fe, or even the Los Angeles area, for that matter.

They went back to Julian's house to relax and collect their thoughts. Mostly to relax. They were all very tired. Julian fought the urge to lie down and close his eyes. Instead, he peered out at Caldera through the picture window. Saney approached and put an arm around him.

"What are you thinking about?" she asked.

"It doesn't look like anything has changed out there."

Saney looked out and saw the same thing as Julian.

"Just tell me again how what we did today was any different from what they did in Salem, or from what the inquisitors did in the Middle Ages, or from any other incident throughout history in which self-serving religious subjectivism was resolved with bloodshed."

"To paraphrase Bubin's philosophical canon," Saney said, "'It requires a strong will, and faith, to accomplish anything in life.'"

"Saney, tell me honestly, are you truly convinced that there is a global organization like the one Bubin described. Or do you think he might have been just another religious fanatic, and we were taken in by it all for some reason, or for various reasons?"

"I just think we needed to find each other, for whatever reason, and Bubin helped us do that. Anything more than that, I don't think we'll ever know for sure."

Julian studied Saney's face. He could see in her eyes that she believed what she had said.

"While we were driving back here," Julian began, "I remembered what you told me one time about evil being in all of us. Then I started to think what it would be like if that evil was somehow released, or unleashed, as it were, by everyone in Caldera *at the same time?*"

Saney signed at the thought of it, then said, "I know that it's a statistical fact that violence, domestic and otherwise, increases dramatically with the stress of city living. But to think that *everyone* could be affected by it in the exact same way simply flies in the face of all that we know about the diversity of individual personality. But it does make you wonder if perhaps there may have been some other influence in Caldera that could not be written into the actuarial equation. Something off the chart. Something that could not be predicted?"

"You mean Deluder?"

"What if there's a Deluder in every big city, in every nation of the world, silently amassing followers of lawlessness and disorder, and waiting for the right day to make a final assault on humanity?"

Julian thought about that for a moment, but seemed distracted by something else that was on his mind. "I got one other insight on the drive over here?" he said.

"Oh. And what was that?"

"Well, it involves a church and priest . . . and a pair of elephant shoes."

Saney's face lit up in anticipation.

"What is it with these elephant shoes you keep talking about?" Chris suddenly asked. "Is it something I'm too young to understand?"

"It's something you can never be too young to understand," Saney said.

Then Julian removed a small box from his shirt pocket and gave it to Saney. She took it, tears already welling up behind her eyes. She hesitated before she popped the top of the velvety box and revealed a diamond engagement ring that had been roughly cut into the shape of a tiny elephant. She put a hand to her mouth to conceal a scream.

Julian paused and took a deep breath. Looking deeply into her eyes, he said, "I've been waiting for the right time to do this. This sure seems like it. So here goes . . . Will you marry me, Xenia Wieland?"

Saney looked from the ring to Julian, disbelieving what she was seeing and hearing, unable to speak.

"I wish you would tell me soon," he said. "I've wasted enough of my life already."

He put the ring on her finger and Saney immediately threw her arms around him. She held him in a tight bear hug and would not let go. When she finally did release him, she started to kiss him all over his face.

"Should I take this as a 'yes?'"

"Yes, yes, yes," she finally said, hastening the words from her mouth.

Chris got up to join them in their celebration. Even though they had all met only a few days before, with all they had been through, it seemed like they had known each other much longer. It was just one unlikelihood in a week of unlikelihoods.

"This calls for a celebration," Julian said. "I'm sure, like me, you're both as hungry as you are tired."

"I can eat," Chris said.

"You sure can," said Saney. "I've seen you."

They quickly got ready, but Saney took the longest time because she kept staring down at the ring on her finger every few moments, expecting it to not be there the next time she looked. Then, just as they were about to leave, Saney noticed Chris staring at the picture of his mother.

"Is there something wrong, Chris?" she asked.

"No," Chris said, "it's just funny. It never occurred to me that my mother might be wearing a nun's habit in this picture."

Saney closely inspected the photograph. "Well, I'll be. I think you're right."

Julian came over and had a look. "And isn't that a cross around her neck?" he asked.

"Yeah. It's so obvious now."

Julian said, "Sometimes the most obvious things are the most difficult to see."

"Do you know what you're going to do next?" Saney asked the boy.

"Well," Chris said, "first I thought I might find some lepers, cure them, and then maybe turn the water in the state reservoirs into wine for all the winos in New Jersey. That should keep me busy for awhile."

Saney laughed. Chris had a wonderful sense of humor and she knew that it would serve him well. It would not allow him to take what he had done too seriously. Maybe that was why he had been chosen. Regardless of what he had just been through, he was still just a sixteen-year-old boy like any other, and that was all he wanted to be. Whatever else came his way in life, Saney knew he would be just fine.

"After that," Chris continued in a more serious tone, "I thought I might go to Spain to find my mom."

"That sounds like a good idea. Moms always know what's best."

"Do you ever go see your mom?"

She looked at him for a long moment, then said, "I never really got along with my mother," she said. "It's a complicated relationship."

"I'm sorry," Chris said.

"Don't be. She's in Hungary and I haven't been back since my father died."

"What's she like?"

"She's a very religious woman. She didn't like the fact that I was studying psychiatry. She thought the basic philosophies of the discipline were the reason that I no longer shared the same beliefs she did. Then, when my father died, I drifted further away from my faith *and* my mother. Now I'm afraid the gap between us has become too wide to bridge." Suddenly her eyes started to gloss over and she had to blink to keep back the tears. "Not long ago, my Aunt Edith wrote me and told me that my mother had been diagnosed with ovarian cancer. I just acted as if I never got the letter and that I didn't care. Then my mother left a message on my answering machine last week. She wanted to talk. I've been planning on calling her back, but I keep putting it off. Now that this whole thing is over, I plan on going to see her. After the experience we just had, I don't think I can ever allow another relationship to deteriorate to that point. Not for any reason. It's not worth it."

"You can take Julian with you so he can meet her," Chris said with a smile.

"I've always wanted to go to Hungary," Julian said, smiling back.

Saney joined them, and then they left together. They enjoyed a nice meal together and shared a bottle of wine at a fine Mexican restaurant named *Los Corrompos* in downtown Caldera. They talked and laughed, enjoying each other's company, knowing that this would be the last time all three of them would be together. And it was.

After they finished eating, Chris went to play a video game on the other side of the restaurant. As Saney sipped her wine, Julian was staring off absently.

"What's on your mind now, Julian?"

He hesitated. What he had been wondering was what was going to become of them now that the Deluder business had been taken care of. But it was one of those questions that would probably have to wait to be answered. Like the rest of the world, their relationship would depend not on fate or destiny, but on the quantity and quality of what each of them put into it. Instead of telling her all that, he kissed her on the nose and said, "I was just thinking how wonderful our life is going to be together."

That evening, they bought Chris a one-way ticket to Madrid and saw him off at the airport, providing him with ample pocket money to get around and to return to the U.S. when he was ready. On the drive back from the airport, Julian and Saney decided to pack up only what they really needed and get out of Caldera as soon as possible.

From that moment on, the details of the whole ordeal began to push themselves, like living things, away from their conscious memories at an increasingly accelerated rate. Just the next morning, even what should have been the most indelible recollections of the previous week were perceived as having happened decades ago.

Maybe it was a protective mechanism. Maybe it was something more. But with each passing day, it all became that much more unreal, until finally it seemed as if none of it had ever happened, and whatever importance it did have at one time was now lost and could not be regained or understood in the same way again.

The following week Julian and Saney were married and living in an exclusive apartment in uptown Manhattan. After a year, as they got caught up in the day to day routines of life, paying bills and raising a family, they forget about it entirely. To even think about such a scenario as Armageddon, infused with enigmatic situations and characters like Bubin and Deluder, seemed merely fantastic and indulgent. Neither of them could have seriously entertained the notion that they had saved the world from the wrath of the Arch Fiend. They were mere mortals, after all, and they did not believe that anything of this world could be called upon to perform such a task, because that would surely result in failure. Such an undertaking would require the concerted effort of supernatural or mythical beings such as Zeus, Sir Lancelot, Moses, or even Tiger Woods, but certainly not Xenia and Julian Bloom. Had they been able to recall anything at all about a city of faceless greed and faithlessness, whose citizenry was led astray by a satanic baker, they would have thought it was a movie they had seen on Pay-Per-View. And whenever one of them was asked how the two of them had met, they would stop and think about it for a moment before answering, "We met through a friend," and then Chris's face would come to mind and a good feeling would come over them.

Epilogue

Not long after the first tremor that morning, the U.S. Geological Survey had been notified. By midmorning, a host of geophysicists, volcanologists, and scores of other scientists had converged on Caldera. For several weeks afterward, very small magnitude earthquakes began to occur on a regular basis. It was soon discovered that most of the trembling had actually been the result of the movement of magma within its chamber far beneath the surface of the city.

The data collected during these weeks paralleled much of what Julian's own studies had revealed previously, such as a decline of wild life, a rise in air and barometric pressures, heightened levels of sulfur dioxide and CO_2 gases in the air as well as the presence of rats, which were being driven up from their underground burrows. Now, these findings were all being interpreted as a precursor to what experts were calling a *major seismic event*. Together with the further diagnostic conclusions of seismometers, magnetometers, tiltmeters, rock samples and gas measurements, all indicators pointed conclusively at a huge magma reservoir a mile below Caldera. More detailed observation of rapid subsurface magma expansion was a sure sign that an eruption was imminent. Of course, no time frame could be given, but an immediate and total evacuation was ordered for the entire city of Caldera and surrounding suburbs.

Tragically, few people took heed of this direct imperative, or were too slow in coming to a decision. For the most part, Calderians were unwilling to give up their indulgent lifestyle or let anything get in the way of their earning potential, including the looming likelihood of a cataclysmic volcanic eruption. The local economy was far better than elsewhere in the country, and the financial opportunities were too good to pass up for the mere doomsday ballyhooing of a modern day *Chicken Little*. That was their collective sentiment anyway, and they were sticking to it.

Meanwhile, the U.S.G.S. continued to register steady, low rumblings throughout the course of each day. Then, without warning, at 1:32 PM on January 17, the mighty upward thrust of magma produced the first stress-relieving cinder cone. The vent blossomed from the ground on tenth street, right in the middle of the sidewalk in front of Walgreens. It started out about the size of a road pylon, only it was gray and releasing noxious sulfur dioxide gas and magma fragments. Smaller cinder cones began to sprout up elsewhere, one a half a block away, on Twelfth, and still another on Glenmere, in the heart of the city's theater district.

The huge magma chamber began to undermine the crust. Soon after that, the roof of the reservoir began to crumble. The pressure caused the gas-filled magma to erupt from the various cinder cones around the city with tremendous explosive power. Ring fractures began to appear all across the surface of Caldera. These perfect concentric circles radiated outward from the area of the city where the most prominent cinder cone had appeared, encompassing a diametric area of nearly ten miles. The fractures gaped as wide as fifty feet and carved down nearly a mile. They spewed superheated gases and ejected molten, plastic-skinned bombs and angular glowing blocks of all sizes across the landscape. These deadly volcanic projectiles traveled at speeds that exceeded 500 feet per second, destroying buildings, setting hundreds of fires and claiming thousands of lives. More powerful quakes followed, triggered by the resulting shock waves, which caused buildings to crumble and fall as the death toll steadily climbed.

The expanding gases quickly drove a turbulent ground-hugging froth of pumice and ash skyward, shrouding the entire city in a gray pall.

Shortly after the initial explosions, viscous gas-rich magma began to roll slowly out of the newborn volcanic cinder cone, which had formed in the center of what had previously been downtown Caldera. The buildings that were not destroyed by the initial forces of the blasts or set ablaze by catapulted lava bombs, were suffocated under a thick blanket of tephra that was still falling to the ground like black snow in a twenty mile radius from the crater.

The lava flow continued to advance through the transformed streets, eventually cooling and hardening. Some of it found its way into the old sewage overflow pipe, sending the vast population of rats scampering for their lives.

As more molten rock was ejected from the crater, the volcanic cone grew both upward and outward. A thick gray wall of soot and ash now towered tens of thousands of feet into the stratosphere, rising upward toward the heavens like the finger of some malevolent deity.

By daybreak the following morning, the volcano had reached a height of fifty feet and a quarter mile in diameter. The final death toll could only be estimated at that point, and would not be known for quite some time. It was still too dangerous to send rescue crews in and it was the consensus of the authorities that few people, if any, had survived what was being called one of the worst natural disasters in the history of humankind.

A hot, glowing wall of lava continued to move slowly over the rubble-strewn ruins toward a burnt-out portion of a commercial building, which was covered almost to the roof with black tephra. Partially protruding from the pitch was a sign for DELUDER BAKE SHOPS. And then the rolling lava engulfed it too.

The lava flow that swept across the devastated region also entombed a mystery that would never to be uncovered. Under layers of cooled, encrusted lava and fallen ash, yards deep, the only bit of physical evidence that could have marked Satan's presence in Caldera was effectively destroyed.

The rat population had proliferated there because of the endless numbers of human corpses that were being served to them in the runoff pipe. In fact, the rodents could not digest the raw flesh fast enough. So many bodies filled the pipe that they began to putrefy before they could be scavenged. Men, women, boys, girls, the very young and the decrepit and old were all featured in this subterranean All-You-Can-Eat human buffet. What the rats liked most, of course, were the delicate internal organs, which remained intact despite the dime-sized hole, black around the edges, that was burnt into the center of every chest, where their souls had been harvested like so many vintage wine grapes. But the rats did not care about that, it was not a flesh organ, and did not have any taste.

When the lava initially entered the rat's sanctum, their feast unceremoniously ended. They abandoned the succulent red meat and fled to ensure the survival of their kind. They, too, would take up residence elsewhere.

As the red-hot channel of lava advanced through the pipe at about a mile per hour, it engulfed the bodies left behind, incinerating the remains in its two thousand degree embrace. Claybert was there. So was Tasker, Tana and, Henry Todd, the motel owner. A.J. was next to his wife, Jeanie.

Among the countless others, lying beside one other, with holes freshly bored into their chests, were the bodies of Julian and Saney.

THE END

A Spectral Visions Imprint

Now Available

Riverwatch

by

Joseph M. Nassise

From a new voice in horror comes a novel rich in characterization and stunning in its imagery. In his debut novel, author Joseph M. Nassise weaves strange and shocking events into the ordinary lives of his characters so smoothly that the reader accepts them without pause, setting the stage for a climactic ending with the rushing power of a summer storm.

When his construction team finds the tunnel hidden beneath the cellar floor in the old Blake family mansion in Harrington Falls, Jake Caruso is excited by the possibility of what he might find hidden there. Exploring its depths, he discovers an even greater mystery: a sealed stone chamber at the end of that tunnel.

When the seal on that long forgotten chamber is broken, a reign of terror and death comes unbidden to the residents of the small mountain community. Something is stalking its citizens; something that comes in the dark of night on silent wings and strikes without warning, leaving a trail of blood in its wake. Something that should never have been released from the prison the Guardian had fashioned for it years before.

Now Jake, with the help of his friends Sam Travers and Katelynn Riley, will be forced to confront this ancient evil in an effort to stop the creature's rampage. The Nightshade, however, has other plans.

Ask for it at your local bookseller!

ISBN 1931402191

www.barclaybooks.com

A Spectral Visions Imprint

Now Available

Psyclone

by

Roger Sharp

Driven by the need to recreate the twin brother who had been abducted more than twenty years ago and using himself as a model, renowned geneticist David Brooks develops the ability to clone an adult human being. His partner, Dr. Williams, is closing in on a break-through that will let them implant a false set of memories, thoughts, and emotions into the newly formed clone's mind to give it a sense of the past. Before Williams succeeds, however, an ancient demon possesses the clone's empty shell and takes the doctors hostage. Is what the demon reveals about the fate of his brother true? Can they escape and stop the demon clone's rampage before too much damage is done?

Ask for it at your local bookseller!

ISBN 193140019

www.barclaybooks.com

A Spectral Visions Imprint

Now Available

Phantom Feast
by
Diana Barron

A haunted antique circus wagon.

A murderous dwarf.

A disappearing town under siege.

The citizens of sleepy little Hester, New York are plunged into unimaginable terror when their town is transformed into snowy old-growth forests, lush, steamy jungles, and grassy, golden savannas by a powerful, supernatural force determined to live...again

Danger and death stalk two handsome young cops, a retired couple and their dog, the town 'bad girl', her younger sister's boyfriend, and three members of the local motorcycle gang. They find themselves battling the elements, restless spirits, and each other on a perilous journey into the unknown, where nothing is familiar, and people are not what they at first appear to be.

Who, or what, are the real monsters?

Ask for it at your local bookseller!

ISBN 193140213

www.barclaybooks.com

A Spectral Visions Imprint

Now Available

Night Terrors
by
Drew Williams

He came to them in summer, while everyone slept....

For Detective Steve Wyckoff, the summer brought four suicides and a grisly murder to his hometown. Deaths that would haunt his dreams and lead him to the brink of madness.

For David Cavanaugh, the summer brought back long forgotten dreams of childhood. Dreams that became nightmares for which there would be no escape.

For Nathan Espy, the summer brought freedom from a life of abuse. Freedom purchased at the cost of his own soul.

From an abyss of darkness, he came to their dreams and whispered his name.

"Dust"

Ask for it at your local bookseller!

ISBN 193140248

www.barclaybooks.com

A Spectral Visions Imprint

Now Available

Spirit Of Independence
by
Keith Rommel

Travis Winter, the Spirit of Independence, was viciously murdered in World War II. Soon after his untimely death, he discovers he is a chosen celestial knight; a new breed of Angel destined to fight the age-old war between Heaven and Hell. Yet, confusion reigns for Travis when he is pulled into Hell and is confronted by the Devil himself—the saddened creature who begs only to be heard.

Freed by a band of Angels sent to rescue him, Travis rejects the Devil's plea and begins a fifty year long odyssey to uncover the true reasons why Heaven and Hell war.

Now, in this, the present day, Travis comes to you, the reader, to share recent and extraordinary revelations that will no doubt change the way you view the Kingdom of Heaven and Hell. And what is revealed will change your own afterlife in ways you could never imagine …

Ask for it at your local bookseller!

ISBN 1931402078

www.barclaybooks.com